A Garland Series

Classics of Children's Literature 1621-1932

A collection of 117 titles
reprinted in photo-facsimile
in 73 volumes

Selected and arranged by
Alison Lurie
and
Justin G. Schiller

The History of Tom Thumbe

with a preface
for the Garland edition by

Michael Patrick Hearn

ঌ

Robin Hood's Garland

with a preface
for the Garland edition by

Bennett A. Brockman

ঌ

The History of
Jack and the Giants

[in two parts]

with a preface
for the Garland edition by

Michael Patrick Hearn

ঌ

Traditional Faery Tales
Sir Henry Cole

with a preface
for the Garland edition by

Margaret Maloney

Garland Publishing, Inc., New York & London
1977

The prefaces to *The History of Tom Thumbe* and *Jack and the Giants*
are copyright © 1977 by Michael Patrick Hearn

The preface to *Robin Hood's Garland*
is copyright © 1977 by Bennett A. Brockman

The preface to *Traditional Faery Tales*
is copyright © 1977 by Margaret Maloney

Library of Congress Cataloging in Publication Data

Tom Thumb.
    The history of Tom Thumbe.

    (Classics of children's literature, 1621-1932)
    Reprint of 4 works, the 1st originally printed in
1621 for T. Langley, London; the 2d originally printed
in 1789, London; the 3d originally printed by J. Turner,
Coventry; and the 4th originally published in 1845 by
J. Cundall, London, under title: The traditional
faëry tales of Little Red Riding Hood, Beauty and the
beast & Jack and the bean stalk.
    Includes bibliographies.
    SUMMARY: A collection of tales reprinted from
early editions.
    1. Tales, English. 2. Fairy tales. 3. Robin Hood--
Juvenile literature. [1. Folklore--England. 2. Fairy
tales. 3. Robin Hood] I. Title. II. Series.
PZ6.T593Hk6   398.2'08   75-32133
ISBN 0-8240-2250-5

Printed in the United States of America

The History of
Tom Thumbe

This facsimile has been made
from a copy in
The Pierpont Morgan Library
(45444).

Preface

*Tom Thumb! whose very Name must Mirth incite
And fill each merry Briton with Delight.*

Henry Fielding, *Tom Thumb* (1730)

The classics of childhood are largely an inherited literature. For nearly every beloved book written specifically for children there is an equally popular title composed with no thought of the child. *Robinson Crusoe, Gulliver's Travels, A Christmas Carol, Huckleberry Finn*, all written for an adult audience, now have an undisputed place in the nursery. Prior to the awakening of the Western mind to the special needs of the child, nearly all literature read by children was watered-down adult fiction and fable. Of course there were a few books designed for the consumption of the young; these were generally intended to teach reading or morality through the frightening example of Christian martyrs. However, the works most avidly absorbed by young readers were stories of high fancy. Rousseau described in his *Confessions* how he developed a love of reading in childhood when he went over popular French romances with his father.[1]

Until the beginning of the nineteenth century, the form of literature most accessible to children was the chapbook. These cheaply printed, crudely illustrated pamphlets, bound in paper covers, were widely hawked in the provinces by the numerous chapmen. Their subject matter was general popular literature, ballads and romances, fairy tales and fables.[2] Many of the books, often taken from classical and medieval sources, had long been snubbed by the aristocracy (and later by the growing middle class) in favor of more contemporary works. But the peasantry and children adopted this literature as their own. Many eminent educators denied the suitability of such "vulgar" literature for young minds. Lord Chesterfield condemned such works for the young, and Hugh Rhodes in his *Book of Nurture* (1554) advised parents to protect their children "from reading feigned fables, vain fantasies, and wanton stories, and songs of love, which bring much mischief to youth." This disapproval was likely as much a matter of class as of literary consciousness, but the chapbooks were also condemned on religious grounds. The Puritan John Bunyan wrote his own pious *Book for Boys and Girls* (1686) in part as a reaction to the popular fare of the nursery, "to shew them how each Fingle-fangle,/On which they doting are, their Souls entangle." The children, however, disregarded such well-meaning complaints and continued to read these cheap books, even if they had to rely on the kindness of a nurse or other servant to provide them.

In addition to printing abridgements and (often crude) translations of popular works, the chapbooks also provided the first appearance in print of important folk material. These pamphlets largely replaced the broadside ballad (as the newspaper eventually did the chapbook) as easily available reading matter, and, like the ballads, they relied on previously unpublished material from the English oral tradition. The many anonymous authors (most merely hacks) generally did not transcribe the old tales and songs (as the Grimm Brothers did in their *Kinder-und-Hausmärchen*) directly from the storytellers. Most often their works combined the old legends with allusions to other literature and with the author's own fancy.

The History of Tom Thumbe, the Little, for his small stature surnamed, King Arthurs Dwarfe was among the most enduring of these chapbooks. Its author, "R.I.," has been identified as one Richard Johnson (1573-1659?), an undistinguished author of much popular literature. It has not been determined how much of his "first part of our ancient story of Sir Thomas Thumbe" comes from the author's own imagination and how much from folklore. Evidently a host of legends about the boy no bigger than a miller's thumb was

PREFACE

current in the Elizabethan age. The author remarks in his introduction that "these merry tales" were a Yuletide tradition, and likely there were many such stories told by bachelor and maid, shepherd and plowman, about the hearth in the past several hundred years. Tom Thumb was certainly a household name at the time. He is mentioned in English literature as early as 1579, in *D. Heskins . . . overthrowne* by William Fulke, and in 1592, in Thomas Nashe's *Pierce Pennilesse.* Reginald Scot in his *The Discouverie of witchcraft* (1584) classified "Tom Thombe" among "changlings, Incubus, Robin good-fellowe, . . . the man in the oke, . . . the puckle, . . . hob gobblin, tom tumbler, boneles, and such other bugs." There is indeed something of Robin Goodfellow in the pranks of Tom Thumb described in the chapbook, and perhaps the two were interchangeable (like Puck and Robin in Shakespeare) in the hearthside stories. Soon after this printing of *The History of Tom Thumbe*, he appeared as a minor character in Ben Jonson's masque *The Fortunate Isles, and their Union* (1624) and as the fairy page in Michael Drayton's mock-romance *Nimphidia; the court of fayrie* (1627).

By the Elizabethan age, Tom Thumb had firmly established himself in English tradition, but these "ancient" legends were not all native born. Although it has been argued that Tom Thumb originated from a dwarf at the court of King Edgar (the chapbook calls the boy "Little Tom of Wales"), more likely he entered English folklore with the coming of the Saxons. The Grimm Brothers collected a version of Tom Thumb, the German "Daumesdick"; but the British character was perhaps more directly inspired by the Danish "Svend Tomling" (which was also in part the source for Hans Christian Andersen's "Tommelise," or "Thumbelina" in the popular English form, 1836). English tradition explained that the real Tom Thumb was buried in Lincoln (one of several Danish towns in Great Britain), where his grave was once marked by a blue stone.

Certainly Johnson borrowed liberally from these legends

and other literary sources. The cow's swallowing of the boy is similar to an episode in Grimm. The discussion of "How Tom Thumbe fell into his Mothers pudding Bowle: and of the first originall of those Puddings now called Tom Thumbs" is obviously from a legend well-known to Johnson's contemporaries. Some verses by Jacobus Field that prefixed *Coryats Crvdities* (1611) mentioned this tradition:

> Tom Thumbe is dumbe, vntill the pudding creepe
> In which he was intom'd then out doth peepe.

This legend may have been then the most popularly known concerning Tom Thumb; Ben Jonson refers to it in *The Fortunate Isles* when a character says:

> Or you may haue come
> In, Thomas Thumbe,
> In a pudding fatt
> With Doctor Ratt.

The "Rime made amongst the Schoole-boyes" was perhaps a standard nursery rhyme which Johnson found convenient to add to his narrative and which may or may not have been originally coupled with the tale of the boy's hanging "black Pots and Glasses on the beames of the Sunne, as vpon a line or cord." The game itself comes from the Middle Ages, being a part of the legend of St. Columbanus long before it was told in this chapbook.

Giants had long had a place in the Arthurian legends, and it is not surprising that Tom Thumb, King Arthur's knight, should encounter them. In this chapbook appears the earliest known printing of the traditional cry of blood-thirsty giants, now better remembered from *Jack the Giant-Killer* and *Jack and the Beanstalk* than from *Tom Thumb*. The doggerel "fi, fee, fau, fan" was well-known to Johnson's contemporaries; Nashe in *Haue with you to Saffron-vvalden*, 1596 ("Fy, fa, fum, I smell the bloud of an Englishman") and Shakespeare in *King Lear* ("fie, foh, fumme,/ I smell the blood of a Brittish man") both facetiously note the old phrase, and

PREFACE

S. Rowlands in his *Knave of Clubbes* (1609) employed "Fee, fa, fum" as a mock-invocation of the Devil. Obviously the simple verse was current in the English nurseries of 1621, and Johnson easily borrowed this popular piece of doggerel for his own tale. The rhyme has had a life of its own beyond the tales of giants: in the American *Tommy Thumb's Song-Book* (1794), a collection of common nursery rhymes, "fee, faw, fum" was printed separately from a giant story. Another English tradition Johnson adapted in his chapbook was the tribe of Pygmies ruled by King Twaddle;[3] the author obviously thought it appropriate that his diminutive hero should meet so famous and so small a race of men. The marvelous gifts bestowed upon Tom Thumb by his fairy godmother are the archetypal magical instruments of Northern mythology often given by supernatural guardians to their mortal charges. *The History of Tom Thumbe* was apparently the first published nursery tale to mention these treasures, a staple in many later fairy stories.

To flesh out these legends, Johnson depended heavily on contemporary literary sources. The most obvious example is that of the giant Gargantua, the Rabelais character. Although the French classic had not been completely translated into English by the printing of this chapbook, the monster was already familiar to Johnson's contemporaries. He is mentioned by Shakespeare in *As You Like It* ("You must borrow me Gargantua's mouth first") and by Ben Jonson in *Every Man in His Humour* ("Your Gargantua breech cannot carry it away so"); Nashe used the term "gargantuan" in *Haue with you*. Certainly something of the actual story was known to English men of letters: Drayton in *Nimphidia* mentions, among the old romances, those told by "Mad Rabelais of Pantagruel." Gargantua had already made his appearance in popular English jestbooks, as early as 1547, in *The Boke of Marchauntes*. In referring to "Garragantua that monster of men" in his introduction along with the folk heroes Guy of Warwicke and Robin Hood, Johnson suggests that part of Rabelais' story had already established itself in English folklore and had likely been included in chapbooks, none of which are known to have survived.[4]

Another of Johnson's embellishments is his introduction of King Arthur and his Knights of the Round Table. The Grimm tale has no references to the English monarch; the German character remains a country character and is not adopted by a royal court. Johnson apparently employed a literary convention by opening his old story in a Golden Age of English history when "the World was in a better frame then it is now." (Chaucer similarly begins his *Wif of Bathes tale* with the following:

> In th'olde dayes of the Kyng Arthour,
> Of which that Bretons speken greet honour,
> Al was this lond fulfild of fayerye.)

By the time of Johnson's chapbook it was as conventional to open an English folk tale with a reference to the age of Arthur as to begin a continental fairy tale with "once upon a time." Among the later chapbooks, both *The History of Jack and the Giants* (earliest known printing, 1711) and *The King of Colchester's Daughters* (commonly called "The Three Heads in the Well") are prefixed with a reference to the former lord of Camelot.[5]

Although Tom Thumb's history begins "In the old time, when King Arthur ruled this land," the world described is not that in Malory. It is not an era of Excaliburs and Holy Grails. The traditional wizard Merlin of the medieval romances would not waste his time impregnating a miller's wife with a son no bigger than his father's thumb.[6] *The History of Tom Thumbe* is clearly a product of the Elizabethan age. Although his hero originated in ancient legend, the author's attitude towards fairy lore is that of the Tudor period. Chaucer had anticipated this declining respect for the realm of faerie when he wrote:

> But now kan no man se none elves mo,
> For now the grete charitee and prayeres

PREFACE

Of lymytours and othere hooley freres, . . .
This maketh that ther ben no fayeryes.

By Elizabeth's time, many of the old legends were recognized as vain superstition. Scot argued in *The Discouverie of witchcraft* that such creatures as elves, fairies, sylvans, nymphs, and changelings were old wives' fancies, created to terrify children so "that we are afraid of our owne shadowes"; even the Devil himself "hauing hornes on his head, fier in his mouth, and a taile in his breech, eies like a bason, fanges like a dog, clawes like a beare, a skin like a Niger, and a voice roring like a lion" was a mere conceit of nurses "whereby we start and are afraid when we heare one crie Bough." Elizabethans viewed fairy legend skeptically, and little changed with the arrival of the Stuarts on the British throne.[7] Although there were then many examples of fairy literature, their subjects were not always treated reverentially; they were depicted more often in burlesque than in high romance.[8] Morgan le Fay would never be found in the medieval romances romping about the forest engaged in so silly a pursuit as Titania's love for the ass-headed Bottom. The actions of the fairies were no longer in the heroic traditions of Celtic folklore. Medb, the great fairy queen of Irish storytellers, was reduced to Mab, the fairy midwife described in *Romeo and Juliet*. The Elfin Queen was no longer the same creature who ravished "the bonniest knight" Tam-a-lane, no longer the Lady of the Lake who befriended King Arthur. She was no longer even of the same stature as mortals. Instead, she comes

> In shape no bigger than an agot stone
> On the fore finger of an alderman,
> Drawn with a team of little atomi
> Over men's noses as they lie asleep.

She became the vain, silly Queen Mab of *Nimphidia*, who

dwells in a palace in the air with its walls of spider's legs,

> The windowes of the eyes of Cats,
> And for the roofe, instead of Slats,
> Is cover'd with the skinns of batts,
> With Mooneshine that are guilded.

She became merely a pixie who flits about the roses and joined "that long line of flower-fairies and fluttering sprites with antennae" that J.R.R. Tolkien "so disliked as a child, and which my children in their turn detested."[9]

Tom Thumb belongs to this tradition. He is the perfect hero for this decadent world of faerie. While the ancient heroes were conceived in the union of gods and mortals, this new protagonist, the child of a miller and his wife, arrived under a pixie spell. The detailed description of his miraculous birth shows more influence of the whimsical than of the divine. Tom Thumb is a perfect godson for Queen Mab. He rides in a coach "made of halfe a Walnut-shell, the wheeles were made of foure button-mouldes, and foure blew flesh-flyes drewe it"; it is of the same make as Mab's hazel-nut chariot, as described in *Romeo and Juliet*:

> Her wagon spokes made of long spinners' legs;
> Her cover, of the wings of grasshoppers;
> Her traces, of the smallest spider's web.

His princely raiment,

> a Hat made of an Oken Leafe, with one feather of a Titti-mouse tayle sticking in the same for a plume: his Band and Shirt being both sowed together, was made of a Spiders Cobweb . . . : his cloth for his Doublet and Hose, the tenth part of a dramme of Thistledowne weaued together: his Stockings the outward Rinde of a greene Apple: his Garters two little hayres pulled from his Mothers eyebrowes: as for his Shooes and Bootes, they were made of a mouses skin, tan'd into Leather. . . .

is as fine as that worn into battle by Lord Pigwiggen in

PREFACE

Nimphidia: a coat of mail of a fish's scales, his rapier a hornet's sting, his shield a small cockleshell, his helmet a beetle's head with a horse's hair as a plume. Tom Thumb was a fitting hero of an Elizabethan fairy tale.

Although he entertained and feasted with kings, Tom Thumb remained a domestic spirit, a favorite of the lower classes with their legends of the hearth and field. They had kept his legend alive, as explained in a verse version of his story,

> Whose fame still liues in England here,
>   Amongst the countrey sort;
> Of whom our wives and children small
>   Tell tales of pleasant sport.

The ancient heroes of the Celts were still remembered in the countryside at the time of the chapbook, even if they had shrunk to the size of a miller's thumb.

This diminutiveness has endeared Tom Thumb to children. In Johnson's time, as he admits in his introduction, Tom Thumb's history was "the onely Story that (at noone dayes) may in time become the awaker of sleepy Youth." It may have been the most universal nursery tale of the period, and by the eighteenth century Tom Thumb was the undisputed champion of an Englishman's childhood. "It is needless to mention the popularity of the following story," Joseph Ritson wrote of Tom Thumb's history in *Pieces of Popular Poetry* (1791). "Every city, town, village, shop, stall, man, woman, and child, in the kingdom, can bear witness to it." His name became a common pseudonym for authors of juvenile literature, whether they composed books of games (*Tom Thumb's Folio*, 1768) or of reading instruction (*Tom Thumb's Play-Book*, 1755). Not surprisingly, the earliest known collection of English nursery rhymes was not the melodies of Mother Goose (that great lady immortalized in French literature) but rather *Tommy Thumb's Pretty Song Book* (1744). The tale's popularity increased when it was turned into a metrical version, *Tom Thumbe, His Life and*

Death: Wherein is declared many Maruailous Acts of Manhood, full of wonder, and strange merriments: which little Knight liued in King Arthurs time, and famous in the Court of Great Brittaine, published in 1630;[10] and as early as 1687, Tom's fame spread across the Atlantic. He quickly made his appearance on the stage as well: Henry Fielding's satirical *Tom Thumb* (later *The Tragedy of Tragedies*, 1731) was produced in London in 1730, and eventually Tom's story became an annual event as one of the popular Christmas pantomime harlequinades.[11]

By the early nineteenth century, when the suitability of all fairy tales for children was questioned, Tom Thumb had undergone a transformation. The protest against such literature grew so great that many children subjected to Victorian progressive education became Gradgrinds (described by Dickens in *Hard Times*, 1854), who never "associated a cow in the field with that famous cow . . . who swallowed Tom Thumb: [they] had never heard of those celebrities, and had only been introduced to a cow as a graminivorous ruminating quadruped with several stomachs." Even if such a child were given a copy of *Tom Thumb* (available in many editions as a toybook), he would likely not find the episode described by Dickens: in many versions, the cow no longer swallowed the boy; he was now saved by his mother before the mistake could occur. The metrical version had already somewhat cleaned up the story, and it is probable this version and not the earlier chapbook was the source of these late editions; but further liberties were taken in Victorian retellings of the old tale. The giants were generally dropped, perhaps because they were too similar to those in *Jack the Giant-Killer*; and a new ending explaining Tom Thumb's death replaced that of the metrical version. According to one toybook, Tom was out hunting one day on his steed, a mouse, when it was attacked by a cat. Tom tried to fight off the beast, but it killed the rodent, and threatened him. Alighting on a butterfly, he made his escape to a wall outside King Arthur's castle, but on dismounting, he was caught in a web and killed by a spider. The court grieved for him, and built a tomb to honor the small champion, with an epitaph:

> Here lies Sir Thomas Thumb, a knight,
> Who died by a cruel spider's bite.

This version survived into the twentieth century, notably in the adaptions illustrated by W. W. Denslow and L. Leslie Brooke.

Certainly the Victorians would have been taken aback if they had read the unexpurgated chapbook. Evidently parents were more liberal (or lax) in the less genteel seventeenth and eighteenth centuries about what literature should be consumed by the young. For example, Mary Cooper unblushingly included in the second volume of her *Tommy Thumb's Pretty Song Book* such a crude verse for children as

> Piss a Bed,
> Piss a Bed,
> Barley Butt,
> Your Bum is so heavy
> You can't get up.[12]

Adults of this period apparently thought nothing of giving their young unexpurgated editions of such popular literature as *Gulliver's Travels* (1724), with its many references to bodily functions.

The History of Tom Thumbe does share with the Swift classic numerous scatological jokes; the humor in both books is in part Rabelaisian. Both Gargantua's boast that "I can drowne a whole Towne with my pisse" and Gulliver's injudicious ability to "extinguish the fire, by discharge of urine in her Majesty's apartment . . . [which] might, at another time, raise an inundation by the same means, to drown the whole palace" likely came from the French Gargantua's actual drowning of 260,418 people, not counting women and children, by the same means.

Gulliver among the Lilliputians perhaps does owe something to Johnson's chapbook. Tom's interview with the giant is reminiscent of Gulliver's meeting with the Emperor of Lilliput. Although the sizes are reversed (Gulliver being a giant, Tom the size of a Lilliputian), the hero on going out for fresh air by chance comes upon the other character on horseback. Gargantua's announcement that "I can eate more then a hundred, I can drinke more than a hundred" is echoed in Gulliver's consumption of Lilliputian food and drink: "Twenty of them were filled with meat, and ten with liquor; each of the former afforded me two or three good mouthfuls, and I emptied the liquor of ten vessels . . . into one vehicle, drinking it off at a draught."

It is, however, among the Brobdingnagians (where Gulliver like Tom Thumb can be picked up by a farmer "by the middle between his forefinger and thumb") that the Swift classic most resembles the chapbook. "A Voyage to Brobdingnag" follows the same course as the life of Tom Thumb: the hero's origins in a farmer's household and his inevitable acceptance at a royal court. Gulliver among this race of giants soon learns, like Tom Thumb, the dangers of being so small; he is likewise threatened by birds and other animals, and falls into a large bowl of cream as easily as Tom fell into his mother's pudding. Both recognize the hazards of the dunghill for one so tiny. Gulliver's ride with an eagle echoes Tom's journey with a raven. Both, as members of a great court, quickly discover that the fair ladies do not appear so lovely from their angle: Gulliver is offended by the ladies' smell and the state of their complexions; Tom falls into a swoon after one maid's particularly prodigious blowing of her nose. Gulliver in his breeches made from a mouse's skin even resembles Tom Thumb; the philosophers of Brobdingnag suspect him to be "an embryo, or abortive birth" echoing Tom's origin. Each is favored by his court with the gift of a gold finger-ring, which Tom wears as a girdle, Gulliver as a collar. It seems impossible not to conclude after reading these two stories that Jonathan Swift must have had something of the history of Tom Thumb, King Arthur's dwarf, in mind

PREFACE

when he penned the voyages of Lemuel Gulliver.

From Thumbelina to the Borrowers, Tom Thumb has undoubtedly affected the diminutive heroes of juvenile literature. Yet the original chapbook remains a marvellous antique, a curiosity in the history of children's books. Its composition is fragmentary, with only a few spots of brilliance among its many (perhaps too many) diverting episodes.[13] It lacks motivation beyond the inclusion of everything its author knew about the character from folklore and popular literature. The narrative falls apart dismally towards the end with the introduction of the magic gifts (which are never fully exploited) and in the knight's unnecessary visits to King Twaddle and Gargantua. This book is not even the whole story, as Johnson concludes the fragment: "So ending this first part of our ancient story of Sir Thomas Thumbe: where if it like the Reader, the second shall be followed with tales of some marvell, by the Author hereof." No copy of this second part has survived, if indeed it was written by "R.I." More sustained in tone is the Grimm "Daumesdick" which now seems more appropriate for children. In trying to entertain bachelor and maid, shepherd and plowboy, Johnson through his base jokes has lost the interest of sleepy youth.

The History of Tom Thumbe has returned to the adult, to the scholar and student of the antiquities of juvenile reading. The present edition reproduces the earliest known printing from a unique copy in the Pierpont Morgan Library of New York. Certainly this was not the first appearance of this chapbook; the wear of the plates, both text and cover, suggests that it, like most such pamphlets, had already been often reprinted by 1621. In its pages one may once again find the crude but fascinating beginnings of a unique literature for children.

Michael Patrick Hearn

PREFACE

MICHAEL PATRICK HEARN is the author of The Annotated Wizard of Oz *and* The Annotated Christmas Carol *and is currently completing a history of children's book illustration.*

Notes

1. Rousseau, however, characterized this instruction as a "dangerous method." In *Emile*, he called reading "the curse of childhood"; he advised the withholding of all books (with the possible exception of *Robinson Crusoe*) from children until they reached puberty.

2. In his introduction, the author of the Tom Thumb chapbook refers to the most popular of these stories, Robin Hood, Guy of Warwicke, Adam Bell, and others.

3. See Joseph Ritson's essay on Pygmies in *Fairy Tales, now first collected* (London 1831).

4. It has been argued that Johnson was inconsistent in first stating in his introduction that he would not mention "Garragantua that monster of men" and then introducing him later in the body of the narrative. Johnson, however, is likely referring to a particular story of the giant (probably a portion of the Rabelais work) then current in the chapbooks, which did not relate to his history of Tom Thumb.

5. The second title actually begins "Long before King Arthur and the Knights of the Round Table," but the effect of this introduction is the same as that of the other English tales.

6. Johnson does explain that it was a time when "an vngarded Plowman might come vncontrolled to a Royal Princes presence, and in those dayes the Country Husbandman was of the Kings Counsell," so it does not seem so odd that Merlin would bother with a lowly farmer's complaint. But this weak justification seems merely an excuse to add Arthur and his court to an originally non-Arthurian story. By the nineteenth century, the farmer is no longer given such

privileges; the miller's wife has no place at the court, and to avoid embarrassment when returning her son to the nobles, she blows him over the castle wall.

7. One is reminded of the lament of Richard Corbet (d. 1635): "Farewell rewards and fairies!" He writes in his poem:

> But, since of late Elizabeth,
>   And later Iames, came in,
> They never daunc'd on any heath,
>   As when the Time hath bin. . . .
>
> But now, alas, they all are dead,
>   Or gone beyond the Seas,
> Or Farther for Religion fled,
>   Or elce they take theyre Ease.

8. With one supreme exception: Edmund Spenser's *Faerie Queene*. Spenser, however, was writing in an archaic tradition; his poem during its own time was as old-fashioned in its way as were the romances read by Don Quixote.

9. "On Fairy Stories," *Tree and Leaf* (Boston: Houghton Mifflin, 1965).

10. This retelling of the chapbook follows closely the 1621 edition; it does, however, replace most of the latter portion of the story, before the gifts of the fairy queen, with a description of Tom Thumb's final sickness and death:

> Now at these sports he toyld himselfe
>   That he a sicknesse tooke,
> Through which all manly exercise
>   He carelessly forsooke.
>
> Where lying on his bed sore sicke,
>   King Arthurs doctor came,
> With cunning skill, by physicks art,
>   To ease and cure the same.
>
> His body being so slender small,
>   This cunning doctor tooke
> A fine prospective glasse, with which
>   He did in secret looke

Into his sickened body downe,
  And therein saw that Death
Stood ready in his wasted guts
  To sease his vitall breath.

His armes and leggs consum'd as small
  As was a spiders web,
Through which his dying houre grew on,
  For all his limbes grew dead.

His face no bigger than an ants,
  Which hardly could be seene:
The losse of which renowned knight
  Much grieu'd the king and queene.

And so with peace and quietnesse
  He left this earth below;
And vp into the Fayry Land
  His ghost did fading goe.

Whereas the Fayry Queene receiu'd,
  With heauy mourning cheere,
The body of this valiant knight,
  Whom she esteem'd so deere.

For with her dancing nymphes in greene,
  She fetcht him from his bed,
With musicke and sweet melody,
  So soone as life was fled.

From whom King Arthur and his Knights
  Full forty daies did mourne;
And, in remembrance of his name
  That was so strangely borne,

He built a tomb of marble gray,
  And yeare by yeare did come
To celebrate the mournefull day,
  And buriall of Tom Thum.

Johnson probably intended to relate the circumstances of Tom's death in part two of the history, but no copies of this second chapbook are known to exist. Although records of "The first and 2. parte of Tom Thombe" survive from 1620, the author of the metrical version was likely unfamiliar with this second part (if it ever did exist); the description of the death and burial of Tom Thumb probably originates from the 1630 version. By the Victorian era, Tom had a new cause of death, a spider's bite, perhaps inspired by the earlier author's simile of the hero's stricken limbs "as small as was a spider's web."

11. Fielding was not the only eighteenth-century author who treated this nursery tale irreverently; William Wagstaff's *A Comment upon the History of Tom Thumb* (1711) was a parody of Addison's praise of the old ballad "Chevy Chase." The popularity of Tom Thumb in England was matched in France by that of "Le Petit Poucet" (translated as both "Hop O' My Thumb" and "Tom Thumb") in Charles Perrault's *Histoires ou contes du temps passé* (1697). This later tale shares little with the English story beyond the child's strange birth, described in the first paragraph, and the ogre's cry like the giant's, "I smell fresh meat."

12. This sort of name-calling survives to the present in such common rhymes as

> Fatty, Fatty,
> Two by Four,
> Couldn't get through the bathroom door;
> So he/she did it on the floor,
> Licked it up and did some more.

Most anthologists of "authentic" nursery rhymes prefer to suppress such offensive verses; they choose to ignore the cruelties and crudities of juvenile popular lore.

13. The author on his title page appropriately terms them "many strange and wonderful accidents," which (perhaps unconsciously) reflects on the narrative's composition.

NOTABLE EDITIONS OF *TOM THUMB*

The History of Tom Thumbe, the Little, for his small stature surnamed, King Arthurs Dwarfe. London 1621.

Tom Thumbe, His Life and Death. London 1630. A chapbook rendering in verse.

Tom Thumb's Folio; or, A New Penny Play-thing, for little Giants. London 1768.

The Life, Death and Renovation of Tom Thumb. London 1785. A "legendary burletta."

Wills, Hal. *Thom Thumb.* Illustrated by "Alfred Crowquill" (A. H. Forrester). London 1844.

The Metrical History of Tom Thumb the Little, as issued early in the eighteenth century. Edited by J. O. Halliwell. London 1860.

Blanchard, Edward. *Tom Thumb the Great; or, Harlequin King Arthur and the Knights of the Round Table.* London 1871.

Denslow, W. W. *Denslow's Tom Thumb.* New York 1903.

Brooke, L. Leslie. *Tom Thumb.* London and New York 1904.

The History of Tom Thumb. Illustrated by Hilda Scott. San Francisco 1934.

The History of *Tom Thumbe*, the

Little, for his small stature surnamed, *King* ARTHVRS *Dwarfe:*

Whose Life and aduentures containe many
strange and wonderfull accidents, published for
the delight of merry Time-spenders.

Imprinted at London for *Tho: Langley.* 1621.

THE
HISTORY OF
TOM THVMBE, the Little,
for his small stature, surnamed King Aʀthvʀs
Dwarfe.

M Y merry Muse begets no Tales of Guy of War-wicke, nor of bould Sir Beuis of Hampton; nor will I trouble my Penne with the pleasant glée of Robin Hood, little Iohn, the Fryer and his Marian; nor will I call to minde the lusty Pindar of Wakefield, nor those bold Yeomen of the North, Adam Bell, Clem of the Clough, nor William of Cloudefly, those ancient Archers of all England, nor shal my Story be made of the mad merry

A 2   pranckes

pranckes of Tom of Bethlem, Tom Lin-
colne, or Tom a Lin, the Diuels supposed
Bastard, nor yet of Garragantua that monster of men, but of an older Tom, a Tom
of more antiquity, a Tom of a strange making, I meane Little Tom of Wales, no
bigger then a Millers Thumbe, and therefore for his small stature, surnamed Tom
Thumbe: This is the Subiect that my Pen
meanes to make you merry with, and the
onely Story that (at noone dayes) may in
tune become the awaker of sleepy Youth,
prone to sluggishnesse: The ancient Tales
of Tom Thumbe in the olde time, haue
beene the onely reuiuers of drouzy age
at midnight; old and young haue with
his Tales chim'd Mattens till the Cocks
crew in the morning; Batchelors and
Maides with his Tales haue compassed
the Christmas fire-blocke, till the Curfew
Bell rings candle out; the old Shepheard
and the young Plow boy after their
dayes labour, haue carold out a Tale of
Tom Thumbe to make them merry with:
and who but little Tom, hath made long
nights seeme short, & heauy toyles easie?
Therefore (gentle Reader) considering
with my selfe, that old modest mirth is
turnd

turnd naked out of doores, while nimble
wit in the great Hall sits vpon a soft
cushion giuing dry bobbes; for which cause
I will, if I can, new cloath him in his former liuerp, and bring him againe into the
Chimney Corner, where now you must
imagine me to sit by a good fire, amongst
a company of good fellowes ouer a well
spic'd Wassel-bowle of Christmas Aie,
telling of these merry Tales which hereafter follow.

Of the birth and Parentage of *Tom Thumbe*,
    with his description and bigneffe.

IN the old time, when King Arthur ruled
this Land, the World was in a better
frame then it is now : for then old plain-
neffe and ciuill society were companions
for all companies : then, an vngarded
Plowman might come vncontroled to a
Royal Princes prefence, and in those
dayes the Countrey Husbandman was
of the kings Counfell, and in his ruffet
Coate gaue as found iudgement, as doe
now many of our embroydred vpstarts in
their robes of Tiffue : for as then (in
                    A 3   this

this Land) learning was geason, and the chiefest discipline in the world was Martiall actiuitie.

Amongst many others of the Kings Councell, that attended in Court, there was a plaine Plowman, as then, called old Thomas of the Mountaine, which was the Kings owne Husbandman; for, as then, Princes maintained Shepheards, Neat-heards, Ploughmen, and such like, to keepe their Cattel, & till their grounds, with like busines of houshold Husbandry. This Thomas of the Mountaine, being a man well growne in yeares, long married, hauing a wife (as he thought) sufficient to bring children; but not blessed with that wished happinesse, often complayned to her in this manner: saying, Oh Wife (quoth he) happy were I, if blessed with one Child: one Child though it were no bigger then my thumb, would make me happy: a child, of the very bignes of my thumb would bring me the greatest content in the world: Therfore would I haue thee (my deare wife) go to the Prophet Merlin, and of him learne the cause of thy barrennesse, and our wants in hauing children; he is a man, rather a diuell or spirit,

rit, cunning in all Arts and Profeſsions,
all ſciences, ſecrets and diſcoueries, a con-
iurer, an inchanter, a charmer, hee con-
ſorts with Clues and Fayries, a Com-
maunder of Goblins, and a worker of
Night-wonders: hee can ſhew the ſecrets
of Nature, calculate childrens Birthes,
and no doubt, but diſcouer the cauſe of thy
barrenneſſe, and bee a meanes to procreate
vs children: Away, and of him procure
this good bleſſing of a child, be hee no bigger then my very Thumbe.

These reaſons, and perſwaſions of olde
Thomas, ſo encouraged and whetted on
this longing woman his wife, that vp ſhe
got the next morning betime, and by the
Sunnes riſe, came to the Caue of old Merlin, which was the hollow trunke of a
blaſted Oke, all euer growne with withered moſſe, (for other houſe had hee none)
whom ſhee found, as it were mumbling
ſpels of incantation, making Characters
in ſand, with an Ebone ſtaffe, to the great
wonder of this poore affrighted Woman;
who to ſatiſfie her Huſbands deſire, deliuered the ful effect of her buſineſſe and com-
ming. To whom Merlin with a graue and
ſolid countenance ſaid as followeth:

Ere

The History

Ere thrice the Moone her brightnes change,
A shapelesse child by wonder strange,
Shall come abortiue from thy wombe,
No bigger then thy Husbands Thumbe :
And as desire hath him begot,
He shall haue life, but substance not ;
No blood, nor bones in him shall grow,
Not seene, but when he pleaseth so :
His shapelesse shadow shall be such,
You'l heare him speake, but not him touch :
And till the World to ending come,
There shall be Tales told of *Tom Thumbe*.

This Ænygma, or mysticall Riddle, no
sooner deliuered, but home goes the merry old Wench to her husband, and tels of
her good successe, and of the Oracle thus
reuealed, how that within three moneths
space Merlin had promised her a litle sonne:
against which time, the father not a little
glad thereof, prouided all things fitting,
for such a purpose, so that no necessaries
were wanting against his wiues lying in :
but such a Child-bed lying in was neuer
seene nor heard of : for thither came the
Queene of Fayres to bee her Midwife,
with her attendance the Elues and Dry-
ades, with such like midnight dancing
                    shaddowes,

ſhadowes, who gaue moſt diligent aſſi-
ſtance, at that painfull houre of this wo-
mans deliuerie. The child thus borne by
the help of this midnights Midwife, the
Queene of Fayres, had at the firſt minute
it tooke life, the full and largeſt bignes
that euer it grew to : which was (as his
Father wiſhed) the bigneſſe of his
Thumbe ; and therefore named Tom
Thumbe, who neuer ſeemed older, nor
yonger; bigger,nor ſmaller; ſtronger, nor
weaker: but as he was at the firſt houre
of his birth, ſo continued hee to the laſt
minute of his life.

Of *Tom Thumbs* apparell, and of the ſports
he vſed amongſt other Children.

TOM Thumbe, being thus by miracle
begot & borne, in leſſe then foure minutes grew to be a little man . againſt
which time the Queene of Fayres, his
kind Midwife, & god Godmother, prouided him a very artificiall ſute of apparell. Firſt,a Hat made of an Oken Leafe,
with one feather of a Tittimouſe tayle
ſticking in the ſame for a plume : his Band
and

and Shirt being both sowed together, was
made of a Spiders Cobweb, only for light-
nesse and soft wearing for his body: his
cloth for his Doublet and Hose, the tenth
part of a dramme of Thistle-downe wea-
ued together: his Stockings the outward
kinde of a greene Apple: his Garters two
little hayres pulled from his Mothers eye-
browes: as for his Shooes and Bootes,
they were made of a mouses skin, tan'd into Leather: the largenesse wherof was
sufficiet to make him twelue payre of
Bootes, & as many Shooes and Pantofles.
Thus furnisht forth like a proper young
Gallant, hee aduentured foorth (though
with great danger of the windes blowing
him away) into the streets, amongst other
childzen to play for Pins, Points, Coun-
ters, and such like, but seldome played hee
bankerupt: for like an inuisible knight, he
would at his pleasure (vnseene) diue into
his play-fellows pockets: where (before)
hauing lost, would there againe renew his
stock, and now and then, when hee pleased,
would he creep into their least cherrybags,
and Pin-boxes. But on a time, it so hapned, that for these his nimble flights of actiuitie, he was most grieuously punished,

and

and impriſoned : for one of his play-fel-
lowes kept him faſt pind vp in his pinboxe
the whole time of ſchooling, without either
meate, drinke, ayre, or light though indeed
he could haue faſted for euer without foode
or ſuſtenance, a gift that his God-mother
the Queene of Fayries had giuen him at
the houre of his birth: yet for all this, Tom
Thumbe, hauing a deſperate little ſpirit,
like to his ſmall bigneſſe, purpoſed to quit-
tance theſe his former iniuries done by his
craftie companions ; for indeed many of
them had ſerued him ſo.

How by art *Tom Thumbe* hung black Pots
and Glaſſes on the beames of the Sunne,
as vpon a line or cord : and of the
ſucceſſe.

TOM Thumb, remembring his former
impriſonment in his companions pin-
boxes, and Cherry-bags, beate ſo together
his nimble braines, that he deuiſed a pretty
reuenge: It ſo fell out, as his playfellowes
acquaintance were playing together, hee
got ſome of his mothers blacke Pots and
Glaſſes, and moſt artificially hangd them
vpon

a Sunne-beame, that shone in at the
Schoole-house window, at a little creuice,
that made it seeme like a small straight
line or cord, vpon which hee orderly, to
the others imaginations, hung vp his
Pots and Glasses all on a row. Which
pretty trick when the rest saw, they likewise got of their mothers Pots & glasses,
and in proffering to doe the like, they broke
them all in pieces : for which doings, they
had not onely the mockage of Tom, but
thereby wonne to themselues euery one a
sound breeching : and euer after that, to
their more disgrace, there was a time
made amongst the Schoole-boyes, as hereafter followeth.

If thou wilt from whipping,
   keepe safely thy bum,
Take heed of the pasti nes,
   here taught by *Tom Thumbe* :
Young Schollers are knauish
   and apter to learne
A tricke that's vnhappy,
   then good to discerne.

How

How *Tom Thumbe* fell into his Mothers puḍ
ding Boᵗle : and of the firſt originall
of thoſe Puddings now called *Tom
Thumbs.*

TOm Thumbe for theſe aforeſaid merry trickes, was denied the fellowſhip
of his Schoole-fellowes and companions,
which made him with great griefe ſtay at
home in his fathers houſe, and to be gouer-
ned onely by his mothers direction. But it
ſo fell out, that about Chriſtmas time, his
father had killed a Hogge, and his mother
was to make Puddings. And hauing all
things ready: as Blood, Oatemeale, Suet
Salt and Spice all mingled, and well ſea-
ſoned together in a greate Bowle of wood;
vpon the ſide whereof, Tom was to ſit (in
ſtead of a Candleſticke) to hold the Candle, and giue her light, which he did ſo mannerly, as if hee had bin brought vp a Candle holder. But now marke the euent: ey-
ther Tom fell aſleepe, or elſe being a little
to nimble, or of to light a timberd body,
that of a ſuddaine hee tipt and fell into the
Pudding batter, quite ouer head and eares
Candle and all, the which his mother ſpy-
ing,

ing, made haſt with all ſpeed to recouer
him, but there ſhee found the Candle but
not her Sonne: for whome after ſhe had
ſearched a long time, and not finding him,
ſuppoſed him to be drowned: with griefe
ſhe ouerpaſſed her loſſe in a ſhort time, (I
might ſay a minutes ſpace) eſpecially con-
ſidering him to be a child (for his little-
neſſe,) more diſgraceful, then comfortable.
So falling againe to her buſineſſe, ſhee
tooke vp her ſmall Sonne, and in ſtead of a
piece of fat put him at vnawares into one
of her Puddings, which was of the largeſt
ſize: the which, with many others, ſhe
caſt into a kettle then boyling ouer the fire.
But now Tom feeling the ſcalding liquor,
and being in the middle of this Pudding,
made ſuch a rumbling and tumbling vp
and downe the Kettle, that all the reſt flew
ouer into the fire, chooſing rather to be
roaſted, then ſodden: Some without ſkins,
ſome without faſhion, ſome brok in pieces,
ſome halfe ſod, ſome oneway, ſome another
as if the Diuell and old Merlin had beene
amongſt them.

This accident, or rather hurlyburly, a-
mongſt Toms mothers puddings, made
her thinke that they were either bewitcht
or

or foze-fpoke by fome vnlucky tongue.
Whereupon, at that very inftant time,
comes to the doore, a fturdy beging Tinker, and afked an almes foz good Saint
Iohnsfake: which the Old Woman hearing, (eperceuiugthe vnrulines of thatpud-
ding in the Kettle)runs to the fame, and
gaue it to the Tinker: who being there-
with well pleafed, into his budget he puts
it, and hyes him away as faft as his legs
can beare him. But farre had he not gone,
but the Pudding beganne to rumble and
tumble in the Tinkers budget, as it had
done befoze in the Pudding Kettle: which
fo affrighted the pooze Tinker,that in going ouer a ftile, hee farted foz very feare.
Marry gip,good man Tinker, quoth Tom
Thumbe ; are you farting ripe with a wan-
nion ? hereupon the tinker (as he thought)
hearing the Diuell at his backe, threw
downe budget, Pudding, tooles and all,
and ran away as faft as his legges could
beare him, not once looking backe, till hee
was out of all the hearing of Tom Thumb,
oz the fight of his budget.

The Tinker being thus gone, and Tom
Thumbe freed from his greafie Leather
impzifonment, hee eate himfelfe at liber-

tie

fle from his blacke bondage, and returned
home againe to his mother house : where
afterwards he told what had hapned, and
how he was carryed away bound vp in the
Puddings belly ; which happy escape and
aduenture not a little reioyced his old Father, and Mother, betwixt whom, and a-
mongst many others, there arose a name &
title, belonging to al puddings of the like
roundnesse and thicknesse, and to be called
Tom Thumbes : Which name to the honour of all Puddings, continues to this
day.

How his mothers Red Cow, at one bit ate
vp *Tom Thumbe*, as he sate vnder
a Thistle.

THese fearefull dangers before rehear-
sed, being thus happily ouerpassed,
durst not by his mother of a long time bee
suffered to depart out of her presence, but
either she lockt him in her Cupbord for
feare of losing him, or else tyed him to a
Brickbat with a Packthrid, doubting the
wind should blow him away : or else kept
him in her pocket for his more securitie:
But

But yet for all this, another mischance befell him. For one a time, as his mother
went a milking, Tom had a great desire to
goe with her, and to see that kinde of wo-
manly housewifery: Whereupon, she toke
vp her Sonne and put him into her empty
Milke-payle, and so bore him to the fielde:
where being come, and the day very cold,
shee set him downe vnder a Thistle for a
shelter to keepe him warme, and so goes a
milking of her Kine : but before shee had
dispatched halfe her businesse, there comes
a Red Cow, and at one bit eates vp this
litle man, her Sonne, Thistle and all: But
whether it was for cowardlinesse or valor
to sit still, I knowe not, but poore Tom was
eaten vp at one mouthfull, where without
chewing he went as easily downe into the
Cowes belly, as if he had bene made of a
docke leafe. But now all this while his mother not missing him, but still milked on till
her payle grew full, & then being ready to
goe home, she loked for her sonne Thomas,
where she neither found him nor the thistle
where she left him. Whereupon she went
vp and downe calling for Tom, but no Tom
was heard of. At last with great earnestnes
(being much affrighted with this losse,)

she

she went crying amongst her kine, where
art thou Tom ? Where art thou , Tom ?
Here, Mother (quoth he) in the Red
Cowes belly : in the Red Cowes belly,
mother still cryed he, vntill such time as
she perceiued his place of abiding , where
(no doubt) but Tom was in a pitifull taking, but the poore Cow in a farre worse,
hauing such a nimble timberd fellow dancing Trench-more in her belly. But to
conclude , the poore beast could not be deliuered of her troublesome burthen , till a
laxatiue drinke cast into her belley , had
turned him out in a Cowturd. Who all
besmeared as he was, went home with his
mother to be made cleane. This was another of Tom Thumbes most dangerous aduentures, which he most happily escaped.

How *Tom Tumbe* , in stead of a wheat corne,
was carried away in a Rauens
mouth.

Another time Tom Thumbe, being de-
sirous to helpe his Father driue the
plowe,and in seedes-time to see the manner
of his sowing wheate, the which the olde
man

man agreed to, and taking his litle sonne
vp, he put him into his pocket, and being
come to the field where his land lay, he set
Tom in one of his horses eares, and so
droue all the rest round about the Land, as
if hee had gone by their sides, so propper, so
fine, and so nimble a light fellow was this
Tom Thumbe, that the horses eare serued
for a shelter to keepe him from raine and
foule weather, and likewise preserued him
as well from drowning in a beasts foote-
step, as from the windes blowing him a-
way, and many times from loosing himselfe
in Chaffe and Prouender, where surely he
had beene eaten vp amongst horses : but
yet for all these great cares thus taken by
his Father, another most strange and dangerous euent behappened him, for as his
father went a sowing wheat vp and down
the land, Tom Thumbe was appointed to
scarre away Crowes, who with a cudgell
made of a Barley straw, for that purpose,
stood most manfully in the middle of the
land, crying, Shoe, shoe, Crow, shoe ; but
amongst the rest, there came a huge blacke
Rauen, that instead of a wheate corne, carried poore Tom quite away, where he was
not of a long time heard of, either by Father,

ther or Mother : which great losse of this
their little Son they long time afterward
mourned for, with many a sad and heauy
lamentation, spending whole dayes and
weekes, and weary iourneys in seeking him
vp and downe, but all in vaine ; there was
not a Crowes nest in a whole countrey but
they searched, nor a Church steeple within
ten miles, nor a Pidgeon hole but they looked into, nor a Counterpit amongst boyes,
nor hardly a cherrypit was forgotten : but
all lost labour, Tom was not to be found,
but vtterly lost and gone for euer, without
al hope of recouery to be got againe; whose
want (as I said before) bred in his old Parents hearts most heauy and long lamentations : where wee will leaue them now
mourning, and tell of their lost litle sonnes
succeeding fortunes and aduentures.

How *Tom Thumbe* fell in at a Chimney
top, and what happened to
him there.

TOm Thumbe, being thus taken vp by
a rauen (as you heard) in steed of a
graine of wheat, was carried in her beake

curr

ouer a great forreſt, where in all the way of
this her long flight,   Tom Thumbe did nothing but cry, Shough,   shough Crowe,
shough, in this maner affrighting the poxe
Rauen in her flight, that ſhe durſt neither
ſwallow him downe her maw, nor let him
fall out of her beake, vntill ſuch time, as
what with faintneſſe in flying, or almoſt
ſtarued with hunger , being quite tyred
with this her heauy burthen and long iourney, ſhe was conſtrained to reſt on the top
of an olde Caſtle wall moted round about
with an exceeding deepe riuer, which belonged to an ancient and neuer conquered Giant, that onely there inhabited without a-
ny other company: This Rauen (as I ſaid)
reſting on the top of the Caſtle, and being
ouerwearied, Tom Thumbe with a nimble
ſkip ſuddenly eſcaped both from her beake
and tallons, and with much lightneſſe leapt
vp to the top of the Caſtle chimney, where
being ſet, and looking downe, he eſpied the
Gyant ſitting by his fire, boyling, broyling
and roaſting the ioynts & quarters of men,
deuouring them all one after another, legs
armes & heads bit by bit till they were all
eaten vp at laſt: which fearful ſight ſo amazed Tom Thumbe, that he knew not what to

dee, no2 tell how to get away; to escape
was impossible : fo2 the Castle wall was
too high fo2 him to get downe, and the
riuer too deepe fo2 such a little fellowe to
wade ouer : so, being in these fearefull
and dangerous doubts, of a sodaine came
a puffe of winde, and blew poo2e Tom
downe into the Gyants Chimney, where
he grew almost besides his wits, to see
himselfe by the fire side : whom when the
Gyant saw thinking him to be some Fairy,o2 a spirit come thither by miracle, ran
with an eager fury to catch him ; but so
nimble and quicke was this little fellowe,
that the Gyant had no feeling of him, fo2
when he caught him in his hand, hee slipt
out betweene his fingers, and being in his
armes,he crept out betweene his elbowes;
so that neither strength no2 policy could
take him. Thus fo2 that time escaped
little Tom, where fo2 his mo2e securitie,
he crept into a mouse-hole, and there safely fo2 that night slept hee freely from the
Gyants intended cruelty.

How *Tom Thumbe* became the Gyants man,
and what happened to him in
that seruice

Tom Thumbe being thus safe in lodging, (I meane in the Mouse hole)
put the Gyant in a great wonder, maruelling what was become of him, for
which cause hee went supperlesse to bed,
but could not sleepe all that night following for thinking of Tom Thumbe, which he
deemed to bee some strange creature, in
that he had so nimbly escaped his clutches:
therefore in the middle of the night, hee
rose vp and tooke his clubbe, (which was
the whole arme of an Oke) and went vp
and downe the Castle in the darke, (for
light had he none) crying with a roaring
voyce, in this maner following,

Now fi, fee, fau, fan,
I feele smell of a dangerous man:
Be he aliue, or be he dead,
Ile grind his bones to make me bread.

These fearefull speeches, thus thundred
out by this Gyant, put poore Tom into a

pit

pittifull taking not knowing what to doe,
nor how to behaue himselfe; yet at last con-
sidered, it was but misery to be thus impri-
soned in this litle closet of darknesse, and
thought it better (then to lye there) to aduenture foorth and submit himselfe to the
Gyants mercy, which most willingly he accepted of, and employed this his new litle
man, about his houshold businesse: whereupon Tom became very diligent & seruice-
able: for the Gyant had no other Cat to
catch Mise and Rats, but Tom; no other
browne to sweepe cobwebs from any corner
of his house but Tom, no other key to open
his lockes, but Tom; so Tom was very fitting and nimble for any businesse whatsoe-
uer. But now marke the euent: the Gyant
on a time had a litle roastmeat to be laid to
the fire, & Tom must be the turn-spit: whereupon, sitting in the Chimney-corner vpon a
litle chip of wood to turne the spit, holding
a spoone before him to keepe the heate from
his face, (for indeede the spoone couered his
whole body) the Gyant now thinking to
take Tom at the aduantage, and to know
whether hee was a humane creature, or a
spirit, of a sudden catched at Tom, purpo-
sing to grinde the poore fellowes bones and
body

body into pieces ; but Tom hauing more
then an ordinary nimblenesse in himselfe,
did, (when the Gyant tooke hold of him)
giue a skippe downe (vnchewed) into his
throat, and so into his belly, and there kept
such a rumbling and tumbling in his guts,
as if hee would haue gnawne a hole quite
thorow: it little booted the Gyant to rest in
quiet, for he thought the Diuell or his dam
had plaide at Tennis in his paunch: therefore in a fury hyed he vp to the toppe of his
Castle wall, where he disgorged his sto-
macke, and cast out his burthen, at least
thre miles into the Sea, (vpon the bankes
whereof this Castle stood) where Tom
Thumbe was most brauely entertained by
a Fishe, which swallowed him downe a-
liue, in which watry dwelling he remained, till the same Fishe was taken, and giuen for a present to king Arthurs Table,
where this noble & aduenturous little Gallant was found, and for the strangenesse of
his stature, accepted of for his Highnesse
Dwarfe, and so by this meanes Tom
Thumbe became a Courtier.

Of

Of *Tom Thumbes* behauiour in Court, and
the honours by him atchie-
ued there.

Tom Thumbe being now in Court, became a companion for Ladies and
Gentlewomen, and so braue minded that
not any in King Arthurs Palace gained
more fauours then hee did, insomuch that
the Ladies and Gentlewomen could seldome bee without him ; for his company
was so pleasing , that many times they
gaue him leaue to skippe vpon their knees,
and now and then in their pockets , with
many such like priuate places , and withall to sit vpon their pinpillowes, and play
with their pinnes, and to runne at tilt a-
gainst their bosomes with a bul-rush ; for
bigger weapon was hee not able to ma-
nage. But now marke what happened :
vpon a time King Arthur appointed a roy-
all triumph in his Court , with great reuelling and masking to be holden amongst
his Knights, where Sir Lancelot-du-Lake,
Sir Triamor, and Sir Tristram, all of the
round Table, performed many noble acts
of

of Chenalry: amongst which worthy Gallants, Tom Thumbe would not sit out, and being then in great fauour, to his vtmost skill, would approue himselfe a right Courtier; whereupon, amongst them all, in presence of the king, Queene, and others of the Nobilitie, hee requested one of the Maydes of Honour to hold foorth her hand, where, vpon the Palme thereof he daunced a most excellent Galliard, to the wonderfull and great admiration of all the beholders; for which noble performance, were many rich guifts bestowed vpon him, as well by strangers as Peeres of the Land; amongst the rest, the king himselfe gaue him a gold king from his owne finger, the which Tom Thumbe wore for a girdle, as a fauour about his middle, for it was the iust compasse of his body to hoope it in round.

How *Tom Thumbe* grew daily into more fauour with the King, and of a boone obtained of his Highnesse.

KIng Arthur seldome sate amongst his knights of the round Table, but
Tom

Tom Thumbe was in company, either a-
mongst their spangled feathers, or fitting
vpon the pommel of the Kings own chaire,
such great delight had his Highnesse in his
company, that he seldome rode abroad, but
Tom was cockered vpon his saddle-bow,
where alwaies when it rained, would he
crepe in at a button-hole of the Kings
doublet to keepe himselfe dry; where being
settled so neere his Highnesse heart, that he
continually obtained what her asked for,
and now hauing opportunity sitting to beg
a boone, and withall remembring his old father and mother, whom he had not of a long
time seene, he requested of the King to giue
him a burthen of money, no more then his
backe could carry, from his Treasury,
therewithal to relieue his father & mother
in their old dayes : which request no sooner
obtained, but away goes Tom Thumbe,
and loades himselfe with a burthen of money from the Kings Treasury, which was
in all, no more but a poore three-pence, the
whole waight that his body could carry at
one time: so trauelling two dayes and two
nights, with long labour, he gat some thirty yardes from King Arthurs Court, some
part of the way towards his Fathers
house,

house, that being all the iourney he was able to goe in fourty eight houres, bearing so huge and heauy a burthen vppon his shoulders : so from time to time, and from iourney to iourney, he came at last (though with great wearinesse) to his Fathers dore, not in all distant from King Arthurs Pallace , aboue three quarters of a mile ; whom when his Father and Mother beheld, for very ioy they swouned ; but recouering themselues , his Mother tooke him vp in her handkercher for feare of hurting his bones , and carried him into the great hall, where she set him in a Wal-nut-shell (in stead of a chaire) by a good fire to warme himselfe. Where after a litle refreshing, and much reioycing, hee deliuered vp the great masse of treasure giuen him by King Arthur , which hee had brought with such long iournies, and great paines to his father & mother. The money receiued, they got him to supper , where the cloath was laid vpon his mothers hand , & the seruice was the curnell of a hazell-nut . of which he eate but the third part, and the rest serued him sufficiently for foure meales after. yet grew he sometimes sicke by eating so much at one time.

Thus

Thus after that Tom Thumbe, with his
Father and Mother, had ryoted for cer-
taine moneths. Time called him away to
his charge in Court: but not knowing
how to get thither, by reaſon of a great
Flud that was riſen by a few Aprill drops,
hee grewe into a very great melanchol-
ly, and made moſt heavy lamentations.
Whereupon his Father hiuing a ready,
and quicke fore caſting wit, but a farre
ſtronger breath, tooke a birding trunke of
Wud, and put his ſonne Thomas therein,
and at one blaſt: blew him into King Arthurs Court: Where after this his great
iourney) hee was entertained with Tri-
umphs and much Reuelling.

Of the gifts that the Queene of Fayries gaue her god-ſonne: and of
the rare and excellent ver-
tues thereof.

TOm Thumbes renowne and honours,
growing to the full height of Fame
in this kingdome, cauſed people to come
from all parts of the Land to viſit him:
ſome with one preſent, ſome with another,
to

to bestow vpon him. Amongst the rest, his
olde Godmother the Quæne of Fayries
came for to sée him, and to witnesse what
Fame and good Fortunes had befallen
him.

But so it happened, that she found her
little God-sonne aslæpe (in the Kings
Garden) vpon the toppe of a Red Rose
new blowne. And being then iust high-
noone-tide, (her chiefest time of liberty to
worke wonders in) she stood inuisibly before him, stroaking downe the sweaty
droppes) with her vnfelt hand from his little forehead, which cast him into a most
swéete and pleasurable dreame, and withall bestowed foure of the most rarest guifts
of the world vpon him, which she left there
lying by against his awaking. First, an
inchanted Hat, the which by wearing hee
should know, what was done in all parts
of the world. A Ring likewise inchanted,
that hauing it vpon his finger, hee might
goe if hee pleased into any place vnseene,
and walke inuisible. Thirdly, a Girdle,
that by wearing it, should change him into
what shape soeuer he desired. And lastly,
a payre of shooes, (that being on his fæts)
would in a moment carry him to any part
of

of the earth, and to be any time where hée
pleaſed. Thus with a feruency of loue
bleſſed ſhee him, and departed. Whereupon Tom Thumbe awaked, as out of a golden ſlumber, & found theſe aforeſaid guifts
as his good Godmother had left him, the
which being well conſidered of, (and as it
was reuealed to him in his ſléeps) he firſt
tooke the Hat & put it vpon his head: wher-
upon he was preſently inſpired with the
knowledge of al things in the world: and at
that very inſtant knew, what was done in
K. Arthurs Court, and what the King himſelf was a doing. Next, putting on the ring,
he went as he wiſhed inuiſible, and caught
birds as they ſate in buſhes: fowles in the
ayre, & ſuch like. Then putting on the Girdle, hee wiſht himſelfe a Gyant, then a
Dwarfe, then a fiſh, then a worme, then a
man, &c. Laſtly, putting on the Shoes,
which no ſooner on his féete, but he was
carried as quicke as thought into another
world, where hee ſawe wonders, as men
without heads their faces on their breaſts,
ſome with one legge, ſome with one eye in
the forehead, ſome of one ſhape, ſome of
another: then by and by was he come backe
againe into King Arthurs Court.

How

How *Tom Thumbe* riding forth to take the
ayre, met with the great *Garagantua*,
and of the speach that was
betweene them.

TOm Thumbe on a time being weary,
crept into a Ladies pocket, and there
rested himselfe, this Lady forgetting of
her seruant Thomas, suddenly pulled forth
her handkercher, and with her handkercher Tom Thumbe : she blowing her nose
with it so frighted poore Thomas, that the
little Gentleman fell in a sound, but they
fetched him againe with the hundred part
of an Aquauity drop: yet for all their care
that they tooke hee was troubled with a
great Palsie, and none of the kings Phy-
sitions could cure him. The king grieued
to see his little Gentleman in this taking,
and for his recouery spared no cost, for he
sent for the chiefe Physition to king Twad-
dell, which was king of the Pigmies,
(which king and his subiects are but two
foote high from the ground,) this Physition being litle of body, but great of skill,
soone found out his disease and cured him.

           C   Tom

Tom Thumbe being cured rod foozth in his Coach one day to take the ayre, his Coach was made of halfe a Wal-nut-shell, the wheeles were made of foure button-mouldes, and foure blew flesh-flyes dzewe it: Riding in this maner by the Wood side he chanced to meete the great Garagantua, who was riding also to solace himselfe, his pipe being of that great bignesse, as is described in the booke of his honourable deeds, and himselfe being in height not inferiour to any streple: Tom Thumbe seeing of him, asked what he was? Garagantua answered him, that he was the onely wonder of the world, the terror of the people, and the tamer of man and beast: Stay there said Tom Thumbe, for I am to be wondzed at as much as thy selfe any waies can bee: for I am not onely feared, but also loued: I cannot onely tame men and beastes, but I also can tame thy selfe. Whereat Garagantua fell into such a laughter that the whole earth where hee stood shooke, which made Tom Thumbe in all hast to ride away, and to beate his winged steades into a false Gallop.

Garagantua seeing him in this feare desired him to stay, and they would talke familiarly

miliarly, who was the better man , and could doe the most wonders. Hereto Tom Thumbe consented , and caused his Coach to stand , and they began to dispute dia-logue maner as followeth. Dwarfe, quoth Garagantua, I can blow downe a Steeple with my breath , I can drowne a whole Towne with my pisse , I can eate more then a hundred, I drinke more then a hun-dred, I carry more then a hundred, I can kill more then a hundred: all this can I do, now tell what thou canst doe?

I can doe more then this , saide Tom Thumbe, for I can creepe into a keyhole, and see what any man or woman doe in their priuate chambers, there I see things that thou art not worthy to know . I can saile in an egge-shel, which thou canst not: I can eate lesse then a Wren , and so saue victuals : I can drinke lesse then a Spar-row, therefore I am no drunkard : I can-not kill a Rat with my strength, and there-fore am no murtherer : these qualities of mine are better then thine in all mens iudgements, and therefore great monster I am thy better.

Hereat Garagantua was madde and would with his foote haue kicked downe

the

the whole wood, and so haue buried Tom
Thumbe: Tom seeing of it, with his skill so
inchanted him that he was not able to stur,
but so stood still with one leg vp, till Tom
Thumbe was at his lodging: Hereat Garagantua was much vexed, but knew not how
to helpe himselfe.

How *Tom Thumbe* after conference had with
great *Garagantua* returned, and how he
met with King *Twadle.*

TOm Thumbe being somewhat well at
ease by taking of the fresh aire returned backe againe to the Court of King Arthur, who no sooner being come, but great
preparation was made for the entertaine-
ment of so tall a person, as that the officers of the house with all their seruants
were in a sweat to prouide for this tall Sir
Thomas Thumbe his dinner.

This entertainment being ended, K. Arthur sent for Tom Thumbe, & being come,
withdrew themselues into a priuate roome,
where Tom told King Arthur what strang
acci-

accidents befell to him in meeting of great
Garagantua, and of their conference together, as likewise of their exploits : and afterward how by his skill he enchanted him
in the wood where they met, and there left
him: whereat K. Arthur was wonderfully
amazed, hearing of the strength of that
mighty Gyant Garagantua.

Then he told K. Arthur how he met with
K. Twadle being King of the Pigmes, a
man of mighty stature in comparison of
Tom Thumbe, being not two foote high,
this stout King did he overthrow at Tilt
both horse and man : and all these things
did he performe by vertue that was in the
guifts which his godmother the Quéene
of Fairies did bestow vpon her godsonne
Tom Thumb: which was his Hat of knowledge, his Ring which made him goe inuisible, his Girdle which made him bee what
he wisht to be either man or beast, & lastly
his shoes, which being on his féet was on
a sudden in any part of the world, & in the
twinkling of an eye was in King Arthurs
Court againe.

Where wee will now leaue this little
wonderous Gentleman of all ages, with
these his most precious Reliques of ad-

C 3   mira-

The History
miration, and so ending this first part of
our ancient story of Sir Thomas Thumbe.
where if it like the Reader, the second
part shall be followed with tales
of more maruell, by the
Author hereof.

R. I.

F I N I S.

Robin Hood's Garland

Preface

Among the popular literature that has come down to us from the late Middle Ages, the Robin Hood ballads are notable for their enduring and wide appeal. Fourteenth-century allusions suggest that the merry outlaw was the hero of ballads before 1400; the cycle of stories which his name attracted was sufficiently popular for two of the first English printers to produce an "epic" composite of Robin Hood ballads called *A Lytell Geste of Robin Hode*, printed perhaps as early as 1500. By 1520 broadsides selling at a penny each kept his exploits current. Folk plays of his adventures were popular in the fifteenth century, and Renaissance dramatists produced serious plays on his downfall and death. Before the present century many major writers, among them Ben Jonson, Michael Drayton, John Dryden, John Keats, Leigh Hunt, and Alfred Lord Tennyson, in one way or another made use of the Robin Hood theme. Comic operas on Robin Hood appeared in London and New York at the end of the eighteenth century and as recently as 1912; a "dramatic equestrian spectacle" was staged in 1876. In our own time there have been Robin Hood movies, a television series, countless children's stories and plays, as well as a serious poem cycle on the theme. This latter effort, Daniel G. Hoffmann's "A Little Geste,"[1] reaffirms one of the characteristics of earlier Robin Hood stories: their appeal to adult and child alike.

Robin Hood's Garland represents an urge like that which produced the earlier *Geste*: the wish to print as many tales of the popular hero as possible. From the earliest extant edition of 1663, which contained a dozen ballads, the collection grew

1. *Sewannee Review*, 66 (1958), 633-648.

iii

to the twenty-seven reproduced here. That number remains constant in the later editions of the *Garland*.[2] To judge from the number of surviving editions, the *Garland* seems to have enjoyed remarkable popularity; it was formed by—and helped to form—the popular taste in adventure literature which nineteenth-century reformers found so deplorable.

While the Robin Hood stories have appealed to all classes of society, the lower middle class, the yeomanry and the gentry not far removed from yeomanry, found him particularly attractive. Despite attempts by Renaissance dramatists and eighteenth-century publishers to elevate him to the peerage as the Earl of Huntingdon, he remained identified with the yeomanry. These ballads repeatedly celebrate traits associated with a middle class appropriating and redefining the aristocratic values implicit in medieval romance: loyalty to the king combined with unfaltering self-respect; sentimental love and friendship; love of a good joke at the expense of the false pride of position; love of a good fight fairly fought; and a commonsense notion of right and wrong which demands sympathy for nominal lawbreakers who suffer at the hands of the powerful. The ballads go out of their way to stress that Robin Hood was a yeoman whose deportment was aristocratic; he is, as has been remarked often, the popular analogue of the courtly Gawain.

The Robin Hood ballads themselves are not individually remarkable. They lack the swift movement, the compression of incident, the telling phrase, the understated emotion of many well-known traditional ballads. They lack literary merit in part because they are entirely comic, reporting Robin's easy victories or his inconsequential defeats at the hands of friends or friends-to-be. Their matter-of-factness goes beyond understatement; they convey neither suspense nor a sense of meaningful risk. The title of the ballad reporting the hero's death is indicative: "Robin Hood and the Valiant

2. For his collection in *The English and Scottish Popular Ballads*, F. J. Child definitively edited some thirty-eight Robin Hood ballads. See volume 3, numbers 117-154.

PREFACE

Knight. Together with an Account of his Death and Burial."
Interest is entirely in simple action; there is no exploration of
the tragic emotions which we value in the great ballads.

If we are to prize the Robin Hood ballads for other than
their antiquarian value, we are likely to do so because of their
humor and because they preserve part of the lively
imaginative literature of the folk. They lack the artifices of
style, but they exhibit the virtues of story told for itself. They
preserved "useless" fiction in ages when literary fashion
distrusted fiction and required it (when countenanced at all)
to be morally and philosophically useful; and that turned out
to be of great significance. The greenwood which the
celebrated outlaw and countless unsung others like him
inhabited was from all historical accounts a brutal reality. But
the fictive green world to which these ballads have given
continuous currency is the world of liberated imagination to
which our greatest writers have turned for inspiration.

Bennett A. Brockman

*BENNETT A. BROCKMAN is an Associate Professor of
English at the University of Connecticut and the coeditor of*
Children's Literature. *He is the author of articles on
children's and medieval literature.*

Bibliography

Robin Hood's Garland, Being a complete history of all the notable and merry exploits performed by him and his men, on many occasions. To which is added a preface, giving a more full and particular account of his birth, life &c . . . adorned with twenty-seven neat and curious cuts etc. London 1789.

> British Museum cat. no. 1078. h. 3. The particularly attractive frontispiece was probably taken from an edition of the *Garland* published in London by T. Sabine in 1780, etc. A handwritten note on the reverse of the frontispiece states that "this print was taken out of another edition of Robin Hood the plates of which were the reverses to these and much more worn but did not appear ever to have been better." This 1789 edition carries the signature "I. I. Banks, 1791"; its British Museum stamp records that it was presented by Lady Banks. Its "plates" are in fact the reverses of the T. Sabine edition

Other Collections:

> Ritson, Joseph. *Robin Hood: A Collection of . . . ancient poems, songs, and ballads. . . .* London 1795, etc.

> Gutch, John M. *A Lytell Geste of Robin Hode, with other ancient and modern songs.* 2 vols. London 1847.

> Child, F. J. *The English and Scottish Popular Ballads,* vol. 3. 5 vols. Boston 1882-1888.

> Quiller-Couch, Sir A. T. *The Oxford Book of Ballads.* Oxford 1924, etc.

Robin Hood Ballad Tunes:

> Chappell, William. *A Collection of National English Airs.*

BIBLIOGRAPHY

2 vols. London 1838-1840.

Rimbault, E. F. In Gutch, vol. 2, 431-447.

Macintyre, Robert. *Ballads Ancient and Modern*. London 1929.

Sharp, Cecil. *English Folk Songs*. Selected Edition. London 1959.

Bronson, B. H. *The Traditional Tunes of the Child Ballads*. Princeton 1959.

Selected Reference:

Gable, J. Harris. *Bibliography of Robin Hood*. University of Nebraska Studies in Language, Literature, and Criticism, number 17 (1939).

Bessinger, J.B., Jr. "The Gest of Robin Hood Revisited," in Larry D. Benson, ed., *The Learned and the Lewed*. Harvard English Studies, number 5 (1974), 355-369.

This print was taken out of
another edition of Robin Hood
the Platts of which were the reverse
to these & much more worn.
One did not appear ever to
have been better.

Robin Hood & Little John in the Sherwood Forest.

Published as the Act directs Nov.ᵣ 1 1789.

Robin Hood's Garland.

BEING A COMPLETE

HISTORY

OF ALL THE

NOTABLE and MERRY EXPLOITS

PERFORMED

By HIM and his MEN on many Occasions.

TO WHICH IS ADDED

A PREFACE

GIVING

A more full and particular Account of his BIRTH, &c. than any hitherto Published.

I'll send this Arrow from my Bow,
And in a Wager will be bound,
To hit the Mark aright, although
It were for fifteen hundred Pound.
***Doubt** not I'll make the Wager good,*
Or ne'er believe bold ROBIN HOOD.

Adorned with Twenty-Seven neat and curious CUTS adapted to the SUBJECT of each SONG.

Printed and Sold in London.

TO ALL

GENTLEMEN ARCHERS.

THIS GARLAND has been long out of Repair,
    Some SONGS being wanting, of which we
        give Account ;
For now at laſt, by true induſtrious Care,
    The Sixteen SONGS to Twenty-ſeven we mount.
Which large Addition needs muſt pleaſe, I know,
All the ingenious YEOMEN of the Bow.
To read how ROBIN HOOD and LITTLE JOHN,
    Brave SCARLET, STUTELY, valiant, bold, and
        free,
Each of them bravely, fairly play'd the Man,
    While they did reign beneath the Green Wood
        Tree ;
Biſhops, Friars, likewiſe many more,
Parted with their Gold for to increaſe their Store,
But never would they rob or wrong the Poor.

THE

PREFACE to the READER.

THERE is fcarce any ftory fo little known, for one
fo very popular, as that of ROBIN HOOD and
LITTLE JOHN. Numbers there are who look upon
all that is faid of them as fabulous, and believe them
(like the Heroes and Gods of Homer and Ovid to have
exifted no where but in the fertile brain of an invent-
ing Poet. Nor is this the opinion of an unthinking
people: I have often heard it afferted by men of good
fenfe; but that they are grofly miftaken is very certain: For King Richard the firft, tranfported with
zeal, blindly facrificed every thing to it, and ruined
himfelf and almoft his whole nation, to carry on a war
againft the Infidels in the Holy Land, where he went
in perfon. The inteftine troubles of England were very
great at that time; and even John, the King's brother,
cabaled to dethrone him, and take poffeffion of his
kingdom. This was an opportunity which the Outlaws and Banditti would by no means neglect, and
England was every where infefted with thieves and
robbers. But amongft thofe, none made fo confiderable a figure as ROBIN HOOD; who, as hiftorians
affure us, chiefly refided in Yorkfhire; but who, if
we may give any credit to moft of our Old Songs,
was very converfant in the county of Nottingham.
Befides LITTLE JOHN, he had an hundred Bowmen
in his retinue, but none but the Rich ftood in awe
of him: So far from fpoiling the poor, he did
them all the good that lay in his power. Of the
Rich, he feldom abufed thofe he robbed; and never offered to ftop or rifle any woman. It is not
very pofitively known who he was; but the general opinion of the hiftorians is, that he was a noble-
man; by birth noble, and created an Earl for fome
A 2 confiderable

confiderable fervice done to his country in war.   But
having riotoufly fpent his eftate, he took that way of
living, rather chufing to venture his life, or every thing
he got, than to live in a dependent ftate, and be be-
holden to any body for his bread. Hubert, Archbifhop
of Canterbury, and Chief Jufticiary of England, en-
deavouring all he could to fupprefs thofe Robbers and
Outlaws, fet a very confiderable price upon the head of
Robin Hood. and feveral ftratagems were ufed to ap-
prehend him ; but all their attempts proved fruitlefs.
Force he repelled by force, and art by cunning ; till at
length falling ill, he went (in order to be better taken
care of) to Birkleys, a nunnery in Yorkfhire, where
he defired to be let blood ; but the reward fet upon his
head being very confiderable, it proved a great tempta-
tion to fome who knew him, by whom he was betray-
ed ; and inftead of bleeding as he defired, he was blooded
to death, about the latter end of 1395.—As to the following Song, with which we fhall begin this Collection
I think I need not fay any thing in oommendation of
it, being the moft beautiful, and one of the oldeft ex-
tent on that fubject.   One thing we muft obferve in
reading it, and that is, between fome of the ftanzas we
muft fuppofe a confiderable time to pafs.   Clorinda
might be a very forward girl, if between Robin Hood's
queftion and her anfwer we did not fuppofe two or three
hours to have been fpent in courtfhip.   And between
Robin Hood's being entertained at Gamewell Hall,
and his having ninety-three Bowmen in Sherwood, we
muft allcw fome years.   I know not how our Criticks
will relifh this ; but I would have them remember,
that the poets of old fcorned to curb the poetic fire to
give gave way to dull rule. They had no tedious comment upon Ariftotle to confult ; no Boffus nor Den-
nis to guide them ; or, at leaft, they had too much
fpirit to be guided by them.   Their works were the
firft flight of a lively imagination ; and poets were
looked upon, like other Englifhmen, born to live and
write with freedom.

ROBIN

ROBIN HOOD's GARLAND, &c.

1. The Pedigree, Education, and Marriage of Robin Hood with Clorinda, Queen of Titbury Feast.

Suppofed to be related by the Fiddler who played at the Wedding.

Kind gentlemen will you be filent awhile?
   Aye, and then you fhall hear anon.
A very good ballad of bold Robin Hood,
   And his brave man Little John.
In Lockfley town, in merry Nottinghamfhire,
   In merry fweet Lockfley town,
There bold Robin Hood was born and bred,
   Bold Robin of famous renown.
The father of Robin a forefter was,
   And he fhot with a lufty ftrong bow,
Two north country miles and an inch at a fhoot,
   As the Pinder of Wakefield does know;
For he brought Adam Bell, and Clim of the Clough,
   And William of Clowdel Lee,
To fhoot with a forefter for forty marks,
   And the forefter beat them all three.
His mother was niece to the Coventry knight,
   Which Warwickfhire men call Sir Guy,

A 3

For

For he flew the blue boar that hangs up at the gate,
  Or my hoft at the Bull tells a lie.
Her brother was Gamewell, of Great Gamewell hall,
  A noble houfekeeper was he,
Aye, as ever broke bread in fweet Nottinghamfhire,
  And a 'fquire of famous degree.
The mother of Robin faid to her hufband,
  My Honey, my Love, and my Dear,
Let Robin and I ride this morning to Gamewell,
  To tafte of my brother's good cheer.
And he faid, I grant thee thy boon, gentle Joan,
  Take one of my horfes, I pray:
The fun is arifing, and therefore make hafte,
  For to-morrow will be Chriftmas-day.
Then Robin Hood's father's grey gelding was brought,
  And faddled and bridled was he;
God wot a blue bonnet, his new fuit of cloaths,
  And a cloak that did reach to his knee.
She got on her holiday kirtle and gown,
  They were of a Lincoln green;
The cloth was home-fpun, but for colour and make,
  It might have befeemed our Queen.
And then Robin got on his bafket-hilt fword,
  And his dagger on the other fide;
And faid, My dear Mother, let's hafte to be gone,
  We have forty long miles for to ride.
When Robin was mounted on his gelding fo grey,
  His father without any trouble,
Set her up behind him, bid her not fear,
  For his gelding had oft carried double.
And when fhe was fettled, they rode to their neighbours,
  And drank and fhook hands with them all;
And then Robin gallop'd, and never gave over,
  'Till they lighted at Gamewell-Hall.
And now you may think the right worfhipful 'fquire
  Was joyful his fifter to fee;
For he kifs'd her, and kifs'd her, and fwore a great oath,
  Thou art welcome kind fifter to me.
The morrow, when mafs had been faid at the chapel,
  Six tables were cover'd in the hall,
And in comes the 'fquire, and makes a fhort fpeech,
  t was, Gentlemen, you're welcome all.

                                       But

But not a man here shall taste my March beer,
    'Till a Chriſtmas Carol he does ſing.
Then all clapp'd their hands, and they ſhouted and ſung,
    'Till the hall and the parlour did ring.
Now muſtard and brawn, roaſt beef and plum pies,
    Were ſet upon every table :
And noble George Gamewell ſaid, Eat and be merry,
    And drink to as long as you're able.
When dinner was ended his chaplain ſaid grace ;
    And be merry, my friends, ſaid the 'ſquire ;
It rains and it blows, but call for more ale,
    And lay ſome more wood on the fire.
And now call ye Little John hither to me,
    For Little John is a fine lad,
At gambols and juggling, and twenty ſuch tricks,
    As ſhall make you both merry and glad.
When Little John came, to gambols they went,
    Both gentlemen, yeomen, and clowns :
And what do you think ? Why, as true as I live,
    But bold Robin Hood put them all down.
And now you may think the right worſhipful 'ſquire
    Was joyful this ſight for to ſee ;
For he ſaid, Couſin Robin, thou goeſt no more home,
    But tarry and dwell here with me :
Thou ſhalt have my land when I die, and till then
    Thou ſhalt be the ſtaff of my age.
Then grant me my boon, dear uncle, ſaid Robin,
    That Little John may be my page.
And he ſaid, kind couſin, I grant thee thy boon ;
    With all my heart, ſo let it be,
Then come hither, Little John, ſaid Robin Hood,
    Come hither my page unto me :
Go fetch me my bow, my longeſt bow,
    And broad arrows one, two, or three ;
For when 'tis fair weather we'll into Sherwood,
    Some merry paſtime to ſee.
When Robin Hood came into merry Sherwood,
    He winded his bugle ſo clear ;
And twice five and twenty good yeomen and bold,
    Before Robin Hood did appear.
Where are your companions all ? ſaid Robin Hood,
    For ſtill I want forty and three ;

                         Then

Then, said a bold yeoman, Lo! yonder they stand,
   All under the green wood tree.
As that word was spoke Clorinda came by,
   The queen of the shepherds was she;
And her gown was of velvet as green as the grass,
   And her buskin did reach to her knee:
Her gait it was graceful, her body was strait,
   And her countenance it was free from pride,
A bow in her hand, and a quiver of arrows,
   Hung dangling down by her sweet side,
Her eye-brows were black, aye, and so was her hair,
   And her skin was as smooth as glass:
Her visage spoke wisdom and modesty too;
   Sets with Robin Hood such a lass!
Says Robin Hood, Fair lady, whither away?
   O whither, fair lady, away?
And she made him answer, to kill a fat buck;
   For to-morrow is Titbury-Day.
Said Robin Hood, Lady fair; will you wander with me,
   A little to yonder green bower;
There sit down to rest you; and you shall be sure
   Of a brace or a leash in an hour?
And as we were going towards the green bower,
   Two hundred good bucks we espy'd;
She chose out the fattest that was in the herd,
   And she shot him thro' side and side.
By the faith of my body, said bold Robin Hood,
   I never saw woman like thee;
And com'st thou from east, or com'st thou from west,
   Thou need'st not beg ven'son of me.
However, along to my bower you shall go,
   And taste of a forester's meat:
And when we came thither we found as good cheer
   As any man need for to eat.
For there was hot ven'son, and warden pies cold,
   Cream clouted, and honey-combs plenty;
And the servitures they were, besides Little John,
   Good yeomen at least four and twenty.
Clorinda said, Tell me your name, gentle Sir;
   And he said, 'Tis Bold Robin Hood:
'Squire Gamewell's my uncle, but all my delight
   Is to dwell in merry Sherwood;

                                   For

For 'tis a fine life, and 'tis void of all ſtrife,
  So 'tis, Sir, Clorinda reply'd ;
But oh ! ſaid bold Robin, how ſweet it would be,
  If Clorinda would be my bride ?
She bluſh'd at the motion ; yet, after a pauſe,
  Said, Yes, Sir, and withal my heart :
Then let us ſend for a prieſt, ſaid Robin Hood,
  And be married before we do part.
But ſhe ſaid, It may not be ſo, gentle Sir,
  For I muſt be at Titbury feaſt ;
And if Robin Hood will go thither with me,
  I'll make him the moſt welcome gueſt.
Said Robin Hood, reach me that buck, Little John,
  For I'll go along with my dear ;
And bid my yeomen kill ſix brace of bucks,
  And meet me to-morrow juſt here.
Before he had ridden five Staffordſhire miles,
  Eight yeomen who were too bold,
Bid Robin Hood ſtand deliver his buck,
  A truer tale never was told.
I will not faith, ſaid bold Robin : Come Little John,
  Stand by me, and we'll beat them all.   ('em
Then both drew their ſwords, and ſo cut 'em and flaſh'd
  That five out of the eight did fall.
The three who remained call'd to Robin for quarter,
  And pitiful John begg'd their lives ;
When John's boon was granted, he gave them good counſel
  And ſent them all home to their wives.
This battle was fought near to Titbury town,
  When the bagpipes baited the bull ;
I'm the king of the fiddlers, and I ſwear 'tis a truth,
  And I call him that doubts it a gull.
For I ſaw them fighting, and fiddled the while,
  And Clorinda ſung " Hey derry down !
" The bumkins are beaten, put up thy ſword Bob,
  " And now let's dance into the town."
Before we came in we heard a great ſhouting,
  And all who were in it look'd madly !
For ſome were on bull-back, ſome dancing a morrice,
  And ſome ſinging Arthur-a-Bradley.
And there we ſaw Thomas, our Juſtice's clerk,
  And Mary to whom he was kind ;   For

For Tom rode before her, and call'd Mary Madam,
  And kifs'd her full fweetly behind ;
And fo may your Worfhips.   But we went to dinner
  With Thomas, and Mary, and Nan.
They all drank a health to Clorinda, and told her,
  Bold Robin Hood was a fine man.
When dinner was ended, Sir Roger the parfon
  Of Dunbridge was fent for in hafte,
He brought his mafs book, and bid them take hands,
  And join'd them in marriage full faft.
And then as bold Robin Hood and his fweet bride,
  Went hand and hand unto the green bower,
The birds fung with pleafure in merry Sherwood,
  And it was a moft joyful hour.
And when Robin came in fight of the bower,
  Where are my yeomen ? faid he :
And Little John anfwer'd, Lo ! yonder they ftand,
  All under the greenwood tree.
Then a garland they brought her by two and by two,
  And plac'd it all on the bride's head :
The mufic ftruck up, and they all fell a dancing,
  'Till the bride and the bridegroom were a bed,
And what they did there muft be counfel to me,
  Becaufe they lay long the next day ;
And I made hafte home ; but I got a good piece
  Of bride cake, and fo came away.
Now out, alas ! I had forgotten to tell ye
  That married they were with a ring ;
And fo will Nan Knight, or be buried a maiden ;
  And now let us pray for the king,
That he may get children, and they may get more,
  To govern and do us fome good ;
Then I'll make ballads in Robin Hood's bower,
  And fing them in merry Sherwood.

2. ROBIN HOOD's Progress to NOTTINGHAM, in
which he flew FIFTEEN FORESTERS.
To the Tune of bold ROBIN HOOD, &c.

ROBIN HOOD was a tall young man,
   Derry, derry down,
And Robin Hood was a proper young man,
  Of courage ftout and bold.
    Hey down, derry, derry down.
Robin Hood went unto fair Nottingham,
  With the General for to dine ;
There was he aware of fifteen forefters,
  Drinking beer, ale, and wine.
What news ? What news ? faid bold Robin Hood,
  What news fain wouldft thou know ?
Our king has provided a fhooting match,
  And I'm ready with my bow.
We hold it in fcorn, faid the fifteen forefters,
  That ever a boy fo young,
Should bear a bow befcre our king,
  That's not able to draw one ftring.
I'll hold you twenty marks, faid bold Robin Hood,
  By the leave of our Lady,
That I'll hit the mark an hundred rod,
  And I'll caufe a hart to die.
We'll hold you twenty marks then, faid the forefters,
  By the leave of our Lady,
Thou hits not the mark an hundred rod,
  Nor caufe the hart to die.
Robin Hood bent up a noble good bow,
  And a broad arrow he let fly :
He hit the mark a hundred rod,
  And caufed a hart to die.
Some fay he broke ribs one or two,
  And fome fay he broke three ;

              The

The arrow in the hart would not abide,
  But glanc'd in two or three.
The hart did skip, and the hart did leap,
  And the hart lay on the ground;
The wager is mine, said Robin Hood,
  If it were for a thousand pounds.
The wager is none of thine, said the foresters,
  Altho' thou be'st in haste,
Take up thy bow, and get thee hence,
  Lest we thy sides should baste.
Robin Hood took up his noble good bow,
  And his broad arrows all amain;
And Robin being pleas'd, began for to smile,
  As he went over the plain.
Then Robin he bent his noble good bow,
  And his broad arrows he let fly,
Till fourteen of the fifteen foresters
  Upon the ground did lie.
He who did the quarrel first begin,
  Went tripping over the plain;
But Robin Hood bent his noble good bow,
  And fetch'd him back again;
You said I was no archer, said Robin Hood,
  But say so now again;
With that he sent another arrow after him,
  Which split his head in twain.
You have found me an archer, says bold Robin Hood,
  Which will make your wives to wring,
And wish you had never said the word,
  That I could not have drawn one string.
The people who did live in fair Nottingham,
  Came running out amain,
Supposing to have taken bold Robin Hood,
  With the foresters who were slain.
Some lost legs, and some lost arms,
  And some did lose their blood:
But Robin he took up his noble good bow,
  And is gone to the merry Green Wood.
They carried their foresters to fair Nottingham,
  As many there did know,
They digg'd them graves in their church-yard,
  And bury'd them all on a row,   3. ROBIN

3. ROBIN HOOD and the JOLLY PINDER of WAKEFIELD.

Showing how he fought with ROBIN HOOD, WILL SCARLET and LITTLE JOHN, a long Summer's Day.

To an excellent new Northern Tune.

IN Wakefield there lives a jolly Pinder,
 In Wakefield all on the green,
 In Wakefield all on the green,
There is never a knight nor 'squire, said the Pinder,
 Nor Baron so bold,
 Nor Baron so bold,
Dare make a trespass to the town of Wakefield,
 But his pledge goes to the pinfold,
 But his pledge goes to the pinfold.
All this was heard by three witty young men,
 'Twas Robin Hood, Scarlet, and John ;
With that they espy'd the jolly Pinder,
 As he sat under a thorn.
Now turn again, now turn again, said the Pinder,
 For a wrong way have you gone ;
For you have forsaken the king's highway,
 And made a path over the corn.
O that was a shame, said jolly Robin,
 We being three, and thou but one.
The Pinder leap'd back then thirty good feet,
 'Twas thirty good feet and one.
He lean'd his back fast to a thorn,
 And his foot against a stone,
And there he fought a summer's day,
 And a summer's day so long,
'Till that their swords in their broad bucklers
 Were broken fast in their hands.
Hold thy hand, hold thy hand, said bold Robin Hood,
 And my merry men every one,   B

For this is one of the beſt Pinders,
　That ever I try'd with a ſword.
And wilt thou now forſake thy Pinder's craft,
　And live in the Green Wood with me?
At Michaelmas next my covenant comes out,
　When every man gathers his fee,
Then I'll take my blue blade in my hand,
　And plod to the green wood with thee.
Haſt either meat or drink, ſaid Robin Hood,
　For my merry men and me?
I have both bread and beef, ſaid the Pinder,
　And good ale of the beſt ;
And that's good meat enough, ſaid Robin Hood,
　For ſuch unbidden gueſts.
O, wilt thou forſake thy Pinder's craft,
　And go to the Green Wood with me?
Thou ſhalt have a livery twice in the year,
　The one green and the other brown.
If Michaelmas once was come and gone,
　And my maſter had paid me my fee,
Then would I ſet as little by him,
　As my maſter doth by me.

---

4. ROBIN HOOD and the BISHOP.

Showing how ROBIN HOOD went to an old Woman's
　Houſe and changed cloaths with her to eſcape from
　the BISHOP; and how he robbed him of all his Gold
　and made him ſing Maſs.

　　Tune of ROBIN HOOD and the STRANGER.

COME Gentlemen all, and liſten awhile,
　With a hey down, down, and a down,
And a ſtory to you I'll unfold ;

I'll

I'll tell you how Robin Hood served the bishop,
 When he robbed him of his gold.
As it fell out on a fun-fhiny day,
 When Phœbus was in his prime,
Bold Robin Hood, that archer good,
 In mirth would fpend fome time.
And as he walked the foreft along,
 Some paftime for to fpy,
There he was aware of a proud Bifhop,
 And of all his company.
O what fhall I do, faid Robin Hood then,
 If the Bifhop he doth take me;
No mercy he'll fhow unto me, I know,
 Therefore away I'll flee.
Then Robin was ftout, and turn'd him about,
 And a little houfe there did fpy;
And to an old wife, to fpare his life,
 He aloud began to cry.
Why, who art thou, faid the old woman,
 Come tell to me for good?
I am an Outlaw, as many do know,
 My name it is Robin Hood.
And yonder's the Bifhop and all his men,
 And if that I taken be,
Then day and night he'll work me fpite,
 And hanged I fhall be.
If thou be Robin Hood? faid the old woman,
 As thou doft feem to be,
I'll for thee provide, thy perfon hide,
 From the Bifhop and his company.
For I remember one Saturday night,
 Thou brough.'ft me both fhoes and hofe;
Therefore I'il provide thy perfon to hide,
 And keep thee from tny foes.
Then give me foon thy coat of grey,
 And take thou my mantle of green;
Thy fpindle of twine unto me refign,
 And take thou my arrows fo keen.
And when Robin Hood was thus array'd,
 He went ftraight to his company.
With the fpindle and twin he oft looks behind
 For the Bifhop and his company.

Oh! who is yonder, quoth Little John,
  That now comes over the lee?
An arrow at her I will let fly,
  So like an old witch looks she.
Hold thy hand, hold thy hand, said Robin Hood then,
  And shoot not thy arrows so keen:
I am Robin Hood, thy master good,
  As quickly shall be seen.
The Bishop he came to the old woman's house,
  And called with a furious mood,
Come let me see, and bring unto me,
  The traitor Robin Hood.
The old woman she sat on a milk white steed,
  Himself on a dapple grey;
And for joy he had got Robin Hood,
  He went laughing all the way.
But as they were riding the forest along,
  The Bishop he chance for to see,
A hundred brave bowmen, stout and bold,
  Stand under the green-wood tree.
O! who is yonder, the Bishop then said,
  That's ranging within yonder wood?
Marry, says the old woman, I think it be
  A man called Robin Hood.
Why, who art thou, the Bishop he said,
  Which I have here with me?
Why, I am a woman, they cuckoldly Bishop,
  Lift up my leg and see.
Then woe is me, the Bishop he said,
  That ever I saw this day:
He turn'd him about, but Robin Hood stout,
  Call'd to him, and bid him to stay.
Then Robin took hold of the Bishop's horse,
  And tied him fast to a tree,
Then Little John smil'd his master upon,
  For joy of his company.
Robin Hood took his mantle from his back,
  And spread it upon the ground,
And out of the Bishop's portmantua he
  Soon told five hundred pound.
Now let him go, said Robin Hood:
  Said Little John that must not be,

For

For I vow and proteſt he ſhall ſing us a maſs,
  Before that he goes from me.
Then Robin Hood took the Biſhop by the hand,
  And bound him faſt to a tree;
And made him ſing a maſs, God wot,
  To him and his yeomandry.
And then they brought him through the wood,
  And ſat him on his dapple grey,
And gave him the tail within his hand,
  And bid him for Robin Hood pray.

---

5. ROBIN HOOD and the BUTCHER.
Showing how he robbed the Sheriff of Nottingham.
The . . Robin Hood and the Begger.

COME all you brave gallants, and liſten while,
  With a hey down, down, and a down,
  That are this bower within;
For of bold Robin Hood, that archer good,
  A ſong I intend to ſing.
Upon a time it chanced ſo,
  Bold Robin in the foreſt did 'ſpy,
A jolly butcher with a fine mare,
  With his fleſh to the market did hie.
Good-morrow, good fellow, ſaid jolly Robin,
  What food haſt thou, tell unto me?
Thy trade to me tell, and where thou doſt dwell,
  For I like well thy company.
The butcher he anſwer'd jolly Robin,
  No matter where I dwell;
For a butcher I am, and to Nottingham
  I am going my fleſh to ſell.
What's the price of thy fleſh, ſaid jolly Robin,
  Come tell it unto me?
And the price of thy mare, be ſhe ever ſo dear,
  For a butcher I fain would be?

The price of my flesh, the butcher reply'd,
  I will soon tell unto thee ;
With my bonny mare, they are not too dear,
  Four marks thou must give unto me.
Four marks I will give thee, said Jolly Robin,
  Four marks it shall be thy fee ;
The money come count, and let me mount,
  For a butcher I fain would be.
Now Robin he is to Nottingham gone,
  His butcher's trade to begin ;
With a good intent to the sheriff he went,
  And there he took up his inn.
When the other butchers did open their shops,
  Bold Robin he then begun ;
But how for to sell he knew not well,
  For a butcher he was but young.
When the other butchers no meat could sell,
  Robin he got both gold and fee ;
For he sold more meat for one penny,
  Then others could do for three.
But when he sold his meat so fast,
  No butcher by him could thrive ;
For he sold more meat for one penny,
  Then others could do for five.
Which made the butchers of Nottingham
  To study as they did stand,
Saying, Surely he is some prodigal,
  That has sold his father's land.
The butchers stepped up to jolly Robin,
  Acquainted with him to be ;
Come, brother, one said, we be all of one trade,
  Come will you go dine with me ?
Accurs'd be his heart, said jolly Robin,
  That a butcher will deny,
I will go with you, my brethren true,
  As fast as I can hie.
But when they to the sheriff's house came,
  To dinner they hied apace,
And Robin Hood he the man must be
  Before them all to say grace.
Pray God bless us all, said jolly Robin,
  And our meat with this place: **A cup**

A cup of fack fo good will nourifh our blood,
  And fo I end my grace.
Come fill us more wine, faid jolly Robin,
  Let's be merry while we do ftay,
For wine, and good cheer, be it ever fo dear,
  I vow I the reck'ning will pay.
Come, brothers, be merry, faid jolly Robin,
  Let's drink, and ne'er give o'er?
For the fhot I will pay, ere I go away,
  If it cofts me five pounds or more.
This is a mad blade, the butchers then faid,
  Says the fheriff he's fome prodigal,
Who fome land hath fold for filver and gold,
  And now he doth mean to fpend all.
Haft thou any horn'd beafts, faid the fheriff,
  Good fellow, to fell to me?
Yes, that I have, good mafter fheriff,
  I have hundreds two or three,
And a hundred acres of good free land,
  If you pleafe it for to fee:
And I'll make you as good affurance of it,
  As ever my father did me.
The fheriff he faddled his good palfrey,
  And took three hundred pounds in gold,
And away he went with Robin Hood,
  His horned beafts to behold.
Away then the fheriff and Robin did ride,
  To the foreft of merry Sherwood,
Then the fheriff did fay, God preferve us this day,
  From a man they call Robin Hood.
But when a little farther they came,
  Bold Robin he chanc'd to 'fpy,
An hundred head of good fat deer,
  Came tripping the fheriff full nigh.
How like you my horned beafts, good mafter Sheriff?
  They be fat and fair to fee;
I tell thee good fellow, I would I were gone,
  For I like not thy company.
Then Robin fet his horn to his mouth,
  And blew out blafts three;
Then quickly and anon there came Little John,
  And all his company.   What

What is your will, Master, then said Little John,
  I pray come tell unto me?
I have brought hither the sheriff of Nottingham,
  This day to dine with thee.
He is welcome then to me, said Little John,
  I hope he will honestly pay;
I know he has gold, if it were but well told,
  Will serve us to drink a whole day.
Then Robin Hood took his mantle from his back,
  And laid it upon the ground:
And out of the sheriff's portmantua he
  Soon told five hundred pound.
Then Robin he brought him through the wood,
  And set him on his dapple grey;
O have me commended to your wife at home;
  So Robin went laughing away.

---

6. ROBIN HOOD and the TANNER;
Or, ROBIN HOOD met with his MATCH.

Tune of ROBIN HOOD and STRANGER.

IN Nottingham there lived a jolly tanner,
  With a hey down, down, and a down,
There is never a Squire in Nottinghamshire
  Dare bid bold Arthur to stand.
With a long staff upon his shoulder,
  So well he can clear his way:
By two and by three he made them to flee,
  For he hath no life to stay.
And as he went forth one summer's morning,
  Into the forest of merry Sherwood,
To view the red deer that run here and there,
  There met he bold Robin Hood.
As soon as bold Robin did him espy,
  He thought he the same sport would make,

Therefore out of hand he bid him to ſtand,
  And thus unto him did ſpake.
Why, who art thou, thou bold fellow,
  Who rangeſt ſo boldly here?
In ſooth, to be brief, thou look'ſt like a thief,
  That comes to ſteal our king's deer.
For I am a keeper in this foreſt,
  The king puts me in truſt,
To look to the deer, that run here and there,
  Therefore ſtop thee I muſt.
If thou be'ſt a keeper in this foreſt,
  And haſt ſuch great command,
Yet you muſt have more partakers in ſtore,
  Before you make me to ſtand.
No, I have no more partakers in ſtore,
  Or any that I do need;
But I have a ſtaff of another oak craft,
  I know it will do the deed.
For thy ſword and thy bow I care not a ſtraw,
  Nor all thy arrows to boot,
If thou get'ſt a knock upon thy bear ſcop,
  Thou can'ſt as well ſh—t as ſhoot.
Speak cleanly, good fellow, ſaid jolly Robin,
  And give better terms unto me:
Elſe I'll thee correct for thy neglect,
  And make thee more mannerly.
Marry-gap with a wanton, quoth Arthur-a-Bland,
  Art thou ſuch a goodly man?
I care not a fig for thy looking ſo big,
  Mend yourſelf wherever you can.
Then Robin Hood unbuckled his belt,
  And laid down his bow ſo long:
He took up a ſtaff of another oak craft,
  That was both ſtiff and ſtrong.
I yield to thy weapon, ſaid jolly Robin,
  Since thou wilt not yield to mine,
For I have a ſtaff of another oak craft,
  Not half a foot longer than thine.
But let me meaſure, ſaid jolly Robin,
  Before we begin the fray;
For I will not have mine to be longer than thine,
  For that will be counted foul play.

                                    I paſs

I pass not for length, both Arthur reply'd,
  My staff is of oak so free;
Eight feet and a half, it will knock down a calf,
  And I hope it will knock down thee.
Then Robin could no longer forbear,
  But gave him a very good knock;
But quickly and soon the blood it ran down,
  Before it was ten of the clock.
Then Arthur soon recover'd himself,
  And gave him a knock on the crown,
That from every side of Robin Hood's head,
  The blood ran trickling down.
Then Robin raged like a wild boar,
  As soon as he saw his blood:
Then Bland was in haste, he laid on so fast,
  As if he'd been cleaving of wood.
And about, and about, and about they went,
  Like two wild boars in a chace,
Striving to aim each other to maim,
  Leg, arm, or any other place.
And knock for knock they lustily dealt,
  Which held for two hours or more;
That all the wood rang at every bang,
  They ply'd their work so sore,
Hold thy hand, hold thy hand, said Robin Hood,
  And let thy quarrel fall;
For here we may thrash our bones all to mash,
  And get no coin at all.
And in the forest of merry Sherwood
  Hereafter thou shalt be free:
God ha' mercy for nought, my freedom I bought,
  I may thank my good staff and not thee.
What tradesman art thou, said jolly Robin,
  Good fellow, I prithee me show?
And also me tell, in what place you dwell?
  For both of these fain would I know.
I am a tanner, bold Arthur reply'd,
  In Nottingham long have I wrought;
And if thou'lt come there, I vow and swear,
  I'll tan thy hide for nought.
God-a-mercy, good fellow, said jolly Robin,
  Since thou art so kind and free,

                                        And

And if thou wilt tan my hide for nought,
  I'll do as much for thee.
And if thou wilt forfake thy tanner's trade,
  To live in the green-wood with me,
My name is Robin Hood, I fwear by the wood,
  To give thee both gold and fee.
If thou be Robin Hood, bold Arthur reply'd,
  As I think well thou art.
Then here's my hand, my name's Arthur-a-Bland,
  We two will never part.
Bus tell me, O tell me, where is Little John,
  Of him I fain would hear ;
For we are ally'd by the mother's fide,
  And he is my kinfman dear.
Then Robin Hood blew on his bugle horn,
  He blew both loud fhrill ;
And quick and anon he faw Little John,
  Come triping over the hill.
O what is the matter? then faid Little John,
  Matter, I pray you tell ?
Why do you ftand with your ftaff in your hand,
  I fear all is not well ?
O man I do ftand, and he makes me to ftand,
  The tanner who ftands by fide ;
He is a bonny blade, and mafter of his trade,
  For he has foundly tann'd my hide.
He is to be commended, then faid Little John,
  If fuch a feat he can do ;
If he be fo ftout, we will have a bout,
  And he fhall tan my hide too.
Hold thy hand, hold thy hand, faid Robin Hood,
  For as I do underftand,
He's a yeoman good, and of thy own blood,
  For his name is Arthur-a-Bland.
Then Little John threw his ftaff away,
  As far as he could fling,
And ran out of hand to Arthur-a-Bland.
  And about his neck did cling,
With loving refpect, there was no neglect,
  They were neither nice nor coy ;
Each other did face with a lovely grace,
  And both did weep for joy.   Then

Then Robin Hood took them by the hands,
  And danc'd about the oak tree,
For three merry men, and three merry men,
  And three merry men we be.
And ever hereafter as long as we live,
  We three will be as one :
The wood it ſhall ring, and the old wife ſing,
  Of Robin Hood, Arthur, and John.

---

7. ROBIN HOOD and the Jolly TINKER.
Tune of,—In Summer Time.

In ſummer time, when leaves grow green,
  Down, a down, a down,
  And birds ſing on every tree,
    Hey down, a down,
Robin Hood went to Nottingham,
    Down, a down, a down.
  As faſt he could dree,
    Hey down, a down.
And as he came to Nottingham,
  A Tinker he did meet.
And ſeeing him a luſty blade,
  He did him kindly greet :
Where doſt thou dwell, quoth Robin Hood,
  I pray thee now me tell?
Sad news I hear there is abroad,
  I fear all is not well.
What is that news, the tinker ſaid,
  Tell me without delay ?
I am a tinker by my trade,
  And do live in Banbury.
As for the news, quoth Robin Hood,
  't is but as I hear,
Two tinkers, were ſet in the ſtocks
  For drinking ale and beer.

If that be all, the tinker said,
  As I may say to you,
Your news is not worth a fart,
  Since that we all be true.
For drinking good ale and beer,
  You will not lose your part:
No, by my faith, quoth Robin Hood,
  I love it with all my heart.
What news abroad, quoth Robin Hood,
  Tell me what thou dost hear?
Seeing thou go'st from town to town,
  Some news thou need'st not fear.
All the news I have, the tinker said,
  I hear it is for good,
It is to seek a bold outlaw,
  Who they call Robin Hood.
I have a warrant from the king,
  To take him where I can;
If you can tell me where he is,
  I will make you a man.
The king would give a hundred pounds,
  That he could but him see:
And if we can but now him get,
  It will serve thee and me.
Let me see the warrant, said Robin Hood,
  I will see if it be right;
And I will do the best I can
  For to take him this night.
That I will not, the tinker said,
  None with it I will trust;
And where he is if you'll not tell,
  Take him by force I must.
But Robin Hood perceiving well
  How then the game would go,
If you will go to Nottingham,
  We shall find I him know.
A crab-tree staff the tinker had,
  Which was both good and strong,
Robin he had a good strong blade;
  So they went both along.
And when they came to Nottingham,
  There they took up their inn.

C

And

And they called for ale and wine,
  To drink it was no fin.
But ale and wine they drank fo faft,
  That the the tinker he forgot,
What thing he was about to do,
  It fell fo to his lot;
That, while the tinker fell afleep,
  Robin made hafte away,
And left the tinker in the lurch,
  For the great fhot to pay.
But when the tinker did awake,
  And faw that he was gone,
He called out then for the hoft,
  And thus he made his moan:
I had a warrant from the king,
  Which might have done me good,
This is to feek a bold outlaw,
  Some call him Robin Hood;
But now the warrant and money is gone,
  Nothing I have to pay;
And he who promifed to be my friend,
  Is gone and fled away.
That friend you fpeak of, faid the hoft,
  They call him Robin Hood:
And when that he firft met with you,
  He meant you little good.
Had I but known it had been he,
  When that I had him here,
The one of us fhould have try'd our might,
  Which fhould have paid full dear.
In the mean time I will away,
  No longer here I'll abide,
But I will go and feek him out,
  Whatever me betide.
But one thing I would gladly know,
  What here I have to pay?
Ten fhillings juft, then faid the hoft,
  I'll pay you without delay,
Or elfe take here my working bag,
  And my good hammer too,
And if I light but on the knave,
  I will then foon pay you.

The

The only way, then faid the hoft,
  And not to ftand in fear,
Is to feek him among the parks,
  Killing of the king's deer,
The tinker he then went with fpeed,
  And made then no delay,
'Till he had found bold Robin Hood,
  That they might have a fray.
At laft he 'fpy'd him in a park,
  Hunting then of the deer.
What knave is that, quoth Robin Hood,
  That doth come me fo near?
No knave, no knave, the tinker faid,
  And that you foon fhall know,
Whether of us has done any wrong,
  My crab-tree ftaff fhall fhow.
Then Robin drew his gallant blade,
  Made then of trufty fteel:
But the tinker he laid on fo faft,
  That he made Robin reel.
Then Robin's anger did arife,
  He fought right manfully,
Until he made the tinker,
  Then almoft fit to fly.
With that they laid about again,
  And ply'd their weapons faft;
The tinker thrafh'd his bones fo fore,
  He made him yield at laft.
A boon, a boon, then Robin cry'd,
  If thou wilt grant it me?
Before I do it, the tinker faid,
  I'll hang thee on this tree.
But the tinker looking him about,
  Robin his horn did blow;
Then came unto him Little John,
  And Will Scarlet alfo.
What is the matter, quoth Little John,
  You fit on the highway fide?
Here is a tinker, who ftands by,
  That hath well paid my hide.
What tinker then, faid Little John,
  Fain that blade would I fee?
      C 2   **And**

And I would try what I could do,
  If he'll do as much for me.
But Robin then he wish'd them both
  They would the quarrel ceafe,
That henceforth we may be as one,
  And ever live in peace.
And for the jovial tinker's part,
  A hundred pounds I give
In a year to maintain him on,
  As long as he doth live.
In manhood he is a mettled man,
  And a metal man by trade ;
Never thought I that any man
  Should have made me fo afraid.
And if he will be one of us,
  We will all take one fare,
And whatfoever we do get,
  He fhall have his full fhare.
So the tinker he was content
  With them to go along,
And with them a part to take :
  And fo I end my fong.

---

8. ROBIN HOOD and ALLEN-A-DALE.

Or, The Manner of ROBIN HOOD, refcuing a young
  Lady from an old Knight, to whom fhe was going
  to be married, and reftoring her to ALLEN-A-DALE,
  her former Lover.

   Tune of ROBIN HOOD in the Green Wood.

COME liften to me, you gallants fo free,
  All you who love mirth for to hear,

                    And

And I will tell you of a bold outlaw,
　Who lived in Nottinghamſhire.
As Robin Hood in the foreſt ſtood,
　All under the green wood tree,
There he was aware of a brave young man,
　As fine as fine could be.
The youngſter was cloathed in ſcarlet red,
　In ſcarlet fine and gay ;
And he did friſk it over the plain,
　And chanted a round-de-lay.
As Robin Hood next morning ſtood
　Among the leaves ſo gay,
There did he 'ſpy the ſame young man
　Come drooping along the way.
The ſcarlet he wore the day before,
　It was clean caſt away ;
And at every ſtep he fetch'd a ſigh,
　Alack and a well-a-day !
Then ſtepp'd forth brave Little John,
　And Midge the miller's ſon,
Which made the young man bend his bow,
　When as he ſee them come.
Stand off, ſtand off, the young man ſaid,
　What is your will with me ?
You muſt come before our maſter ſtrait,
　Under the green wood tree.
And when he came bold Robin before,
　Robin aſk'd him courteouſly,
O haſt thou any money to ſpare,
　For my merry men and me ?
I have no money, the young man ſaid
　But five ſhillings and a ring ;
And that I have kept this ſeven long years,
　To have it at my wedding.
Yeſterday I ſhould have married a maïd,
　But ſhe ſoon from me was ta'en,
And choſen to be an old knight's delight,
　Whereby my poor heart is ſlain.
What is thy name, then ſaid Robin Hood,
　Come tell me without fail ?
By the faith of my body, then ſaid the young man,
　My name is Allen-a-Dale.

　　　　　　　　　　　　　　　　　What

What wilt thou give me, said Robin Hood,
  In easy gold or fee,
To help thee to thy true love again,
  And deliver her up to thee ?
I have no money, then quoth the young man,
  No ready gold or fee,
But I will swear upon a book,
  Thy true servant to be.
How many miles is it to thy true love?
  Come tell me without guile;
By the faith of my body, then said the young man,
  It is but five little mile.
Then Robin he hasted o'er the plain,
  He did neither stint nor lint,
Until he came unto the church
  Where Allen should keep his wedding.
What hast thou here, the bishop then said,
  I prithee now tell unto me?
I am a bold harper, quoth Robin Hood,
  And the best in the north country:
O welcome! O welcome! the bishop then said,
  That music best pleaseth me.
You shall have no music, quoth Robin Hood,
  Till the bride and the bridegroom I see.
With that came in a wealthy knight,
  Who was both grave and old,
And after him a finikin lass,
  Did shine like the glittering gold.
This is not a fit match, quoth bold Robin Hood,
  That you do seem to make here
For since we are come unto the church,
  The bride shall choose her own dear.
Then Robin Hood put his horn to his mouth,
  And blew out blasts two or three ;
Then four and twenty bowmen bold
  Came leaping over the lee;
And when they came into the church-yard,
  Marching all on a row,
The first man was Allen-a-Dale,
  To give bold Robin his bow.
This is thy true love, Robin said,
  Young Allen, as I heard say,

                          And

And you fhall be married at the fame time,
  Before we depart away.
That fhall not be, the bifhop he faid,
  For thy word fhall not ftand,
They fhall be three times afk'd in the church,
  As the law is of our land.
Robin Hood pull'd off the bifhop's coat,
  And put it upon Little John;
By the faith of my body, then Robin he faid,
  This cloth doth make thee a man.
When Little John went to the choir,
  The people began to laugh;
He afk'd them feven times in the church,
  Left three times fhould not be enough.
Who gives this maid, faid Little John,
  Quoth Robin Hood, that do I,
And he who takes her from Allen-a-Dale,
  Full dearly fhall her buy.
And thus having ended this merry wedding,
  The bride fhe look'd like a queen:
And fo they return'd to the merry green wood,
  Amongft the leaves fo green.

9. ROBIN HOOD and the SHEPHERD.

Showing how ROBIN HOOD. LITTLE JOHN, and the
SHEPHERD fought a fore COMBAT.

Tune of ROBIN HOOD and QUEEN CATHARINE.

ALL gentlemen and yeomen good,
  Down, a down, a down,
I wifh you to draw near;
For a ftory of bold Robin Hood
  Unto you I will declare.
    Down, a down, a down.

As Robin Hood walk'd the foreſt along,
  Some paſtime for to 'ſpy,
There he was aware of a jolly ſhepherd,
  Who on the ground did lie.
Ariſe, ariſe, ſaid jolly Robin,
  And now come let me ſee
What's in thy bag and thy bottle, I ſay,
  Come tell it unto me.
What's that to thee, thy proud fellow,
  Tell me as I do ſtand?
What haſt thou to do with my bottle and bag?
  Let me ſee thy command.
My ſword that hangeth by my ſide,
  Is at my command I know:
Come let me taſte of thy bottle,
  Or it may breed thee woe.
The devil a drop, thou proud fellow,
  Of my bottle ſhalt thou ſee,
Until thy valour here is try'd,
  Whether thou'lt fight or flee.
What ſhall we fight for? ſaid Robin Hood,
  Come tell it unto me;
Here's twenty pounds of good bright gold,
  Win it, and take it thee.
The ſhepherd ſtood all in amaze,
  And knew not what to ſay;
I have no money, thou proud fellow,
  But bag and bottle I'll lay:
I am content, thou ſhepherd ſwain,
  Fling them down on the ground;
But it will breed thee mickle pain,
  To win my twenty pound.
Come draw thy ſword, thou proud fellow,
  Who ſtandeth too long to prate;
This hook of my mine ſhall let thee know,
  A coward I do hate.
So they fell to it full hard and ſore,
  It was on a ſummer's day,
From ten to four in the afternoon
  The ſhepherd held him in play:
Robin's buckler prov'd his chief defence,
  And ſav'd him many a bang,

For

For every blow the fhepherd ftruck
  Made Robin Hood's fword cry twang.
Many a fturdy blow the fhepherd gave,
  And that bold Robin found,
'Till the blood ran trickling from his head,
  Then he fell to the ground.
Arife, arife, thou proud fellow,
  And thou fhalt have fair play,
If thou wilt yield before thou go,
  That I have won the day.
A boon, a boon, cry'd bold Robin,
  If that a man thou be,
Then let me have my bugle horn,
  And blow out blafts three.
Then faid the fhepherd to bold Robin,
  To that I will agree ;
For if thou fhould'ft blow 'till to-morrow morn,
  I fcorn one foot to flee.
Then Robin he fet his horn to his mouth,
  And he blew with might and main,
Until he 'fpied Little John
  Come tripping o'er the plain.
Who is yonder, thou proud fellow,
  That comes down yonder hill ?
Yonder is John, bold Robin Hood's man,
  Shall fight with thee thy fill.
What is the matter, faid Little John,
  Mafter, come tell unto me ;
My cafe is bad, faid Robin Hood,
  For the fhepherd hath conquer'd me.
I am glad of that, cries Little John,
  Shepherd turn thou to me;
For a bout with thee I mean to have,
  Either come fight or flee.
With all my heart, thou proud fellow,
  For it fhall ne'er be faid,
That a fhepherd's hook, at thy fturdy look,
  Will one jot be difmay'd.
So they fell to it, hard and fore,
  Striving for victory,
I will know, fays John, ere we give o'er,
  Whether thou wilt fight or flee.

The

T e shepherd gave John a sturdy blow,
  With the hook under his chin;
Beshrew thy heart said Little John,
  Thou basely dost begin.
Nay, that is nothing, said the shepherd,
  Either yield to me the day,
Or I will bang thy back and sides,
  Before thou goest thy way.
What dost thou think, thou proud fellow,
  That thou can'st conquer me ?
Nay, thou shalt know before I go,
  I'll fight before I'll flee.
Again the shepherd laid on him,
  The shepherd he begun;
Hold thy hand, cry'd jolly Robin,
  I will yield the wager won.
With all my heart, said Little John,
  To that I will agree;
For he is the flower of shepherd swains,
  The like I ne'er did see.
Thus have you heard of Robin Hood,
  Also of Little John;
How a shepherd swain did conquer them,
  The like was never known.

---

10. The famous Battle between ROBIN HOOD
and the Curtal FRYAR, near FOUTAIN-DALE.

To a NORTHERN Tune.

IN summer time, when leaves grow green,
  And flowers are fresh and gay,
Robin Hood and his merry men
  Were all dispos'd to play.

Then

Then fome would leap, and fome would run,
  And fome ufe artillery;
Which of you can a good bow draw,
  A good archer for to be ?
Which of you can kill a buck,
  Or who can kill a doe;
Or who can kill a hart of Greece
  Five hundred foot him fro'.
Will Scarlet he did kill a buck;
  And Midge did kill a doe ?
And Little John kill'd a heart of Greece
  Five hundred foot him fro'.
God's bleffing on thy heart, faid Robin Hood,
  That fhot fuch fhot a for me ;
I would ride my horfe a hundred miles,
  To find one could match thee.
That caufed Will Scarlet to laugh,
  He laugh'd full heartily :
There lives a fryar in Fountain Abbey
  Will beat both him and thee.
The Curtal Fryar in Fountain Abbey
  Well can a ftrong bow draw,
He will beat you and your yeomen,
  Set them all on a row.
Robin Hood took a folem'n oath,
  It was by Mary free,
That he would neither eat nor drink,
  'Till he the fryar he did fee.
Robin Hood put on his harnels good,
  And on his head a cap of fteel,
Broad fword and buckler by his fide,
  And they became him well.
He took his bow into his hand,
  It was of a trufty tree,
With a fheaf of arrows by his fide,
  And to Fountain-Dale went he.
And coming to fair Fountain-Dale,
  No farther would he ride ;
There he was aware of a curtal fryar,
  Walking by the water fide,
The fryar had on a harnefs good,
  And on his head a cap of fteel,

                                        Bread

Broad fword and buck'er by his fide,
　And they became him well.
Robin Hood alighted from off his horfe,
　And tied him to a thorn;
Carry me over the water thou curtal fryar,
　Or elfe thy life's forlorn.
The fryar took Robin Hood on his back,
　Deep water he did betide,
And neither fpoke good word nor bad,
　'Till he came to the other fide.
Lightly ftept Robin off the fryar's back,
　The fryar faid to him again,
Carry me over the water, thou fine fellow,
　Or it will breed thee pain.
Robin Hood took the fryar on his back,
　Deep water he did betide,
And fpoke neither good word nor bad,
　'Till he came on the other fide.
Lightly leap'd the fryar off Robin Hood's back,
　Bold Robin faid to him again,
Carry me over the water, thou curtal fryar,
　Or it fhall breed thee pain.
The fryar took Robin on his back again,
　And ftept up to his knee,
And 'till he came to the middle ftream,
　Neither bad nor good fpoke he.
And coming to the middle ftream,
　Then he threw Robin in;
And chufe thee, chufe thee, fine fellow,
　Whether thou wilt fink or fwim.
Robin fwam to a bufh of broom,
　The fryar to the willow wand;
Bold Robin Nood is gone to the fhore,
　And took his bow in his hand.
One of his beft arrows under his belt
　To the fryar he let fly;
The curtal fryar with his fteel buckler
　Did put his arrow by.
Shoot on, fhoot on, thou fine fellow,
　Shoot as thou haft begun,
If thou fhoot here a fummer's day,
　Thy mark I will not fhun.

Robin

Robin fhot on fo paffing well,
  'Till his arrows all were gone;
They took their fwords and fteel bucklers,
  And fought with might and main,
From ten o'clock that very day,
  'Till four in the afternoon.
Then Robin Hood came on his knee;
  Of the fryar to beg a boon.
A boon, a boon, thou curtal fryar,
  I beg it on my knee;
Give me leave to fet my horn to my mouth,
  And to blow blafts three.
That I will do, fays the curtal fryar,
  Of thy blafts I have no doubt;
I hope thou wilt blow fo paffing well,
  'Till both thy eyes drop out.
Robin Hood fet his horn to his mouth,
  And blew out blafts three;
Half a hundred yeomen, with their bows bent,
  Came ranging over the lee.
Whofe men are thefe, faid the fryar,
  That come fo haftily?
Thofe are mine, faid Robin Hood,
  Fryar, what's that to thee?
A boon, a boon, faid the curtal fryar,
  The like I gave to thee;
Give me leave to fet my fift to my mouth
  And to whute whutes three.
That will I do, faid Robin Hood,
  Or elfe I were to blame;
Three whutes in a fryar's fift
  Would make me glad a fain.
The fryar fet his fift to his mouth,
  And whuted him whutes three;
Half an hundred good bay dogs
  Came running over the lee.
Here is for every man a dog,
  And I myfelf for thee.
Nay, by my faith, faid Robin Hood,
  Fryar, that may not be.
Two dogs at once to Robin did go,
  The one behind, the other before;

D

Robin

Robin Hood's mantle of Lincoln green,
  From off his back they tore.
And whether his men fhot eaft or weft,
  Or they fhot north or fouth,
The curtal dogs fo taught were they,
  They caught their arrows in their mouths.

Take up thy dogs, faid Little John,
  Fryar, at my bidding thee:
Whofe man art thou? faid the curtal fryar,
  Comes here to prate to me?

I am Little John, Robin Hood's man,
  Fryar, I will not lie:
If thou take not thy dogs anon,
  I'll take them up and thee.

Little John had a bow in his hand,
  He fhot with might and main:
Soon half a fcore of the fryar's dogs
  Laid dead upon the plain.

Hold thy hand, good fellow, faid the curtal fryar,
  Thy mafter and I will agree,
And we will have new orders taken
  With all the hafte that may be.

If thou wilt forfake fair Fountain Dale,
  And Fountain Abbey free,
Every Sunday throughout the year
  Chang'd fhall thy garment be.

And if thou wilt go to fair Nottingham,
  And there remain with me.
The curtal fryar had kept Fountain-Dale
  Seven long years and more;
There was never knight, lord, nor earl
  Could make him yield before.

11. ROBIN HOOD newly revived; Or,
His meeting and fighting with his COUSIN SCARLET.
To a New Tune.

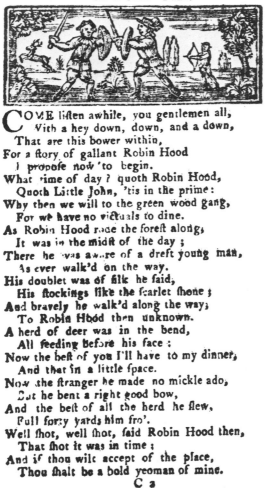

COME liſten awhile, you gentlemen all,
   With a hey down, down, and a down,
That are this bower within,
For a ſtory of gallant Robin Hood
   I propoſe now 'to begin.
What time of day? quoth Robin Hood,
   Quoth Little John, 'tis in the prime:
Why then we will to the green wood gang,
   For we have no victuals to dine.
As Robin Hood rode the foreſt along,
   It was in the midſt of the day;
There he was aware of a dreſt young man,
   As ever walk'd on the way.
His doublet was of ſilk he ſaid,
   His ſtockings like the ſcarlet ſhone;
And bravely he walk'd along the way,
   To Robin Hood then unknown.
A herd of deer was in the bend,
   All feeding before his face:
Now the beſt of you I'll have to my dinner,
   And that in a little ſpace.
Now the ſtranger he made no mickle ado,
   But he bent a right good bow,
And the beſt of all the herd he ſlew,
   Full forty yards him fro'.
Well ſhot, well ſhot, ſaid Robin Hood then,
   That ſhot it was in time:
And if thou wilt accept of the place,
   Thou ſhalt be a bold yeoman of mine.

C 3

Go play the chivan, the stranger then said,
  Make haste and quickly go,
Or with my fist, before of this,
  I'll give thee buffets sto'.
Thou hadst not best buffet me, quoth Robin Hood,
  For altho' I am forlorn,
Yet I have those will take my part,
  If I do blow my horn.
Thou had'st not best wind thy horn, the stranger said,
  Be'st thou never in so much haste,
For I can draw a good broad sword,
  And quickly cut the blast.
Then Robin Hood bent a very good bow,
  To shoot and that he would fain ;
The stranger he bent a very good bow,
  To shoot at bold Robin again.
Hold thy hand, hold thy hand, quoth Robin Hood,
  To shoot it would be in vain ;
For if we shoot the one at the other,
  The one of us must be slain.
But let's take our swords and broad bucklers,
  And gang under yonder tree :
As I hope to be sav'd, the stranger he said,
  One foot I will not flee.
Then Robin lent the stranger a blow,
  Most scared him out of his wits :
Thou'lt feel a blow, the stranger he said,
  That shall be better quits.
The stranger then with a good broad sword
  Hit Robin upon the crown,
That from every hair of bold Robin Hood's head
  The blood it ran trickling down.
God-a-mercy, good fellow, quoth Robin Hood then,
  And for this that thou hast done,
Tell me good fellow, who thou art,
  Tell me where thou do'st won ?
The stranger than answer'd bold Robin Hood,
  I'll tell thee where I do dwell :
In Maxwell town I was born and bred,
  My name is young Gamewell.
For killing of my father's steward,
  Am forc'd to the English wood,

And

And for to feek an uncle of mine,
  Some call him Robin Hood.
But art thou a coufin of Robin Hood, then
  The fooner we fhall have done.
As I hope to be fav'd, the ftranger then faid,
  I am his own fifter's fon.
But, Lord! what kiffing and courting were there,
  When thefe two coufins did meet!
And they went all that fummer's day,
  And Little John did not meet.
And when they met with Little John,
  He then unto him did fay;
O mafter, pray where have you been,
  You have tarry'd fo long away?
I met with a ftranger, quoth Robin Hood,
  Full fore he hath beaten me.
Then I'll have a bout with him, faid Little John,
  And try if he can beat me.
O no, O no, quoth Robin Hood then,
  Little John it muft not be fo;
For he is my own dear fifter's fon,
  And coufins I have no mo'.
But he fhall be a bold yeoman of mine,
  My chief man next to thee;
And I Robin Hood, and thou Little John,
  And Scarlet he fhall be.
And we will be three of the braveft outlaws
  That live in the north country,
If thou wilt hear more of bold Robin Hood,
  In the fecond part it will be.
Then b Id Robin Hood to the north he went,
  With valour and mickle might,
With fword by his fide, which oft had been try'd,
  To fight and recover his right.
The firft that he met was a bonny bold Scot,
  His fervant he faid he would be;
No, quoth Robin Hood, it cannot be good,
  For thou wilt prove falfe unto me.
Thou haft not been true to fire or cuz,
  Nay, marry, the Scot he faid,
As true as your heart, I'll never part.
  Good mafter be not afraid.

Then

Then Robin turned his face to the east,
  Fight on my merry men stout,
Our case is good, quoth Robin Hood,
  And we shall not be beaten out.
The battle grew hot on every side,
  The Scotchmen made great moan ;
Quoth Jockey, Geud faith, they fight on each side,
  Would I were with my wife Joan.
The enemy compass'd brave Robin about,
  'Tis long ere the battle ends ;
There's neither will yield, nor give to the field,
  For both are supplied with friends.
This song it was made in Robin Hood's days ;
  Let's pray unto Jove above,
To give us true peace that mischief may cease,
  And war may give place unto love,

---

12. RENOWNED ROBIN HOOD ;

Or, His famous Archery truly related in the worthy
Exploits he performed before Queen CATHARINE.

To a New Tune.

GOLD ta'en from the King's harbingers,
  Down, a down, a down,
As seldom hath been seen,
  Down, a down, a down,
And carried by bold Robin Hood,
  For a present to the Queen.
    Down, a down, a down.
If that I live one year to an end,
  Thus did Queen Catharine say,
Bo'd Robin Hood, I'll be thy friend,
  And all thy yeomen gay.

The

The Queen is to her chamber gone,
 As faſt as ſhe could wen ;
She calls unto her lovely page,
 His name was Richard Partington.
Come hither to me, thou lovely page,
 Come thou hither to me ;
For thou muſt poſt to Nottingham,
 As faſt as thou can'ſt dree ;
And as thou go'ſt to Nottingham,
 Search every Engliſh wood,
Inquire of one good yeoman or another,
 That can tell thee of Robin Hood.
Sometimes he walk'd, ſometimes he ran,
 As faſt as he could wen,
And when he came to Nottingham,
 There he took up his inn.
He cals for a bottle of Rheniſh wine,
 And drinks a health to the Queen,
Wiſhing he might now ſpeedily
 Find out jolly Robin.
There ſet a yeoman by his ſide,
 Who ſaid, ſweet page, tell me
What is thy buſineſs and thy cauſe,
 So far in the north country ?
This is my buſineſs, and my cauſe,
 Sir, I'll tell it you for good,
To inquire of one good yeoman or another,
 To tell me of Robin Hood.
I'll get my horſe by times in the morn,
 Be't by the break of day,
And I will ſhow thee bold Robin Hood,
 And all his yeomen gay.
When that he came to Robin Hood's place,
 He fell down on his knee,
Queen Catharine ſhe doth greet you well,
 She greets you well by me.
She bids you poſt to fair London court,
 Not fearing any thing :
For there ſhall be a little ſport,
 And ſhe has ſent you a ring.
Robin Hood took his mantle from his back,
 It was of Lincoln green,
And ſent it by this lovely page,
 For a preſent to the Queen.

In fummer time, when leaves grow green,
  'Twas a comely fight to fee,
How Robin Hood had dreft himfelf,
  And all his yeomandree.
He cloathed his men in Lincoln green,
  And himfelf in fcarlet red :
Black hats, white feathers, all alike,
  Now told Robin Hood is rid.
And when he came to London court,
  He fell down on his knee.
Thou art welcome, Lockfley, faid the Queen,
  And all thy yeomandree.
Come hither, Tepus, faid the King,
  Bow bearer, after me ;
Come meafure me out with a line,
  How long our mark muft be.
What is this wager ? faid the Queen ;
  For that I muft know here ;
Three hundred tons of Rhenifh wine,
  Three hundred tons of beer,
Three hundred of the fatteft harts
  That run on Dallen lee ;
That's a princely wager, faid the Queen,
  That I muft needs tell thee.
With that befpoke one Clifton then,
  Full quickly and full foon,
Meafure no mark for us, moft Sovereign Leige,
  We will fhoot at fun and moon.
Full fifteen fcore your mark fhall be,
  Full fifteen fcore fhall ftand ;
I'll lay my bow, faid Clifton then,
  I'll cleave the willow wand.
With that the King's archers led about,
  'Till it was three to one ;
With that the ladies began to fhout,
  Madam, your game is gone.
A boon, a boon, Queen Catharine cries,
  I crave it on my knee ;
Is there never a knight of your privy council,
  On Queen Catharine's fide will be ?
Come hither to me Sir Robert Lee,
  Thou art a knight full good ;

                                    For

For I do know thy pedigree,
  Thou fprang'ft from Gower's blood.
Come hither to me thou bifhop of Herefordfhire,
  For a noble prieft was he:
By my filver mitre, faid the bifhop then,
  I'll not bet one penny.
The king has archers of his own,
  Full ready and full right;
And thefe be ftrangers every one,
  No man knows what they height,
What wilt thou bet? faid Robin Hood,
  Thou fee'ft our game's the worfe;
By my filver mitre, then faid the bifhop,
  All the money in my purfe.
What is in thy purfe? faid Robin Hood,
  Now throw it on the ground;
Ninety-nine angels, faid the bifhop,
  'Tis near a hundred pound.
Robin Hood took his bag from his fide,
  And threw it on the green;
Will. Scarlet then went fmiling away,
  I know who this money muft win.
With that the king's archers led about,
  While it was three to three;
With that the ladies gave a fhout,
  Woodcock beware thy knee.
It is three to three now, faid the King,
  The next three pays for all;
Robin Hood went and whifper'd the Queen,
  The King's part is but fmall.
Then Robin Hood did leap about,
  He fhot it under hand;
And Clifton with a bearing arrow,
  He clove the willow wand.
And little Midge the miller's fon,
  He fhot not much the worfe;
He fhot within a finger of the prick,
  Now bifhop beware thy purfe.
A boon, a boon, Queen Catharine cries,
  I crave it on my bare knee,
That you will angry be with none
  That are of my party.

                                   They

They shall have forty days to come,
    And forty days to go,
And three times forty days to sport and play,
    Then welcome friend or foe.

Thou art welcome, Robin Hood, said the Queen,
    And so is Little John,
And so is Midge the miller's son:
    Thrice welcome every one.

Is this Robin Hood? the King then said,
    For it was told to me,
That he is slain in the palace gate,
    So far in the north country.

Is this Robin Hood? quoth the bishop then,
    As it seems well to be;
Had I known it had been that bold outlaw,
    I would not have let one penny.

He took me late one Sunday night,
    And bound me fast to a tree,
And made me sing a mass, god wot,
    To him and his yeomandree.

What, and if I did, says Robin Hood,
    Of that mass I was full fain;
For recompense of that, he says,
    Here's half thy gold again,

Now nay, now nay, says Little John,
    Master that may not be,
We must give gifts to the king's officers,
    That gold will serve thee and me.

---

13. ROBIN HOOD's CHACE;
Or, A Merry Progress between ROBIN HOOD and
KING HENRY.
Tune of ROBIN HOOD and the BEGGAR.

COME you gallants all, to you I call,
    With a hey down, down, and a down,

That are now in this place;
For a song I will sing of Henry our king,
  How he did bold Robin chace.
Queen Catharine she then a match did make,
  As plainly doth appear,
For three hundred tons of wine,
  And three hundred tons of beer.
But she had her archers to seek,
  With their bows and arrows so good;
But her mind was bent with a full intent,
  To send for bold Robin Hood.
But when bold Robin Hood he came there,
  Queen Catharine she did say,
Thou art welcome, Locksley, unto me,
  And thou on my part must be.
If I miss the mark, be it light or dark,
  And all my yeomen gay,
For a match of shooting I have made,
  Then hanged I will be,
But when the game began to be play'd,
  Bold Robin won it with grace;
But after the King was angry with him,
  And vow'd he would him chace.
What tho' his pardon granted was,
  While he did with him stay;
But yet the King was vex'd at him,
  When he was gone away.
Soon after the King from court did hie,
  In a furious angry mood,
And often inquired both far and near
  After bold Robin Hood,
But when the King to Nottingham came,
  Bold Robin was in the wood:
O come, said he, and let me see
  Who can find bold Robin Hood.
But when bold Robin did hear,
  The King had him in chace;
Then said Little John, 'tis time to be gone,
  And that to another place.
And away they went to merry Sherwood,
  And into Yorkshire he did hie;
And the King did follow with a hoop and a hallo,
  But could not him come nigh.

Yet jolly Robin he paſſed along,
   And went ſtrait to Newcaſtle town,
And there they ſtaid hours two or three,
   And he to Berwick is gone.

When the King did ſee how Robin did flee,
   He was vexed wond'rous ſore;
With a hoop and a hallo he vow'd to follow,
   And take him, or ne'er give o'er.

Come now let's away, ſays Little John,
   Let any man follow who dare;
To Carliſle we'll hie, with our company,
   And ſo then to Lancaſter.

From Lancaſter than to Cheſter he went,
   And ſo did good King Henry;
But Robin went away, for he durſt not ſtay,
   For fear of ſome treachery.

Says Robin come let us for London go,
   To ſee our royal Queen's face,
It may be ſhe wants our company,
   Which makes the King us chace.

When Robin he came Queen Catharine before,
   He fell upon his knee;
If it pleaſe your Grace, I am come to this place,
   To ſpeak with King Henry.

Queen Catharine anſwer'd bold Robin again,
   The King is gone to merry Sherwood,
And when he went away to me he did ſay,
   He would go and ſeek Robin Hood.

Then fare you well my gracious Queen,
   For to Sherwood I'll hie apace;
For fain would I ſee what he d have with me,
   If I could but meet with his grace.

But when King Henry he came home,
   Full weary and vex'd in mind;
And that he did hear that Robin had been there,
   He blam'd dame fortune unkind.

You're welcome home, Queen Catharine cry'd,
   Henry, my Sovereign Liege;
Bold Robin Hood, that archer good,
   Your perſon hath been to ſeek.

A boon, a boon, Queen Catharine cry'd,
   I beg it here of your Grace,
To pardon his life, and ſeek not ſtrife;
   And ſo ends Robin Hood's chace.

14. ROBIN HOOD's GOLDEN PRIZE.

Showing how he robbed two PRIESTS of FIVE
HUNDRED POUNDS.

Tune of Robin Hood was a tall young Man, &c.

I HAVE heard talk of Robin Hood,
  Derry, derry down,
  And of brave Little John,
Of fryar Tuck, and Will. Scarlet,
  Lockfley, and maid Marrian.
But fuch a tale as this before
  I think was never known;
For Robin Hood difguifed himfelf,
  And from the wood is gone.
Like to a fryar bold Robin Hood,
  Was accoutred in his array:
With hood, gown, beads, and crucifix,
  He paffed upon the way.
He had not gone pafs miles two or three,
  But it was his chance to efpy,
Two lufty priefts clad all in black,
  Come riding gallantly.
Benedicite, then faid Robin Hood,
  Some pity on me take;
Crofs my hand with a fingle groat,
  For our dear Lady's fake.
For I have been wand'ring all this day,
  And nothing could I get;
Not fo much as one poor cup of drink,
  Nor bit of bread to eat.
Now, by our holy Dame, the priefts reply'd,
  We never a penny have;
For we this morning have been robb'd,
  And could no money fave.

E

I am

I am much afraid, faid bold Robin Hood,
  That you both tell a lie ;
And now before you do go from hence,
  I am refolved to try.
When as the priefts heard him fay fo,
  Then they rode away amain ;
But Robin Hood betook to his heels,
  And foon overtook them again.
Then Robin Hood laid hold of them both,
  And pulled them down from their horfe,
O fpare us, fryar, the priefts cry'd out,
  On us have fome remorfe.
You faid, you had no money, quoth Robin Hood,
  Wherefore, without delay,
We three will fall down on our knees,
  And for money we will pray.
The priefts they could not him gain fay,
  But down they kneel with fpeed :
Send us, O fend us, then quoth they,
  Some money to ferve our need.
The priefts did pray with mournful cheer,
  Sometimes their hands did wring ;
Sometimes they wept and tore their hair,
  Whilft Robin did merrily fing.
When they had been praying for an hour's fpace,
  The priefts did ftill lament ;
Then quoth Robin, now let us fee
  What money heaven hath fent.
We will be fharers all alike
  Of money that we have :
And there is never a one of us
  That his fellow will deceive.
The priefts their hands in their pockets put
  But money could find none : .
We will fearch ourfelves, faid Robin Hood,
  Each other, one by one.
Then Robin Hood took pains to fearch them,
  And found good ftore of gold,
Five hundred pieces prefently
  Upon the grafs he told.
Here is a brave fhow, faid Robin Hood,
  Such ftore of gold to fee,
And you each one fhall have a part,   Becaufe

Becaufe you prayed fo heartily.
He gave them fifty pounds apiece,
    And the reft himfelf did keep :
The priefts they durft not fpeak one word.
    But fighed wond'rous deep.
With that the priefts rofe up from their knees,
    Thinking to have parted fo ;
Nay, nay, fays Robin Hood, one thing more,
    I have to fay ere you go.
You fhall be fworn, fays bold Robin Hood,
    Upon this holy grafs.
That you will never tell lies again,
    Which way foever you pafs.
The fecond oath that you here muft make,
    That all the days of your lives,
You never fhall tempt maids unto fin.
    Nor lay with other men's wives.
The laft oath you fhall take, is this,
    Be charitable to the poor:
Say you met with a holy fryar,
    And I defire no more.
He fet them on their horfes again,
    And away then they did ride ;
And he return'd to the merry green wood,
    With great joy, mirth, and pride.

---

15. ROBIN HOOD Refcuing WILL. STUTELY from
the SHERIFF and his MEN, who had taken him
Prifoner, and were going to hang him.
    Tune of, ROBIN HOOD and Queen CATHARINE.

WHEN Robin Hood in the green wood ftood,
    Under the green wood tree,
Derry, derry down,

Tidings

Tidings there came to him with speed,
　　Tidings for certainty.
　　　　Hey down, derry, derry down.
That Will. Stutely furprifed was,
　　And eke in prifon lay ;
Three varlets that the king had hir'd,
　　Did bafely him betray.

Ay, and to-morrow hang'd muft be ;
　　To-morrow as foon as 'tis day ;
Before they could the victory get,
　　Two of them did Stutely flay.

When Robin Hood did hear this news,
　　Lord ! it did grieve him fore ;
And to his merry men he did fay,
　　Who altogether fwore,

That Will. Stutely fhould refcued be,
　　And be brought back again,
Or elfe fhould many a gallant wight
　　For his fake there be flain.

He cloathed himfelf in fcarlet then,
　　His men were all in green ;
A finer fhow throughout the world
　　In no place could be feen.

Good Lord ! it was a gallant fight
　　To fee them all on a row ;
With every man a good broad fword,
　　And eke a good yew bow.

Forth of the green wood they are gone,
　　Yea all courageoufly,
Refolving to bring Will. Stutely home,
　　Or every man to die.

And when they came the caftle near,
　　Wherein Will. Stutely lay ;
I hold it good, faid Robin Hood,
　　We here in ambufh ftay,

And fend one forth fome news to hear,
　　To yonder palmer fair,
That ftands under the caftle wall,
　　Some news he may declare.

With that fteps forth a brave young man,
　　Who was of courage bold,
Thus did he fpeak to the old man,
　　I pray thee palmer old.

　　　　　　　　　　　　　　　　　　Tell

Tell me, if thou rightly ken,
  When muſt Will. Stutely die;
Who is one of bold Robin Hood's men,
  And here doth priſoner lie?
Alas! alas! the palmer ſaid,
  And for ever woe is me!
Will. Stutely hang'd will be this day,
  On yonder gallows tree.
O! had his noble maſter known,
  He would ſome ſuccour ſend;
A few of his bold yeomandree,
  Full ſoon would fetch him hence.
Ay, that is true, the young man ſaid;
  Ay, that is true, ſaid he;
Or if they were near to this place,
  They ſoon would ſet him free.
But fare thee well, thou good old man,
  Farewel, and thanks to thee;
If Stutely hanged be this day,
  Reveng'd his death will be.
No ſooner was he from the palmer gone,
  But the gates were open'd wide,
And out of the caſtle Will. Stutely came,
  Guarded on every ſide.
When he was forth of the caſtle come,
  And ſaw no help was nigh;
Thus he did ſay to the ſheriff,
  Thus he ſaid gallantly;
Now ſeeing that I needs muſt die,
  Grant me one boon, ſaid he,
For my noble maſter ne'er had a man,
  That yet was hang'd on a tree.
Give me a ſword all in my hand,
  And let me be unbound,
And with thee and thy men I'll fight,
  'Till I lay dead on the ground.
But this deſire he would not grant,
  His wiſhes were in vain;
For the ſheriff ſwore he hang'd ſhould be,
  And not by the ſword be ſlain.
Do but unbind my hands, he ſaid,
  I will no weapon crave,
E 3

And

And if I hanged be this day,
  Damnation let me have.
O no, no, no, the sheriff said,
  Thou shalt on the gallows die,
Ay, and so shall thy master to,
  If ever in me it lie.
O dastard coward! Stutely cries,
  Faint hearted peasant slave!
If ever my master doth thee meet,
  Thou shalt thy payment have.
My noble master doth thee scorn,
  And all thy cowardly crew;
Such silly imps unable are,
  Bold Robin to subdue.
But when he was to the gallows gone,
  And ready to bid adieu,
Out of a bush steps Little John,
  And comes Will. Stutely to,
I pray thee Will. before thou die,
  Of thy dear friends take leave;
I needs must borrow him awhile,
  How say you, master shreeve?
Now, as I live, the sheriff said,
  That varlet will I know;
Some sturdy rebel is that same,
  Therefore let him not go.
Then Little John most hastily
  Away cut Stutely's bands;
And from one of the sheriff's men,
  A sword twitch'd from his hands.
Here, Will. take thou this same,
  Thou can'st it better sway;
And here defend thyself awhile,
  For aid will come straitway.
And there they turn'd them back to back,
  In the midst of them that day,
'Till Robin Hood approached near,
  With many an archer gay.
With that an arrow from them flew,
  I wist from Robin Hood;
Make haste, make haste, the sheriff said,
  Make haste for it is not good.

                                    The

The fheriff is gone, and his doughty men
  Thought it no boot to ftay,
But, as their mafter had them taught,
  They ran full faft away.
O ftay! O ftay! Will. Stutely faid,
  Take leave ere you depart :
You ne'er will catch bold Robin Hood,
  Unlefs you dare him meet.
O ! ill befide you, faid Robin Hood,
  That you fo foon are gone ;
My fword may in the fcabbard reft,
  For here our work is done.
I little thought, Will. Stutely faid,
  When I came to this place,
For to have met with little John,
  Or feen my mafter's face.
Then Stutely was at liberty fet,
  And fafe brought from his foe ;
O thanks! O thanks! to my mafter,
  Since here it was not fo.
And once again my fellows all,
  We fhall in the green wood meet,
Where we'il make our bow-ftrings twang,
  Mufic for us moft fweet.

---

16. The NOBLE FISHERMAN.
Or, ROBIN HOOD's PREFERMENT.

IN fummer time, when leaves grow green,
  When they do grow both green and long,
Of a bold outlaw, call'd Robin Hood,
  It is of him I fing this fong.

When

When the lilly leaf, and cowslip sweet,
  Both bud and spring with merry cheer,
This outlaw was weary of the wood side,
  And a chasing of the king's deer.
The fishermen brave, more money have,
  Than any merchant, two or three;
Therefore I will to Scarborough go,
  That a fisherman I may be.
This outlaw called his merry men all,
  As they sat under the green wood tree;
If any of you have gold to spend,
  I pray you heartily spend it with me.
Now, quoth Robin Hood, I'll to Scarborough go,
  It seems to be a very fine day:
He took up his inn at a widow woman's house,
  Hard by the waters grey.
Who asked him, where wert thou born?
  O tell me where thou didst fare?
I am a poor fisherman, said he then,
  This day entrapped all in care.
What is thy name, thou fine fellow,
  I pray thee heartily tell to me?
In mine own country, where I was born,
  Men call me Simon over the Lee.
Simon, Simon, said the good wife,
  I wish thou may'st well brook thy name.
The outlaw was aware of her courtesy
  And rejoic'd he'd got such a dame.
Simon, wilt thou be my man?
  And good round wages I'll give thee;
I have as good a ship of my own,
  As any that sails on the sea.
Anchors and planks thou shalt want none,
  Masts and planks that are so long:
And if that thou so furnish me,
  Said Simon, nothing shall go wrong.
They pluck'd up anchor, and away did sail,
  More of a day than two or three;
When others cast in their baited hooks,
  The bare lines into the sea cast he.
It will be long, said the master then,
  Ere this great lubber do thrive on the sea.

He

He shall have no share in our fish,
   For in truth he is in no part worthy.
O woe is me, said Simon then,
   This day that ever I came here!
I wish I were in Plumpton park,
   Chasing of the fallow deer.
For every clown laughs me to scorn,
   And by me set nothing at all;
If I had them in Plumpton park,
   I would set as little by them all.
They pluck'd up anchor, and away did sail,
   More of a day than two or three:
But Simon espy'd a ship of war,
   That sail'd towards them vigorously.
O woe is me, said the master then,
   This day that e'er I was born;
For all the fish that we have got,
   Is every bit lost and forlorn!
For these French robbers on the seas,
   They will not spare of us one man,
But carry us to the coast of France,
   And lay us in a prison strong.
But Simon said, do not fear them,
   Neither, master, take you care,
Give me a bent bow in my hand,
   And never a Frenchman will I spare.
Hold thy peace, thou long lubber,
   For thou art nought but brass and boast,
If I should cast you overboard,
   There is but a simple lubber lost.
Simon grew angry at these words,
   And so angry then was he;
Then he took his bent bow in his hand,
   And in the ship hatch goeth he.
Master, tie me to the mast, he said,
   That at my mark I may stand fair,
Then give my bent bow in my hand,
   And never a Frenchman will I spare.
He drew his arrow to the head,
   And drew it with might and main,
And strait in the twinkling of an eye,
   To the Frenchman's heart the arrow gain.

The

The Frenchman fell down on the fhip's hatch,
　And under the hatches down below :
Another Frenchman that him efpy'd,
　The dead corpfe into the fea did throw.
O mafter, loofe me from the maft, he faid,
　And for them all take you no care,
For give me my bent bow in my hand,
　And never a Frenchman will I fpare.
Then ftrait they boarded the French fhip,
　They laying dead all in their fight ;
They found within the fhip of war,
　Twelve thoufand pounds in money bright,
The one haif of the fhip, faid Simon then,
　I'll give to my dame and children fmall ;
The other haif of the fhip I'll give,
　To you that are my fellows all.
But now befpoke the mafter then,
　For fo Simon it muft not be,
For you have won it with your hands,
　And the owner of it you fhall be.
It fhall be fo as I have faid,
　And with this gold for the oppreft,
An habitation will I build,
　Where they fhall live at peace and reft.

_____

17. ROBIN HOOD's DELIGHT;

Or. A new Combat fought between ROBIN HOOD,
LITTLE JOHN, and WILL. SCARLET, with three
ftout KEEPERS, in Sherwood Foreft.

Tune of ROBIN HOOD and Queen CATHARINE.

THERE's fome will talk of lords and knights,
　Down, a down, a down,
And fome of yeomen good :

　　　　　　　　　　　　　　　But

But I will tell you of Will. Scarlet,
  Little John, and Robin Hood.
They were outlaws it is well known,
  And men of noble blood,
And many times their valour was fhown
  In the foreft of merry Sherwood.
Upon a time it chanced fo,
  As Robin Hood would have it be,
They all three would a walking go,
  The paftime for to fee.
And as they walk'd the foreft along,
  Upon a Midfummer day,
There was he aware of three forefters,
  All clad in green array.
With brave long falchions by their fides,
  And foreft bills in their hand,
They called aloud to thofe outlaws,
  And charged them to ftand.
Why, who are you, cried bold Robin,
  That fpeak fo boldly here?
We three belong to King Henry,
  And are keepers of his deer.
The devil you are, faid Robin Hood,
  I am fure it is not fo;
We be the keepers of this foreft,
  And that you foon fhall know.
Your coats of green lay on the ground,
  And fo we will all three,
And take your fwords and bucklers round,
  And try the victory.
We be content, the keepers faid,
  We be three, and no lefs,
Then why fhould we of you be afraid,
  As we never did tranfgrefs?
Why if you be the keepers of this foreft,
  We be three rangers good,
And will make you know, before you do go,
  You met with bold Robin Hood.
We be content, thou bold outlaw,
  Our courage here to try,
And will make you know before you do go,
  We will fight before we will fly.

Then

Then come draw your fwords, you bold outlaws,
   No longer ftand to prate,
But let us try it ftrait with blows,
   For cowards we do hate.
Here is one for thee Will. Scarlet,
   And another for Little John,
And I myfelf for Robin Hood,
   Becaufe he is ftout and ftrong.
So they fell to it hard and fore,
   It was on a Midfummer day;
From eight of the o'clock, 'till two and peft,
   They all fhow'd gallant play.
There Robin, Will, and Little John,
   They fought moft manfully,
'Till all their wind was fpent and gone,
   Then Robin Hood aloud did cry,
O hold! O hold! cries bold Robin,
   I fee you be ftout men,
Let me blow one blaft on my bugle horn,
   Then I'll fight with you again.
That bargain is to make Robin Hood,
   Therefore we it deny;
Thy blaft upon thy bugle horn,
   Cannot make us fight or fly.
Therefore fall on, or elfe begone,
   And yield to us the day:
It never fhall be faid that we are afraid
   Of thee, or thy yeomen gay.
If that be fo, cries Robin Hood,
   Let me but know your names,
And in the foreft of merry Sherwood,
   I fhall extol your fames.
And with our names, one of them faid,
   What haft thou here to do?
Except that thou wilt fight it out,
   Our names thou fhalt not know.
We'll fight no more, faid bold Robin Hood,
   You be men of valour ftout;
Come and go with me to Nottingham,
   And there we will fight it out.
With a But of fack we will bang it about,
   To fee who wins the day.

                           And

And for the cost make you no doubt,
  I have gold enough to pay.
And ever hereafter as long as we live,
  We all will brethren be:
For I love those men with heart and hand,
  That will fight and never flee.
So away they went to Nottingham,
  With fack to make amends;
For three days they the wine did chace,
  And drank themselves good friends.

---

18. ROBIN HOOD and the BEGGAR

Showing how he and the BEGGAR fought and changed
  Cloaths; how he went a begging to Nottingham;
  and how he saved three Brethren from hanging for
  stealing the King's Deer:
Tune of, ROBIN HOOD and the STRANGER.

COME and listen, you gentlemen all,
  With a hey down, down, and a down,
That mirth do love for to hear,
And a story true, I'll tell unto you,
  If that you will but draw near.
In elder times, when merriments were,
  And archery was holden good,
There was an outlaw, as many do know,
  Which men call Robin Hood.
Upon a time it chanced so,
  Bold Robin-Hood was merry dispos'd,
His time for to spend, he did intend,
  Either with friends or foes.
Then he got upon a gallant steed,
  The which was worth angels ten,
With a mantle of green, most brave to be seen,
  He left all his merry men.

F   And

And riding towards Nottingham
  Some paftime for to 'fpy,
There was he aware of a jolly beggar,
  As e'er he beheld with his eye.
An old patch'd coat the beggar had on,
  Which he did daily ufe to wear;
And many a bag about him did wag,
  Which made Robin Hood to him repair.
God fpeed, God fpeed, faid Robin Hood then,
  What countryman tell unto me ?
I am Yorkfhire, Sir, but ere you go far,
  Some charity give unto me.
I have no money, faid Robin Hood then,
  But a ranger within the wood;
I am an outlaw, as many do know,
  My name it is Robin Hood.
But yet I muft tell thee bonny beggar,
  That a bout with thee I muft try;
Thy coat of grey lay down I fay,
  And my mantle of green fhall lie by.
Content, content, the beggar he cry'd,
  Thy part it will be the worfe;
For I hope this bout to give thee the rout,
  And then have at thy purfe.
The beggar he had a mickle long ftaff,
  And Robin had a nut brown fword;
The beggar drew nigh, and at Robin let fly,
  But gave him ne'er a word.
Fight on, fight on, faid Robin Hood then,
  This game well pleafeth me,
For every blow that Robin gave,
  The beggar gave buffets three.
And fighting there full hardy and fore,
  Not far from Nottingham town,
They never fled 'till from Robin Hood's head
  The blood it ran trickling down.
O hold thy hand, faid Robin Hood,
  And thou and I will agree;
If that be true, the beggar he faid,
  Thy mantle come give unto me.
Now a change, a change, faid Robin Hood,
  Thy bags and coat give me;

                                        And

And this mantle of mine I'll to thee resign,
  My horse and my bravery.
When Robin Hood had got the beggar's cloaths,
  He looked round about;
Methinks, said he, I seem to be,
  A beggar brave and stout.
For now I have a bag for my bread;
  So I have another for my corn;
I have one for salt, and another for malt,
  And one for my little horn.
And now I will a begging go,
  Some charity for to find;
And if any more of Robin you'll know,
  In the second part 'tis behind.
Now Robin he is to Nottingham bound,
  With his bag hanging down to his knee,
His staff and his coat scarce worth a groat,
  Yet merrily passed he.
As Robin he passed the streets along,
  He heard a pitiful cry;
Three brethren dear, as he did hear,
  Condemned were to die.
Then Robin he hied to the sheriff's house,
  Some relief for to seek;
He skipp'd, he leap'd, and caper'd full high,
  As he went along the street.
But when to the sheriff's house he came,
  There a gentleman fine and brave,
Thou beggar, said he, come tell unto me,
  What is it thou would'st have?
No meat nor drink, said Robin Hood then,
  That I come here to crave;
But to get the lives of yeomen three,
  And that I fain would have.
That cannot be, thou bold beggar,
  Their fact it is so clear;
I tell to thee, they hang'd must be,
  For stealing our king's deer.
But when to the gallows they did come,
  There were many a weeping eye;
O hold your peace, said Robin Hood then,
  For certain they shall not die.

Then

Then Robin he fet his horn to his mouth,
  And he blew out blafts three,
'Till an hundred bold archers brave
  Came kneeling down to his knee.
What is your will, Mafter ? faid they,
  We are at thy command ;
Shoot eaft, fhoot weft, faid Robin then,
  And fee you fpare no man.
Then they fhot eaft, and they fhot weft,
  Their arrows were fo keen ;
The fheriff he, and his company,
  No longer could be feen.
Then he ftept to thofe brethren three,
  And away he has them ta'en ;
The fheriff he was croft, and many a man loft,
  That lay dead on the plain.
And away they went to the merry green wood,
  And fung with a merry glee,
And Robin Hood took thefe three brethren bold,
  To be of his yeomandree.

---

19. ROBIN HOOD, WILL. SCARLET, and LITTLE JOHN.

Or, A Narrative of the Victory obtained againft the
  Prince of ARRAGON and the two GIANTS ; and
  how WILL. SCARLET married the PRINCESS.
  Tune of, ROBIN HOOD ; Or, Hey down, a down.

NOW Robin Hood, Will. Scarlet, and Little John,
  Are walking over the plain,
With a good fat buck, which Will. Scarlet
  With his ftrong bow had flain.
Jog on, jog on, cries Robin Hood,
  The day it runs full faft,

                                 For

For tho' my nephew me a breakfast gave,
  I have not broke my fast.
Then to yonder lodge let us take our way,
  I think it wond'rous good,
Where my nephew, by my bold yeomen,
  Will be welcom'd unto the green wood.
With that he took the bugle horn,
  Full well he could it blow;
Strait from the woods came marching down
  One hundred tall fellows and mo.
Stand, stand to your arms, says Will. Scarlet,
  Lo, the enemies are within ken.
With that Robin Hood he laughed aloud,
  Crying, they are my bold yeomen.
Who when they arriv'd, and Robin espy'd,
  Crying, Master, what is your will?
We thought you had in danger been,
  Your horn did sound so shrill.
Now nay, now nay, quoth Robin Hood,
  The danger is past and gone;
I would have you welcome my nephew here,
  That has paid me two for one.
In feasting and sporting they spent the day,
  'Till Phœbus sunk into the deep;
Then each one to his quarters hy'd,
  His guard for to keep.
Long had they not walk'd within the green wood,
  But Robin he soon espy'd,
Of a beautiful damsel all alone,
  That on a black palfry did ride.
Her riding suit was of a sable hue black,
  Cyprus over her face,
Thro' which her rose-like cheeks did blush,
  All with a comely grace.
Come tell me the cause, thou pretty one,
  Quoth Robin, and tell me right,
From whence thou com'st, and whither thou go'st,
  All in this mournful plight?
From London I came, the damsel reply'd,
  From London upon the Thames,
Which circled is, O grief to tell!
  Besieg'd with foreign arms.

         By

By the proud Prince of Arragon,
　　Who swears by his martial hand,
To have the princess to his spouse,
　　Or else to waste this land.

Except such champions can be found,
　　That dare fight three to three,
Against the prince and giants twain,
　　Most horrid for to see;

Whose grisly looks and eyes like brands,
　　Strike terror where they come,
With serpents hissing on their helms,
　　Instead of feather'd plume.

The princess shall be the victor's prize,
　　The King hath vow'd and said;
And he that shall the conquest win,
　　Shall have her to his bride.

Now we are four damsels sent abroad,
　　To East, West, North, and South,
To try whose fortune is so good,
　　To find these champions out.

But all in vain we have fought about,
　　For none so bold there are,
Who dare adventure life and blood,
　　To free a lady fair.

When is the day? quoth Robin Hood,
　　Tell me this and no more?
On Midsummer next, the damsel said,
　　Which is June the twenty-four.

With that the tears trickl'd down her cheeks,
　　And silent was her tongue.
With sighs and sobs she took her leave,
　　And away her palfry sprung.

The news struck Robin to the heart,
　　He fell down on the grass,
His actions and his troubl'd mind,
　　Show'd he perplexed was.

Where lies your grief? quoth Will. Scarlet,
　　O master! tell to me?
If the damsel's eyes have pierc'd your heart,
　　I'll fetch her back to thee.

Now nay, now nay, quoth Robin Hood,
　　She does not cause my smart;

　　　　　　　　　　　　　　　But

But 'tis the poor diſtreſs'd princeſs,
　That wounds me to the heart :
I'll go fight the giants all,
　To ſet the lady free,
The D —— take my ſoul, quoth Little John,
　If I part with thy company.
Muſt I ſtay behind ? quoth Will. Scarlet,
　No, no, that muſt not be ;
I'll make the third man in the fight,
　So we ſhall be three to three.
Theſe words cheer'd Robin to the heart,
　Joy ſhone upon his face,
Within his arms he hugged them both,
　And kindly did embrace.
Quoth he we'll put on motley grey,
　And long ſtaves in our hands,
A ſcrip and bottle by our ſides,
　As come from the Holy Lands.
So may we paſs along the highway,
　None will aſk us from whence we came.
But take us pilgrim for to be,
　Or elſe ſome holy men :
Now they are on their journey gone,
　As faſt as they may ſped,
Yet for all their haſte, ere they arriv'd,
　The princeſs forth was led,
To be delivered to the prince,
　Who in the liſt did ſtand,
Prepar'd to fight, or elſe receive
　His lady by the hand.
With that he walk'd about the liſt,
　With giants by his ſide ;
Bring forth, quoth he, your champions,
　Or bring me forth my bride :
This is the four and twentieth day,
　The day prefix'd upon ;
Bring forth my bride, or London burns,
　I ſware by Alcoran.
Then cries the King and Queen likewiſe,
　Both weeping as they ſpake,
Lo! we have brought our daughter dear,
　Whom we are forc'd to forſake.

Wih

With that ſtept out bold Robin Hood,
   Cries, my Liege, it muſt not be ſo,
Such beauty as the fair princeſs
   Is not for a tyrant's mow.

The prince he then began to ſtorm,
   Cries fool, fanatic, baboon!
How dare thou ſtop my valour's prize,
   I'll kill thee with a frown.

Thou Tyrant, Turk, thou Infidel,
   Thus Robin began to reply,
Thy frowns I ſcorn: lo! here's my gage,
   And thus I thee defy.

And for thoſe two Goliaths there,
   That ſtand on either ſide,
Here are two little David's by,
   That ſoon can tame their pride.

Then the King did for armour ſend,
   For lances, ſwords and ſhields;
And thus all three in armour bright,
   Came marching into the field.

The trumpets began to ſound a charge,
   Each ſingled out his man;
Their arms in pieces ſoon were hew'd,
   Blood ſprang from every vein.

The Prince reach'd Robin Hood a blow,
   He ſtruck with might and main,
Which made him reel about the field,
   As though he had been ſlain.

God-a-mercy, quoth Robin Hood, for that blow,
   The quarrel ſhall ſoon be try'd,
This ſtroke ſhall ſhow a full divorce,
   Betwixt thee and thy bride.

So from his ſhoulders he cut his head,
   Which on the ground did fall,
And grumbled ſore at Robin Hood,
   To be ſo dealt withal.

The giants then began to rage
   To ſee their prince lay dead;
Thou wilt be next, ſaid Little John,
   Unleſs thou guard thy head.

With that his falchion he whirl'd about,
   It was both keen and ſharp;

He

He clave the giant to the belt,
 And cut in twain his heart.
Will. Scarlet well had play'd his part,
 The giant he had brought to his knee;
Quoth Will. the Devil cannot break his faft,
 Unlefs he has you all three,
So with his falchion he run him through,
 A deep and ghaftly wound ;
Who damn'd and foam'd, curs'd and blafphem'd,
 And then fell to the ground.
Now all the lifts with fhouts were fill'd,
 The fkies they did refound,
Which brought the princefs to herfelf,
 Who had fallen into a fwoon.
The King, and Queen, and Princefs fair,
 Came walking to the place,
And gave the champions many thanks,
 And did them further grace.
Tell me, quoth the King, whence you are,
 That thus difguifed came,
Whofe valour fpeaks that noble blood,
 Doth run through every vein.
A boon, a boon, quoth Robin Hood,
 On my knees I beg and crave ;
By my crown, quoth the king, I grant,
 Afk what, and thou fhalt have.
Then pardon I beg for my merry men,
 Which are in the green wood,
For Little John, and Will Scarlet,
 And for me bold Robin Hood.
Art thou Robin Hood ? Quoth the King ;
 For the valour thou haft fhown,
Your pardon I do freely grant,
 And welcome every one.
The Princefs I promis'd the victor's prize,
 She cannot have you all three ;
She fhall chufe, quoth Robin ; faid Little John,
 Then little fhare falls to me.
Then did the Princefs view all three,
 With a comely lovely grace,
And took Will. Scarlet by the hand,
 Saying here I make my choice.

With

With that a noble Lord ſtept forth,
  Of Maxwell earl was he,
Who look'd Will. Scarlet in the face,
  And wept moſt bitterly.
Quoth he, I had a ſon like thee,
  Whom I lov'd wond'rous well,
But he is gone, or rather dead,
  His name is young Gamewell.
Then did Will. Scarlet fall on his knees,
  Crying father! father! here,
Here kneels your ſon, your young Gamewell,
  You ſaid you lov'd ſo dear.
But, lord! what embracing and kiſſing were there,
  When all theſe friends were met!
They are gone to the wedding, and ſo to the bedding,
  And ſo I bid you good night.

---

20. LITTLE JOHN and the four BEGGARS.
Showing how he went a BEGGING, and fought with
four BEGGARS, and what a Prize he got from them.
Tune of, ROBIN HOOD and the BEGGAR.

ALL you that delight for to ſpend ſome time,
    With a hey down, &c.
  A merry ſong for to ſing,
Unto me draw near, and you ſhall hear,
  How Little John went a begging.
As Robin Hood walked the foreſt along,
  And all his yeomandree,
Says Robin, ſome of you muſt a begging go,
  And, Little John, it muſt be thee.
Says John, if I muſt a begging go,
  I will have a palmer's weed,

                                        With

With a ftaff and a coat, and bags of all fort,
  The better than fhall I fpeed.
Come now give me a bag for my bread,
  And another for my cheefe,
And one for a penny, if I get any,
  That nothing I may leefe.
Now Little John he is a begging gone,
  Seeking for fome relief;
But of all the beggars he met on the way,
  Little John he was the chief.
But as he was walking himfelf alone,
  Four beggars he chanc'd to 'fpy,
Some deaf, fome blind, fome came behind;
  Says John, Here is a brave company.
Good-morrow, fays John, my brethren dear,
  Good fortune I had you to fee:
Which way do you go, pray let me know,
  For I want fome company.
O what is here to do? faid Little John:
  Why ring all thefe bells? faid he,
What dog is hanging? Come, let us be ganging,
  That we the truth may fee.
Here is no dog, one of them faid,
  Good fellow, I tell unto thee;
But here is one dead, that will give us cheefe and bread,
  And it may be one fingle penny.
We have brethren in London, another faid,
  So we have in Coventry,
In Berwick and Dover, and all the world over,
  But ne'er a crooked Carl like thee.
Therefore ftand thee back, thou crooked Carl,
  And take that knock on the crown;
Nay, fays Little John, I'll not be gone,
  For a bout I will have of you round.
Now have at you all, faid Little John,
  If you be fo full of your blows,
Fight on all four, and never give o'er,
  Whether you be friends or foes.
John nipp'd the dumb, and made him to roar,
  And the blind that could not fee;
And he that a cripple had been for feven years,
  He made him run fafter than he.

                              And

And flinging them all againſt the wall,
  With many a ſturdy bang,
It made John to ſing, to hear the gold ring,
  And againſt the walls cry twang.

Then he got out of the beggars cloaks
  Three hundred pounds in gold ;
Good fortune had I, ſaid Little John,
  Such a ſight for to behold.

But found he in the beggars' bag
  But three hundred pounds and three ;
If I drink water while this doth laſt,
  Then an ill death may I die.

And my begging trade I will now give o'er,
  My fortune hath been ſo good :
Therefore I will not ſtay, but I will away,
  To the foreſt of merry Sherwood ;

And when to the foreſt of Sherwood he came,
  He quickly there did ſee,
Bold Robin Hood, his maſter good,
  And all his company.

What news ? what news ? ſaid Robin Hood,
  Come, Little John, tell unto me,
How do'ſt thou ſped with thy beggar's trade,
  For that I fain would ſee ?

No news, but good, ſaid Little John,
  With begging full well I have ſped ;
Three hundred and three have I here for thee,
  In ſilver and gold ſo red.

Then Robin Hood took Little John by the hand,
  And danced round the oak tree ;
If we drink water while this doth laſt,
  Then an ill death may we die.

So to conclude my merry new ſong,
  All you that delight to ſing,
'Tis of Robin Hood, that archer good,
  And how Little John went a begging.

21. ROBIN HOOD and the RANGER.

Or, True Friendship after a Fierce Fight.
Tune of, Arthur-a-Bland.

WHEN Phœbus had melted the fickles of ice,
   With a hey down, &c.
And likewise the mountains of fnow,
Bold Robin Hood he would ramble to fee,
   To frolick abroad with his bow.
He left all his merry men waiting behind,
   Whilft through the green vallies he pafs'd,
Where he did behold a forefter bold,
   Who cry'd out, Friend, whither fo faft?
I am going, quoth Robin, to kill a fat buck,
   For me and my merry men all;
Befides, ere I go, I'll have a fat doe,
   Or elfe it fhall coft me a fall.
You'd beft have a care, faid the forefter then,
   For thefe are his Majefty's deer;
Before you fhall fhoot, the thing I'll difpute,
   For I am head forefter here.
Thefe thirteen long fummers, faid Robin, I'm fure,
   My arrows I here have let fly,
Where freely I range; methinks it is ftrange
   You fhould have more power than I.
This foreft, quoth Robin, I think is my own,
   And fo are the nimble deer too;
Therefore I declare, and folemnly fwear,
   I'll not be affronted by you.
The forefter he had a long quarter ftaff,
   Likewife a broad fword by his fide;
Without more ado, he prefently drew,
   Declaring the truth fhould be try'd.

G

Bold Robin Hood had a ſword of the beſt,
    Thus ere he would take any wrong,
His courage was fluſh, he'd venture a bruſh,
    And thus they went to it ding dong.
The very firſt blow the foreſter gave,
    He made his broad weapon cry twang;
'Twas over the head, he fell down for dead,
    O that was a damnable bang!
But Robin he ſoon recovered himſelf,
    And bravely fell to it again;
The very next ſtroke their weapons they broke,
    Yet never a man there was ſlain.
At quarter ſtaff then they reſolved to play,
    Becauſe they would have the other bout;
And brave Robin Hood right valiantly ſtood,
    Unwilling he was to give out.
Bold Robin he gave him very hard blows,
    The other return'd them as faſt;
At every ſtroke their jackets did ſmoke;
    Three hours the combat did laſt.
At length in a rage the bold foreſter grew,
    And cudgell'd bold Robin ſo ſore,
That he could not ſtand, ſo ſhaking his hand,
    He ſaid, Let us freely give o'er.
Thou art a brave fellow, I needs muſt confeſs
    I never knew any ſo good;
Thou art fit to be a yeoman for me,
    And range in the merry green wood.
I'll give thee this ring as a token of love,
    For bravely thou haſt acted thy part:
That man that can fight in him I delight,
    And love him with all my whole heart.
Then Robin Hood ſetting his horn to his mouth,
    A blaſt he merrily blew;
His yeomen did hear, and ſtrait did appear,
    A hundred with ſturdy long bows.
Now Little John came at the head of them all,
    Cloath'd in a rich mantle of green;
And likewiſe the reſt were gloriouſly dreſt,
    A delicate ſight to be ſeen!
Lo! theſe are my yeomen, ſays Robin Hood,
    Thou ſhalt be one of the train;

                    A mantle

A mantle and bow, and quiver alſo,
  I give them whom I entertain.
The foreſter willingly entered the liſt,
  They were ſuch a beautiful fight ;
Then with a long bow they ſhot a fat doe,
  And made a rich ſupper at night.
What ſinging and dancing was in the green wood,
  For the joy of another new mate ;
With might and delight they ſpent all the night,
  And liv'd at a plentiful rate.
The foreſter ne'er was ſo merry before,
  As when he was with theſe brave ſouls,
Who never would fail, in beer, wine, and ale,
  To take off their cheriſh bowls.
Then Robin Hood gave him a mantle of green,
  Broad arrows, and a curious long bow :
This done the next day, ſo gallant and gay,
  He marched them all on a row.
Quoth he, my bold yeomen be true to your truſt,
  And then we may range the woods wide ;
They did all declare, and ſolemnly ſwear,
  They'd conquer, or die by his ſide.

---

22. ROBIN HOOD and LITTLE JOHN.
Being an Account of their firſt meeting, their fierce
  Encounter and Conqueſt. To which is added, their
  friendly Agreement, and how he came to be called
  LITTLE JOHN.
     Tune of ARTHUR-A-BLAND.

WHEN Robin Hood was about twenty years old
  With a hey down, down, and a down,
He happened to meet Little John,
A jolly briſk blade, right fit for the trade,
  For he was a luſty young man.

Tho' he was call'd little, his limbs they werelrge,
   And his ftature was feven feet high :
Wherever he came, they quak'd at his name,
   For foon he would make them fly.
How they came acquainted I'll tell you in brief,
   If you will but liften awhile,
For this very jeft among all the reft,
   I think may caufe you to fmile.
For Robin Hood faid to his jolly bowmen,
   Pray tarry you here in this grove,
And fee that you all obferve well my call,
   While thorough the foreft I rove.
We have had no fport thefe fourteen long days,
   Therefore now abroad will I go ;
Now fhould I be beat, and cannot retreat,
   My horn I will prefently blow.
Then did he fhake hands with his merry men all,
   And bid them at prefent good-bye :
Then as near the brook his journey he took,
   A ftranger he chanc'd to efpy.
They happen'd to meet on a long narrow bridge,
   And neither of them would give way.
Quoth bold Robin Hood, and fturdily ftood,
   I'll fhow you right Nottingham play.
With that from his quiver an arrow he drew,
   A broad arrow with a goofe wing :
The ftranger reply'd, I'll licker thy hide,
   If thou offer to touch the ftring.
Quoth bold Robin Hood, thou deft prate like an afs,
   For were I but to bend my bow,
I could fend a dart quite through thy proud heart,
   Before thou could'lt ftrike me one blow.
Thou talk'lt like a coward, the ftranger reply'd,
   Well arm'd with a long bow you ftand,
To fhoot at my breaft, while I, I proteft,
   Have nought but a ftaff in my hand.
The name of coward, quoth Robin, I fcorn,
   Therefore my long bow I'll lay by ;
And now for thy fake a ftaff I will take,
   The truth of thy manhood to try.
Then Robin Hood ftept to a thicket of trees,
   And chofe him a ftaff of ground oak ;

                                                Now

Now this being done, away he did run
  To the stranger, and merrily spoke:
Lo! see my staff is lusty and tough,
  Now here on this bridge we will play;
Whoever falls in, the other shall win
  The battle, and so we'll away.
With all my whole heart, the stranger reply'd,
  I scorn in the least to give out;
This said, they fell to it, without more dispute,
  And their staffs they did flourish about.
At first Robin Hood gave the stranger a bang,
  So hard that it made his bones ring:
The stranger he said, this must be repaid,
  I'll give you as good as you bring.
So long as I am able to handle a staff,
  To die in your debt, friend, I scorn.
Then to it both goes, and follow their blows,
  As if they'd been threshing of corn.
The stranger gave Robin a crack on the crown,
  Which caused the blood to appear;
Then Robin enrag'd more fiercely engag'd,
  And follow'd his blows more severe.
So thick and so fast he did lay it on him,
  With a passionate fury and ire;
At every stroke he made him to smoke,
  As if he had been all on fire.
O then in a fury the stranger he grew,
  And gave them a damnable look,
And with it a blow, which laid him full low,
  And tumbled him into the brook.
I prithee, good fellow, where art thou now?
  The stranger in laughter he cry'd;
Quoth bold Robin Hood, good faith, in the flood,
  And floating along with the tide.
I needs must acknowledge thou art a brave soul,
  With thee I'll no longer contend;
For needs must I say, thou hast got the day,
  Our battle shall be at an end.
Then unto the bank he did presently wade,
  And pull'd himself out by a thorn;
Which done, at the last he blew a loud blast
  Straitway on his fine bugle horn:

The echo of which thro' the vallies did ring,
  At which his ftout bowmen appear'd,
All cloath'd in green, moft gay to be feen,
  So up to their mafter they fteer'd.
O what is the matter! quoth Will. Stutely,
  Good mafter, you are wet to the fkin?
No matter, quoth he, the lad that you fee,
  In fighting hath tumbled me in.
He fhall not go fcot free, the others reply'd,
  So ftrait they were feizing him there,
To duck him likewife; but Robin Hood cries,
  He is a ftout fellow, forbear.
There's no one fhall wrong thee, friend, be not afraid,
  Thefe bowmen upon me do wait;
There's threefcore and nine; if thou wilt be mine,
  Thou fhalt have my livery ftrait.
And other accoutrements fitting alfo,
  Speak up jolly blade, never fear:
I'll teach you alfo the ufe of the bow,
  To fhoot at the fat fallow deer.
O here is my hand, the ftranger reply'd,
  I'll ferve you with all my whole heart;
My name is John Little, a man of good mettle,
  Ne'er doubt me, for I'll play my part.
His name fhall be alter'd, quoth Will. Stutely,
  And I will his god-father be;
Prepare than a feaft, and none of the leaft,
  For we will be merry, quoth he.
They prefently fetched him a brace of fat does,
  With humming ftrong liquor likewife;
They lov'd what was good; fo in the green wood
  This pretty fweet babe they baptiz'd.
He was, I muft tell you, but feven feet high,
  And may be an ell in the waift;
He was a fweet lad; much feafting they had,
  Bold Robin the chriftening grac'd,
With all his bowmen, which ftood in a ring,
  And were of the Nottingham breed;
Brave Stutely came then with feven yeomen,
  And did in this manner proceed:
This infant was call'd John Little quoth he,
  Which name fhall be changed anon;

                                    The

The words we'll tranſpoſe ; ſo wherever he goes,
   His name ſhall be called Little John.
They all with a ſhout made the elements ring ;
   So ſoon as the offi.e was o'er,
To feaſting they went, with true merriment,
   And tippled ſtrong liquors gallore.
Then Robin he took the pretty ſweet babe,
   And cloath'd him from top to toe,
In garments of green, moſt gay to be ſeen,
   And gave him a curious long bow.
Thou ſhalt be an archer as well as the beſt,
   And range in the green wood with us,
Where we will not want gold or ſilver, behold,
   While biſhops have ought in their purſe.
We live here like 'ſquires or lords of renown,
   Without e'er a foot of free land ;
We feaſt on good cheer, with wine, ale, and beer,
   And every thing at our command.
Then muſick and dancing did finiſh the day,
   At le h when the ſun wax'd low,
Then all the whole train the grove did refrain,
   And unto their caves they did go.
And ſo ever after, as long as they liv'd,
   Altho' he be proper and tall,
Yet nevertheleſs, the truth to expreſs,
   Still Little John they did him call.

---

23. The Bishop of Hereford's Entertainment by
   Robin Hood and Little John, &c. in Merry
   Barnsdall.

Some they will tak of bold Robin Hood
   And ſome of barons bold ;
But I'll tell you how he ſerv'd the biſhop of Hereford,
   When he robb'd him of his gold.

As it befel in merry Barnſdale,
  And under the green wood tree,
The biſhop of Hereford was to come by,
  With all his company.
Come kill a veniſon, ſaid Bold Robin Hood,
  Come kill me a good fat deer,
The biſhop of Hereford is to dine with me to-day,
  And he ſhall pay well for his cheer.
We'll kill a fat ven'ſon, ſaid bold Robin Hood,
  And dreſs it by the highway ſide.
And we will watch the biſhop narrowly,
  Leſt ſome other way he ſhould ride.
Robin Hood dreſs'd himſelf in ſhepherd's attire,
  With ſix of his men alſo ;
And when the biſhop of Hereford came by,
  They about the fire did go.
O what is the matter, than ſaid the biſhop,
  Or for whom do you make this ado ?
Or why do you kill the king's ven'ſon,
  When your company is ſo few ?
We are ſhepherds, ſaid bold Robin Hood,
  And we keep ſheep all the year,
And we are diſpoſed to be merry this day,
  And to kill of the king's fat deer.
You are brave fellows, ſaid the biſhop,
  And the king of your doings ſhall know,
Therefore make haſte, and come along with me,
  For before the king you ſhall go.
O pardon ! O pardon ! ſaid bold Robin Hood,
  O pardon, I thee pray ;
For it becomes not your lordſhip's coat
  To take ſo many lives away.
No pardon, no pardon, ſays the biſhop,
  No pardon I thee owe ;
Therefore make haſte, and come along with me,
  For before the king you ſhall go.
Then Robin ſet his back againſt a tree,
  And his foot againſt a thorn,
And from underneath a ſhepherd's coat
  He pull'd out his bugle norn.
He put the little end to his mouth,
  And a loud blaſt he did blow,

                      'Till

'Till threefcore and ten of bold Robin's men,
  Came running all on a row :
All making obeyfance to bold Robin Hood,
  'Twas a comely fight to fee.
What is the matter, Mafter, faid Little John,
  That you blow fo haftily ?
O here is the bifhop of Hereford,
  And no pardon we fhall have ;
Cut off his head, Mafter, faid Little John,
  And throw him into his grave.
O pardon ! O pardon ! faid the bifhop,
  O pardon, I thee pray ;
For if I had known it had been you,
  I'd have gone fome other way.
No pardon, no pardon, faid Robin Hood,
  No pardon I thee owe ;
Therefore make hafte, and come along with me,
  For to merry Barnfdale you fhall go.
Then Robin took the bifhop by the hand,
  And led him to merry Barnfdale,
He made him ftay and fup with him that night,
  And to drink, wine, beer, and ale.
Call in the reckoning, faid the bifhop,
  For I think it grows woud'rous high ?
Lend me your purfe, Mafter, faid Little John,
  And I'll tell you bye-and-bye.
Then Little John took the bifhop's cloak,
  And fpread it upon the-ground,
And out of the bifhop's portmantua
  He told three hundred pound.
Here's money enough, Mafter, faid Little John,
  And a comely fight 'tis to fee ;
It makes me in charity with the bifhop,
  Tho' he heartily loveth not me.
Robin Hood took the bifhop by the hand,
  And he caufed the mufic to play ;
And he made the bifhop dance in his boots,
  And glad he could fo get away.

24. ROBIN HOOD rescuing the three SQUIRES
from NOTTINGHAM GALLOWS.

BOLD Robin Hood ranging the forest all round,
   The forest all round ranged he;
O there did he meet with a gay lady,
   She came weeping along the highway.
Why weep you? why weep you? bold Robin he said,
   What weep you for gold or fee?
Or do you weep for your maidenhead,
   That is that is taken from your body?
I weep not for gold, the lady reply'd,
   Neither do I weep for fee;
Nor do I weep for my maidenhead,
   That is taken from my body.
What weep you for then, said jolly Robin,
   I prithee come tell unto me?
Oh! I do weep for my three sons,
   For they are all condemned to die.
What church have they robbed, said jolly Robin,
   Or what parish priest have they slain?
What maids have they forc'd against their will,
   Or with other mens wives have they lain?
No church have they robbed, this lady reply'd,
   Nor parish priest have they slain;
No maids have they forc'd against their will,
   Nor with other mens wives have they lain.
What have they done then, said jolly Robin,
   Come tell me most speedily?
Oh! it is for killing the king's fallow deer,
   And they're all condemned to die.

                              Get

Get you home, get you home, said jolly Robin,
  Get you home most speedily,
And I will unto fair Nottingham go,
  For the fake of the 'squires all three.
Then bold Robin Hood for Nottingham goes,
  For Nottingham town goes he,
O there did he meet with a poor beggar man,
  He came creeping along the highway.
What news, what news, thou old beggar man,
  What news come tell unto me?
O there's weeping and wailing in Nottingham,
  For the death of the 'squires all three.
This beggar man had a coat on his back,
  'Twas neither green, yellow, nor red;
Bold Robin Hood thought 'twas no difgrace,
  To be in the beggar man's ftead.
Come, pull off thy coat, thou old beggar man,
  And thou fhalt put on mine,
And forty good fhillings I'll give thee to boot,
  Befides brandy, good beer, ale, and wine.
Bold Robin Hood then unto Nottingham came,
  Unto Nottingham town came he,
O there did he meet with great mafter fheriff,
  And likewife the 'squires all three.
One boon, one boon, fays jolly Robin,
  One boon I beg on my knee,
That as for the death of thefe three 'squires,
  Their hangman I may be.
Soon granted, foon granted, fays mafter fheriff,
  Soon granted unto thee;
And you fhall have all their gay cloathing,
  Aye, and all their white money.
O, I will have none of their gay cloathing,
  Nor none of their white money;
But I'll have three blafts on my bugle horn,
  That their fouls to heaven may flee.
When Robin Hood mounted the gallows fo high,
  Where he blew loud and fhrill,
Till an hundred and ten of Robin Hood's men,
  Came marching down the green hill.
Whofe men are they, fays mafter fheriff,
  Whofe men are they, come tell unto me?

O they

O they are mine, but none of thine,
 And are come for the 'squires all three.
O take them! O take them, fays great mafter fheriff,
 O take them along with thee;
For there's never a man in fair Nottingham,
 Can do the like of thee.

---

25. The KING's DISGUISE and FRIENDSHIP
 with ROBIN HOOD.

TO A NORTHERN TUNE.

KING RICHARD hearing of the pranks
 Of Robin Hood and his men,
He much admir'd, and more defir'd,
 To fee both him and them.
Then with a dozen of his lords,
 To Nottingham he rode:
When he eame there, he made good cheer,
 And took up his abode.
He having ftaid there fome time,
 But had no hopes to fpeed,
He and his lords, with one accord,
 All put on monks weeds.
From Fountain Abbey they did ride,
 Down to Barnfdale;
Where Robin Hood prepared ftood,
 All company to affail.
The king was higher than the reft,
 And Robin thought he had
An abbot been whom he had feen,
 To rob him he was glad.
He took the king's horfe by the head,
 Abbot, fays he, abide?

I am

I am bound to rue such knaves as you,
   That live in pomp and pride.
But we are messengers from the king,
   The king himself did say;
Near to this place his royal grace,
   To speak with thee does stay.
God save the king, said Robin Hood,
   And all that wish him well;
He that denies his sovereignty,
   I wish he was in hell.
Thyself thou cursed, says the king,
   For thou a traitor art:
Nay, but that you are his messenger,
   I swear you lie in heart.
For I never yet hurt any man,
   That honest is and true;
But those who give their minds to live
   Upon other men's due.
I never hurt the husbandman,
   That use to till the ground;
Nor spill the blood who range the wood,
   To follow hawk or hound.
My chiefest spite to clergy is,
   Who in these days bear great sway;
With friars and monks, and their fine sprunks,
   I make my chiefest prey.
But I am very glad, says Robin Hood,
   That I have met you here;
Come, before we end, you shall, my friend,
   Taste of our green wood cheer.
The king he then did marvel much,
   And so did all his men;
They thought with fear, what kind of cheer,
   Robin would provide for them.
Robin took the king's horse by the head,
   And led him to his tent:
Thou would'st not be so us'd, quoth he,
   But that my king thee sent:
Nay, more than that, quoth Robin Hood,
   For good King Richard's sake,
If you had as much gold as ever I told,
   I would not one penny take.

H

Then

Then Robin fet his horn to his mouth,
  And a loud blaft he did blow,
'Till a hundred and ten of Robin Hood's men,
  Came marching all of a row.
And when they came bold Robin before,
  Each man did bend his knee,
O, thought the King, 'tis a gallant thing,
  And a feemly fight to fee.
Within himfelf the King did fay,
  Thefe men of Robin Hood's
More humble be than mine to me ;
  So the court may learn of the woods,
So then they all to dinner went,
  Upon a carpet green ;
Black, yellow, red, finely mingled,
  Moft curious to be feen.
Venifon and fowls were plenty there,
  With fifh out of the river :
King Richard fwore, on fea or fhore,
  He never was feafted better.
Then Robin takes a cann of ale,
  Come let us now begin,
And every man fhall have his cann,
  Here's a health unto the king.
The king himfelf drank to the king,
  So round about it went :
Two barrels of ale, both ftout and ftale,
  To pledge that health was fpent.
And after that a bowl of wine,
  In his hand took Robin Hood,
Until I die, I'll drink wine, faid he,
  While I live in the green wood.
Bend all your bows, faid Robin Hood,
  And with the grey goofe wing,
Such fport now fhow, as you would do
  In the prefence of the king.
They fhewed fuch brave archery,
  By cleaving fticks and wands,
That the king did fay, fuch men as they
  Live not in many lands.
Well, Robin Hood, then fays the King,
  If I could thy pardon get,

To

To ferve the King in every thing,
  Would'ft thou thy mind firm fet ?
Yes, with all my heart, bold Robin faid,
  So they flung off their hoods,
To ferve the King in every thing,
  They fwore they would fpend their blood.
For a clergyman was firft my bane,
  Which makes me hate them all ;
But if you will be fo kind to me,
  Love them again I fhall.
The King no longer could forbear,
  For he was mov'd with truth.
I am thy King, thy fovereign King,
  That appears before you all :
When Robin faw that it was he,
  Strait then he down did fall.
Stand up again, then faid the King,
  I'll thee thy pardon give,
Stand up my friends, who can contend,
  When I give leave to live ?
So they are all gone to Nottingham,
  All fhouting as they came,
And when the people them did fee,
  They thought the King was flain.
And for that caufe the outlaws were come,
  To rule all as they lift ;
And them to fhun, which way to run,
  The people did not wift.
The plowman left the plow in the fields,
  The fmith ran from his fhop ;
Old folk alfo, that 'fcarce could go,
  Over their fticks did hop.
The King foon did let them underftand,
  He had been in the green wood,
And from that day, for evermore,
  He'd forgiven Robin Hood.
When the people they did hear,
  And the truth was known,
They all did fing, God fave the King,
  Hang care, the town's our own.
What's that Robin Hood ? then faid the fheriff,
  That varlet I do hate,

H 2
                        Both

Both me and mine he caufed to dine,
  And ferved us all with one plate:
Ho! ho! faid Robin, I know what you mean,
  Come, take your gold again;
Be friends with me, and I with thee,
  And fo with every man.
Now mafter fheriff you are paid,
  And fince you are the beginner,
As well as you give me my due,
  For you ne'er paid for that dinner.
But if that fhould pleafe the King,
  So much your houfe to grace;
To fup with you, for to fpeak true,
  Know you ne'er was bafe.
The fheriff could not gainfay,
  For a trick was put upon him;
A fupper was draft, the King was a gueft,
  But he thought it would have undone him.
They are all gone to London court,
  Robin Hood and all his train;
He once was there a noble peer,
  And now he's there again.
Many fuch pranks brave Robin play'd,
  While he liv'd in the green wood;
Now, my friends attend, and hear an end
  Of honeft Robin Hood.

26. ROBIN HOOD and the GOLDEN ARROW.

WHEN as the fheriff of Nottingham,
  Was come with mickle grief;
He talk'd no good of Robin Hood,
  That ftrong and fturdy thief.
    Fal la, dal do.

So

So unto London road he paſt,
    His loſſes to unfold,
To King Richard, who did regard,
    The tale that he had told.
Why, quoth the King, what ſhall I do;
    Art thou not ſheriff for me?
The law is in force, to take thy courſe,
    Of them that injure thee.
Go, get thee gone, and by thyſelf
    Deviſe ſome tricking game,
For to enthral yon rebels all,
    Go, take thy courſe with them.
So away the ſheriff he return'd,
    And by the way he thought
Of th' words of the King, and how the thing
    To paſs might well be brought.
For within his mind he imagined
    That when ſuch matches were,
Thoſe outlaws ſtout, without all doubt,
    Would be the bowmen there.
So an arrow with a golden head,
    And a ſhaft of ſilver white,
Who on the day ſhould bear away
    For his own proper right.
Tiding came to bold Robin Hood,
    Under the green wood tree;
Come prepare you then, my merry men,
    We'll go yon ſport to ſee.
With that ſtept forth a brave young man,
    David of Doncaſter,
Maſter, ſaid he, be rull'd by me,
    From the green wood we'll not ſtir.
To tell the truth, I'm well informed,
    Yon match it is a wile,
The ſheriff I wiſs deviſes this,
    Us archers to beguile.
Thou ſmell'ſt of a coward, ſaid Robin,
    Thy words do not pleaſe me;
Come on't what will, I'll try my ſkill,
    At yon brave archery.
O then beſpoke brave Little John,
    Come, let us thither gang;

H 3

Come liften to me how it fhall be,
   That we need not be ken'd.
Our mantles of Lincoln green
   Behind us we will leave ;
We'll drefs us all fo feveral,
   They fhall not us perceive.
One fhall wear white, another red,
   One yellow, another blue ;
Thus in difguife, in the exercife
   We'll gang whate'er enfue.
Forth from the green wood they are gone,
   With hearts all firm and ftout,
Refolving with the fheriff's men
   To have a hearty bout.
So themfelves they mixed with the reft,
   To prevent all fufpicion ;
For if they fhould together hold
   They thought it no difcretion.
So the fheriff looking round about,
   Amongft eight hundred men,
But could not fee the fight that he,
   Had long fufpected then.
Some faid, if Robin Hood was here,
   And all his men to boot,
Sure none of them could pafs thefe men,
   So bravely they did fhoot.
Ay, quoth the fheriff, and fcratch'd his head,
   I thought he would have been here ;
I thought he would, but tho' he's bold,
   He durft not now appear,
O that word griev'd Robin Hood to the heart,
   He vexed in his blood :
Ere long, thought he, thou fhalt well fee
   That here was Robin Hood.
Some cried Blue Jacket, another cried Brown,
   And a third cried brave Yellow ;
But the fourth man faid, yon man in red,
   In this place has no fellow.
For that was Robin Hood himfelf,
   For he was cloath'd in red ;
At every fhot the prize he got,
   For he was both furo and dead.

So the arrow with the golden head,
  And shaft of silver white,
Brave Robin Hood won, and bore with him,
  For his own proper right.
These outlaws there that very day,
  To shun all kinds of doubt,
By three or four, no less nor more,
  As they went in came out.
Until they all assembled were
  Under the green wood shade,
Where they relate in pleasant sport
  What brave pastime they made.
Says Robin Hood, all my care is,
  How that yon sheriff may
Know certainly that it was I
  That bore his arrow away.
Says Little John, my counsel good
  Did take effect before;
So therefore now, if you'll allow,
  I will advise once more.
Speak on, speak on, said Robin Hood,
  Thy wit's both quick and sound.
This I advise, said Little John,
  That a letter shall be penn'd,
And when it is done, to Nottingham
  You to the sheriff shall send.
That is well advised, said Robin Hood,
  But how must it be sent?
Pugh! when you please, 'tis done with ease,
  Master, be you content.
I'll stick it on my arrow's head,
  And shoot it into the town,
The mark must show where it must go,
  Wherever it lights down.
The project it was well perform'd,
  The sheriff that letter had,
Which when he read he scratch'd his head,
  And rav'd like one that's mad.
So we'll leave him chafing in the grease,
  Which will do him no good:
Now, my friend attend, and hear the end
  Of honest Robin Hood.

27. ROBIN HOOD and the VALIANT KNIGHT.

Together with an Account of his DEATH and BURIAL.

Tune of ROBIN HOOD and the FIFTEEN FORESTERS.

WHEN Robin Hood, and his merio men all,
    Derry down, down,
  Had reigned many a year,
The King was then told that they had been bold
  To his bishops and noble peers.
      Hey down, derry, derry down.
Therefore they called a council of state,
  To know what was to be done,
For to quell their pride, or else, they reply'd
  The land would be over-run.
Having consulted a whole summer's day,
  At length it was agreed,
That one should be sent to try the event,
  And fetch him away with speed.
Therefore a trusty and worthy knight
  The King was pleased to call
Sir William by name, when to him he came,
  He told him his pleasure all.
Go from hence to bold Robin Hood,
  And bid him, without more ado,
Surrender himself, or else the proud elf
  Shall suffer, with all his crew.
Take here a hundred bowmen brave,
  All chosen men of might,
Of excellent art for to take thy part,
  In glittering armour bright.
Then said the knight, My sovereign Liege,
  By me they shall be led ;

I'll venture my blood againſt Robin Hood,
 And bring him alive or dead.
One hundred men were choſen ſtrait,
 As proper as e'er men ſaw:
On Midſummer Day they marched away,
 To conquer that brave outlaw.
With long yew bows, and ſhining ſpears,
 They march'd in mickle pride,
And never delay'd, or halted, or ſtay'd
 'Till they came to the green wood ſide.
Said he to his archers, tarry here,
 Your bows make ready all,
That if need ſhould be, you may follow me,
 And ſee that you obſerve my call.
I'll go in perſon, firſt, he cry'd,
 With the letters of my good King,
Well ſign'd and ſeal'd, and if he will yield,
 We need not draw one ſtring.
He wander'd about 'till at lenght he came
 To the tent of Robin Hood,
The letter he ſhows; bold Robin aroſe,
 And there on his guard he ſtood.
They'd have me ſurrender, quoth bold Robin,
 And lie at their mercy then;
But tell them from me, that never ſhall be,
 While I have full ſeven ſcore men.
Sir William the knight, both hardy and bold,
 Did offer to ſeize him there,
Which William Lockſley by fortune did ſee,
 And bid him that trick to forbear.
Then Robin Hood ſet his horn to his mouth,
 And blew a blaſt or twain,
And ſo did the knight, at which there in ſight,
 The archers came all amain.
Sir William with care he drew up his men,
 And plac'd them in battle array;
Bold Robin, we find, he was not behind,
 Now this was a bloody fray.
The archers on both ſides bent their bows,
 And the clouds of arrows flew,
The very firſt flight that honoured knight,
 Did there bid the world adieu.

Yet neverthelefs their fight did laft
　From morning till almoft noon ;
Both parties were ftout, and loth to give out :
　This was on the laft of June.
At length they went off : one party they went
　For London with free gooa will ;
And Robin Hood he, to the green wood tree,
　And there he was taken ill.
He fent for a monk to let him blood,
　Who took his life away :
Now this being done, his archers they run,
　It was not time to ftay.
Some went on board, and crofs'd the feas,
　To Flanders, France, and Spain,
And others to Rome, for fear of their doom,
　But foon returned again.
Thus he that never fear'd bow nor fpear,
　Was murder'd by letting of blood ;
And fo, loving friends, the ftory doth end
　Of valiant bold Robin Hood.
There's nothing remains but his epitaph now,
　Which, Reader, here you have,
To this very day read it you may,
　As it was upon his grave.

ROBIN HOOD's EPITAPH,

Set on his TOMB

By the Prioress of Birkslay Monastry, in
Yorkshire.

ROBIN, Earl of Huntingdon,
　Lies under this little Stonee
No Archer was like him fo good ;
His Wildnefs nam'd him ROBIN HOOD.
Full thirteen Years, and fomething more,
Thefe Northern Parts he vexed fore.
Such Outlaws as He and his Men,
May England never know again.

A Table

A Table of all the Songs contained in this Book.

A New

A NEW
ROBIN HOOD SONG.
SUNG by Mr. BEARD.

AS blithe as the linnets fing in the green woods,
  So blithe we'll wake, we'll wake the morn,
    So blythe, &c.
And thro' the wide foreſt of merry Sherwood,
  We'll wind the bugle horn.
    We'll wind, &c.

The ſheriff attempts to take bold Robin Hood,
  Bold Robin diſdains to fly;
Let him come when he will, we'll in merry Sherwood,
  Or vanquiſh boys, or die.

Our hearts they are ſtout, and bows they are good,
  And well their maſters know;
They are cull'd in the foreſt of merry Sherwood,
  And never will ſpare a foe.

Our arrows ſhall drink of the fallow deer's blood,
  We'll hunt them all o'er the plain;
And thro' the wide foreſt of merry Sherwood,
  No ſhaft ſhall fly in vain.

Brave Scarlet and John, who ne'er were ſubdu'd,
  Gave each his hand ſo bold,
We'll range thro' the foreſt of merry Sherwood,
  What ſay my Hearts of Gold?
    What ſay, &c.

F I N I S.

The History of
Jack and the Giants

[in two parts]

Preface

What neither yields us profit nor delight
Is like a nurse's lullaby at night;
Guy Earl of Warwick and fair Eleanore,
Or giant killing Jack, would please me more.
                William Cowper, "Conversation" (1782)

"Speaking of English fairy tales," lamented Andrew Lang, the celebrated critic and anthologist, in his column "At the Sign of the Ship" (*Longman's*, March 1889), "one has often marvelled why they are so scarce and so dull, just like the ballads of England." Lang admitted to knowing few English equivalents of the German *märchen* and French *contes populaires*. Only "Tom Hickathrift," "Tom Thumb," "Jack and the Bean Stalk," and "Jack the Giant Killer" came to his mind among the published tales, and even these had been much revised. The same thing is true today. "Tom Hickathrift" is remembered only by folklorists; "Tom Thumb" rarely appears in its original form, as recorded in a chapbook of 1621, and "Jack and the Bean Stalk" only faintly resembles its earliest version, "The Story of Jack Spriggins and the Enchanted Bean" in the pamphlet *Round about Our Coal Fire* (1740). "Jack the Giant Killer" has not fared much better.

With the growth of a genuine literature created for young readers within the genteel tradition of the late eighteenth century, the old popular fare was reevaluated in terms of its suitability for a modern juvenile public. In France, Rousseau advised that Émile be protected from any book of fancy (including La Fontaine's fables) before he reached puberty, for fear it might confuse his young mind. In England, such authors as Thomas Day, Sarah Trimmer, and Maria Edgeworth attempted to provide suitable new works based upon the teachings of Locke and Rousseau. They wrote con-

iii

temporary tales designed for the instruction and elevation of the young. As Maria Edgeworth argued in her preface to *The Parent's Assistant* (1800), "Why should the mind be filled with fantastic visions instead of useful knowledge?" One result of such opinions was an odd combination of the instructional and the entertaining in juvenile literature. For example, in John Newbery's *A Little Pretty Pocket-Book Intended for the Instruction and Amusement of Little Master Tommy and Pretty Miss Polly* (1744), the once mighty hero of the nursery, the celebrated Jack the Giant-Killer, delivers lectures on good and evil with the aid of ball and pincushion that might rival the little lessons of Thomas Day's Mr. Barlow.

Protestations against the "abominable absurdities" of "Jack the Giant Killer" (as described by the popular critic Robert Bloomfield) persisted into the nineteenth century. Not even the outcries of John Ruskin and Charles Dickens against such "fraud on the fairies" could combat the criticism of Samuel Griswold Goodrich, the original "Peter Parley." In his *Recollections of a Lifetime* (1856), Goodrich expressed contempt for these "tales of horror, commonly put into the hands of youth, as if for the express purpose of reconciling them to vice and crime"; and none was more shocking to Goodrich than "Jack the Giant Killer." Even the academic anthologies of old English tales, those edited by Joseph Jacobs and Andrew Lang,[1] had to conform to public opinion by bowdlerizing the old traditional version of the story of Jack and his exploits with the Cornish and Welsh giants and other multiheaded monsters. Not all editions were so judicious. The first volume in the projected "Hugh Thomson's Illustrated Fairy Books" (a picture book series designed to compete with Randolph Caldecott's popular books) was the traditional *Jack the Giant Killer* (1898); it was not a success. Apparently it was far too grisly for late-Victorian tastes, and no additional titles were issued in the projected series. "Jack the Giant Killer" has rarely been published since the turn of the century.

The critics of the old tales might have done well to keep in mind Samuel Johnson's observation: "Babies do not like to hear stories of babies like themselves; . . . they require to have their imaginations raised by tales of giants and fairies, and castles and inchantments." Dr. Johnson objected to giving Newbery's books to children, and he did not feel it beneath his dignity to reread "Jack the Giant Killer" as an adult. As he wrote Mrs. Thrale (March 14, 1768), "Perhaps so noble a narrative may rouse in [me] the soul of enterprise." Among the other "babies" of the eighteenth century to delight in the old chapbook was the good doctor's biographer. "Having when a boy, been much entertained with *Jack the Giant-Killer* and such little story-books, I have always retained a kind affection for them, and recall my early days. . . . I shall certainly some time or other write a little story-book in the style of these. It will not be a very easy task for me; it will require much nature and simplicity and a great acquaintance with the humours and traditions of the English common people. I shall be happy to succeed, for he who pleases children will be remembered with pleasure by men."[2] Boswell's scheme was never realized, but in his mature years, finding a collection of the old chapbooks in Bow Churchyard, he purchased about two dozen of them to be specially bound as *Curious Productions*[3] in order to preserve the tales "which in my dawning years amused me as much as *Rasselas* does now. I saw the whole scheme with a kind of pleasing romantic feeling to find myself where all my old darlings were printed."[4] Boswell's affection for the old English story books was shared by William Cowper who (as he described in his "Conversation") found in "Jack the Giant Killer" qualities he advised modern writers to follow in composing their fictions:

> A tale should be judicious, clear, succinct;
> The language plain, and incidents well link'd;
> Tell not as new what ev'ry body knows;
> And, new or old, still hasten to a close;
> There, cent'ring in a focus round and neat,
> Let all your rays of information meet.

How well the chapbook follows these precepts is arguable, but surely it proves Cowper's other point:

> A story, in which native humour reigns,
> Is often useful, always entertains.

Henry Fielding acknowledged the praise being given to the popular tale by these distinguished contemporary men of letters. As he wrote in the opening argument of his novel *The Adventures of Joseph Andrews* (1742), our "language affords many examples of excellent use and instruction, finely calculated to sow the seeds of virtue in youth, and very easy to be comprehended by persons of moderate capacity. Such [is] the history of John the Great, who, by his brave and heroic actions against the men of large and athletic bodies obtain'd the glorious appellation of the Giant-Killer." How seriously this opinion should be taken is questionable. In the prologue to his burletta *Tom Thumb* (1730), Fielding mockingly invoked the native muse:

> Britons, awake!—Let Greece and Rome no more
> Their Heroes send to our Heroick Shore.
> Let home-bred Subjects grace the modern Muse,
> And Grub-Street from her Self, her Heroes chuse:
> Her Story-Books Immortalize in Fame,
> Hickathrift, Jack the Giant-Killer, and Tom Tram.[5]

As suggested by such a passage, Fielding was as much amused with his contemporaries' defense of the old tales as he was entertained by them.

The earliest recorded printing of "The History of Jack and the Giants" dates from the childhood of Johnson and Fielding.[6] Although no mention of this nursery hero appears in any known source prior to the eighteenth century,[7] the legends preserved in the chapbook surely date from an earlier period. The evocation of the Age of the Knights of the Round Table at the opening hints at a medieval origin to some of the incidents; the author may be referring in part to King Arthur's battle with the giant of St. Michael's Mount, described in the twelfth century by Geoffrey of Monmouth in *Historia Regum Britanniae* and in the fifteenth in the Caxton edition of Sir Thomas Malory's *Le morte D'Arthur.* The adventure of the king's son and his lady suggests the many legends of early Christendom concerning saints and sinners who outwitted the Devil. Local giant legends were known in the sixteenth century,[8] but none has been discovered in either manuscript or print. Nevertheless, Jack was certainly familiar to the English public (if only through nurses' tales) by the early eighteenth century—so familiar that his legend was the basis of several political farces.[9]

Like *Tom Thumb* (1621) and "The Story of Jack Spriggins and the Enchanted Bean" in *Round about Our Coal Fire* (1740), the chapbook accounts of Jack and his adventures are an odd assortment of many legends. One may wonder, as did Dickens, "whether there was more than one Jack (which I am loath to believe possible), or only one genuine original admirable Jack, who achieved all the recorded exploits."[10] The references to specific locales suggest that local legends were gathered from various corners of the commonwealth, and not all of these had completely passed from the popular consciousness. Land's End, the home of Cormilan, was still known in the nineteenth century as "the burial place of giants."[11] Apparently some material was borrowed from other chapbooks: the famous chant of Thunderdel (now more characteristic of the giant in "Jack and the Bean Stalk") appeared earlier in *Tom Thumb.* The imprisonment of the knights and ladies by Galigantus has its parallel in "Jack Spriggins and the Enchanted Bean," where this other Jack discovers "a large Gallery, where several thousand young ladies were tied up like Calves o' fatting, and bemoaning their hard Case, Alas, dear Prince, (say they) to-morrow early shall we be broiled and crushed between the Giant Gogmagog's monstrous teeth, if you do not save us; and there are two thousand Knights below in as bad a Condition." The enchanted talismans giant-killing Jack secures from his uncle, the three-headed giant, were also known to Tom Thumb and

PREFACE

Jack Spriggins,[12] who likely inherited them from Norse mythology.

Many of Jack's adventures obviously came to England with the Saxons. The deception of the Welsh giant has its counterpart in the thirteenth-century Prose Edda of Snorri Sturlson: the cautious Skrymir makes a mound in his bed which Thor, thinking it to be his companion, strikes with his hammer; Skrymir merely asks if a leaf has fallen on his head. Iona and Peter Opie in their *Classic Fairy Tales* (London and New York 1974) describe a Swedish folktale "The Herd-Boy and the Giant" which rephrases this attack on the suspected sleeping hero by the giant and includes a variation of the stomach-slitting trick. The stupidity of giants is not restricted to that race once native to the British Isles: the German giant in the Grimms' "Valiant Little Tailor" (*Das tapfere Schneiderlein*) is easily deceived into thinking a bit of cheese a rock, a bird a stone. The extraneous episode of Lucifer and the lady is an English equivalent[13] to the German "Twelve Dancing Princesses" (*Die zertanzten Schuhe*). This salmagundi of legends from numerous sources has been thrown together haphazardly into a two-part chapbook, a length needed by the anonymous author for all he has to recount. "Both ballads and tales have suffered horribly from chapbook editions," Lang complained. "Very early . . . they were made spoil of by very dull men, who wrote them out with idiotic bits of 'gag' or of parochial moralising for the cheap booksellers on London bridge. These bad printed versions killed the native oral versions." Perhaps the "once grand and traditional" originals were corrupted by cheap printers, but even in the impure form are marvelous bits of fancy.

Still, much of this text is strong meat for the young to digest. Perhaps the beheadings, strangulations, cannibalism, and other such horrors seemed less revolting in those pre-Freudian days when schoolboys were often armed and public executions were still a national pastime. In *The Vicar of Wakefield* (1766), Oliver Goldsmith recorded an amusing

viii

anecdote about the tastes of children. At the request of an adult, the youngest child of the family recounts the following fable he had been reading:

> Once upon a time, ... a Giant and a Dwarf were friends, and kept together. ... The first battle they fought was with two Saracens, and the Dwarf, who was very courageous, dealt one of the champions a most angry blow. It did the Saracen but very little injury, who lifting up his sword fairly struck off the poor Dwarf's arm. ... but the Giant coming to his assistance, in a short time left the two Saracens dead on the plain, and the Dwarf cut off the dead man's head out of spite.

The child goes on to describe in gory detail the bloody exploits of these two friends, adventures that include several more killings and that mark the Dwarf with the loss of an arm, a leg, and an eye. Anyone who has asked a child to relate some adventure he has read or heard can easily conclude that Goldsmith took this incident from life. Little has changed since the eighteenth century. Children will read what they will, whether it be "Jack the Giant Killer," the violent modern Japanese comic book, or the American daily newspaper.

Michael Patrick Hearn

MICHAEL PATRICK HEARN is the author of The Annotated Wizard of Oz *and* The Annotated Christmas Carol *and is currently completing a history of children's book illustrations.*

Notes

1. *English Fairy Tales*, illustrated by J. D. Batten (London 1890); *The Blue Fairy Book*, illustrated by H. J. Ford (London 1889). Jacobs, in his notes, found the second part of the chapbook "a weak and late invention of the enemy, . . . not *volkstümlick* at all"; but he did retain the episode with Galigantus and the conjuror.

2. In a note to *Boswell's London Journal, 1762-1763*, edited by Frederick A. Pottle (London 1951), p. 365.

3. This volume is now in the Child Memorial Collection of Chapbooks, Harvard College Library.

4. *Boswell's London Journal*, July 10, 1763, p. 364.

5. Although Fielding did not realize it, this passage anticipates the late eighteenth-century movement to protest the tyranny of Greece and Rome over German literature. In the work of the Brothers Grimm, the native Muse was invoked through the preservation of the popular legends and fairy tales.

6. Only the second part, printed by J. White of Newcastle in 1711 is recorded, but is now missing from the British Museum.

7. The earliest reference is in *The Weekly Comedy*, January 22, 1708, in which *Jack and the Gyants* is said to be "formerly printed in small Octavo."

8. *The Complaynt of Scotland* (1549) describes a shepherd's "tayl of the giantis that eit quyk men."

9. Among them, a "comi-tragical farce" *Jack the Gyant-Killer*, performed in 1730; and Henry Brooke's *The last Speech of John Good, vulgarly called Jack the Giant-Queller*, published about 1745, along with *The Songs in Jack the Giant-Queller*, derived from the "antique history."

10. In "A Christmas Tree," *Household Words*, December 21, 1850, p. 290.

NOTES

11. See Charles Dickens, *A Christmas Carol*, Stave Three (1843).

12. In "The Story of Jack Spriggins and the Enchanted Bean," the hero receives a fairy ring.

13. A curious British variant of this tale is "The Story of Kate Crackernuts"(published by Lang in *Longman's*, April 1889), in which the heroine saves a dancing prince.

NOTABLE EDITIONS OF *JACK THE GIANT KILLER*

The History of Jack and the Giants [and] *The Second Part* . . . New Castle [c. 1711-1730].

Leigh, Percival. *Jack the Giant Killer*. Illustrated by John Leech. London 1844.

"Summerly, Felix" (Sir Henry Cole). *The Chronicle of the Valiant Feats . . . of Jack the Giant Killer*. Westminster 1845.

The Story of Jack and the Giants. Illustrated by Richard Doyle. London 1851.

Jack the Giant-Killer. Illustrated by W. H. Thwaites. New York 1855.

Jack the Giant Killer; or, Harlequin King Arthur, and ye Knights of ye Round Table. London 1859. Pollock's Toy Theater also issued a *Harlequin Jack the Giant Killer*.

Doyle, Richard. *Jack the Giant Killer*. London 1888. A facsimile of the manuscript of 1842.

Rhys, Grace. *Jack the Giant-killer, and Beauty and the Beast*. Illustrated by R. Anning Bell. London 1894.

Jack the Giant Killer. Illustrated by Hugh Thomson. London 1898.

Jack the Giant Killer. Illustrated by H. M. Brock. London and New York 1916.

Jacobs, Joseph. *Jack the Giant-Killer*. Illustrated by Fritz Wegner. New York 1970.

[de Regniers, Beatrice Schenk]: *Jack the Giant Killer*. Illustrated by Edward Gorey. New York 1973.

THE
HISTORY
OF
Jack & the Giants.

Part the First.

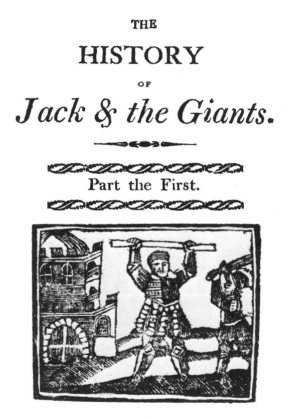

COVENTRY:
Printed and Sold by J. TURNER.

THE FIRST PART OF

HISTORY OF

JACK and the GIANTS.

CHAP. I.

Of his Birth, Parentage, and Discourse
with a country Vicar when but seven
Years old.

IN the reign of King Arthur, near to
the Land's End of England, in the
county of Cornwall, lived a worthy farmer, who had a son named Jack. He
was a brisk lad, and of ready wit, so
what he could not perform by force
and strength, he compleated by wit and
policy; never was any person heard of
that could worst him. Nay, the very
learned many times he has baffled with
his cunning and sharp inventions;—
For instance, when he was no more
than seven years of age, his father (the

farmer) sent him to the field, to look after his oxen, which were then feeding in a pasture. A country vicar (by chance) coming across the field called to Jack, and asked him how many commandments there was? Jack told him nine. The parson replied, there are ten. Nay, says Jack, Mr. Parson, you are out in that, it is true there was ten, but you have broke one of them with your maid Margery.

The parson replied, thou art an arch wag, Jack. Well, Mr. Parson, quoth he, you have asked me one question, and I have answered it: I beseech you let me ask you another: Who made these oxen? The parson replied, God, my dear child, Why now you are wrong again, says Jack, for God made them bulls, but my father and his man Hobson, made them oxen. These were the witty answers of Jack.

The parson seeing himself thus fooled, this witty boy trudged away, leaving him in a laughter.

CHAP. II.

Of a Giant inhabiting the Mount of
Cornwall, and what Spoil he made
in the Neighbourhood.

IN those days, the Mount of Cornwall was kept by a large and monstrous Giant, of eighteen feet high, and
about three yards in circumference,
and of a fierce and grim countenance,
the terror of the neighbouring towns
and villages,

His habitation was in a cave in the
midst of the mount; never would he
suffer any living creatures to come near
him. His feeding was of other men's
cattle, which often were his prey; for
when he wanted food he would often
wade over to the main sand, where he
would well furnish himself with what
he could find; for the people at his approach would all forsake their habitations. Then would he seize on their
cows and oxen, of which, he would

make nothing to carry over upon his
back half a dozen at once; and as for
their sheep and hogs, he would tie them
round his waist like a bunch of can-
dles; this he practised for many years,
so that a great part of the county of
Cornwall was very much impoverish-
ed by him.

CHAP. III.

Of Jack slaying this Monster, and from that time obtaining the name of Jack the Giant Killer.

JACK having undertaken to destroy this voracious monster, he furnished himself with a horn, a shovel, and a pick-axe, and over to the Mount he goes, in the beginning of a dark winter's evening, when he fell to work, and digged a pit twenty-two feet deep, and almost as broad, covering it over with long sticks and straw, and then strewing a little of the mould over it, appeared like plain ground. Then putting the horn to his mouth, he blew tantivy, tantivy; which noise awaked the Giant, who came roaring towards Jack, crying out, you incorrigible villain, you shall pay dearly for disturbing me, for I will broil you for my break-

fast!! These words were no sooner
spoke but he tumbled headlong into
the pit, and his heavy fall made the
foundation of the mountain shake.—

Oh! Mr. Giant, quoth Jack, where
are you now? Faith you are in Lob's
pound, where I will plague you for
your threatened words. What do you
think now of broiling me for your
breakfast? Will no other diet serve
you but poor Jack? Having thus tan-
talized the Giant for a while, he struck
him a terrible blow upon the crown
with his pole-ax, as he tumbled down,
and with a groan expired. This done,

Jack threw the dirt upon him, and so buried him. Then searching the cave, he found much treasure.

Now when the magistrates who employed Jack, heard that the job was over, they sent for him, declaring he should henceforth be called Jack the Giant Killer, and in honour thereof, presented him with a sword and embroidered belt, upon which, these words were written in letters of gold :—

" Here's the valiant Cornish man,
" Who slew the Giant Cormorant !"

CHAP. IV.

JACK is surprized by a Giant, while asleep, and the danger he underwent to gain his liberty.

THE news of Jack's victory was soon spread over the western parts, so that another Giant called

Blunderbeard hearsng of it, vowed to
be revenged on Jack, if ever it was his
fortune to light on him. This Giant
kept an enchanted castle, situated in
the midst of a lonesome wood, About
four months after, as Jack was walking by the borders of the wood, in his
journey towards Wales, he grew weary,
and sat himself down by the side of a
pleasant fountain, when a deep sleep
suddenly seized him. At this time
the Giant coming there for water,
found him, and by the lines upon his
belt immediately knew him to be Jack,
so without any words, he took him
upon his shoulders to carry him to his
enchanted castle. As he passed through
a thicket, the rustling of the boughs
awaked Jack, who finding himself in
the clutches of the Giant was much
surprised, though it was but the beginning of his terrors, for entering the
walls of the castle he found the floor
covered with the skulls and other bones
of dead men, when the Giant told him,

bis bones should enlarge the number of
what he saw. He then brought him
into a large parlour, where lay the
blood and quarters of some lately slain,
and in the next room were hearts and
livers; when the Giant (to terrify him)
said, that mens hearts were his favorite
diet, which, he said, he most commonly eat with pepper and vinegar; add-
ing, that he did not question but his
heart would make him a curious breakfast. This said, he locks poor Jack up
in a upper room, leaving him there
while he went to fetch another Giant,
who lived in the same wood, that he
might partake in the pleasures they
should have in the destruction of poor
honest Jack. While he was gone,
dreadful shrieks and cries affrighiened
Jack, especially a voice which con-
tiually cried :—

Do what you can to get away,
Or you'll become the Giant's prey;
He's gone to fetch his brother, who
Will likewise kill and torture you!

This dreadful noise so affrighted poor Jack that he was ready to run distracted. Then going to the window, he opened the casement, and beheld afar off, the two Giants coming together. So now, quoth Jack, to himself, my death or deliverance is at hand. There were two strong cords in the room by him, at the end of which he made a noose, and as the Giants were unlocking the iron gates, he threw the ropes over each of the Giants heads, and then threw the other ends across a beam, where he pulled with all his might till he had throttled them. And then fastening the ropes to a beam, he returned to the window, whence he beheld the two Giants both black in the face, and so sliding down the ropes, he came to the heads of the helpless Giants, who could not defend themselves, and drawing his own sword he slew them both, and so delivered himself from their intended cruelty. Then taking the bunch of keys he entered the castle, where, upon strict search, he there found three ladies tied up by the hair of their heads, and almost starved to death, who told Jack, that their husbands had been slain by the Giant, and they had been kept there many days without food, in order to force them to eat the flesh of their murdered husbands, which they could not do if they were to be starved to death. Sweet ladies, said Jack, I have destroyed the monster and his brutish brother, by which means I have obtained your liberties. This said, he presented them with the keys of the castle, and proceeded on his journey to Wales.

CHAP. V.

Jack travels into Flintshire, and of what
happened there.

JACK having but little money, he
thought it prudent to make the
best of his way by travelling hard; and
at length losing his road he was benighted, and could not get a place of
entertainment, till coming to a valley
between two hills, he found a large
house in a lonesome place, and by reason of his present necessity he took
courage to knock at the gate, but to
his amazement, there came forth a
monstrous Giant with two heads, yet
he did not seem so fierce as the other
two, for he was a Welch Giant, and
all he did was by private and secret
malice, under the false shew of friendship. Jack telling his condition, he
bid him welcome, shewing him into
a room with a bed, where he might

take his night's rest. Upon this, Jack
undresses himself, and as the Giant was
walking towards another apartment,
Jack heard him say these words to
himself :—

Tho' here you lodge with me this night,
You shall not see the morning light,
My club shall dash your brains out quite.

Say you so, says Jack, is this one of
your Welch tricks? I hope to be as
cunning as you. Then getting out of
bed he found a thick billet, and laid it
in the bed in his stead, and hid himself
in a dark corner of the room. In the
dead time of the night came the Giant,
with his club, and struck several blows
on the bed, where Jack had artfully
laid the billet, and then he returned to
his own room, supposing that he had
broken all his bones. Early in the
morning Jack came to thank him for
his lodging. O! said the Giant, how
have you rested? did you feel any thing

in the night? No, said Jack, but a rat gave me three or four slaps with his tail.

Soon after the Giant went to breakfast on a great bowl of hasty pudding, giving Jack but a little quantity; he being loath to let him know that he could not eat with him, got a leather bag, putting it artfully under his coat, in which he put what he should have eat. After breakfast, he told the Giant he would shew him a trick, so taking a large knife, he ripped open the bag; which the Giant thought was his belly, and out came the hasty pudding, which the Welch Giant seeing, cried out,—" Cots splutter, hur can do that hurself;" and taking up the knife, he ripped open his belly from top to bottom, and out dropped his tripes and trillybubs, so that he immediately fell down dead.

Thus Jack outwitted the Welch Giant and proceeded on his journey to Wales.

CHAP. VI.

King Arthur's son goes to seek his fortune, meets Jack; and the wonderful things performed by him while
they were together.

KING Arthur's only son desired his
father to furnish him with a
certain sum of money, that he might
go and seek his fortune in the princi-
pality of Wales, where a beautiful lady
lived, who (he had heard) was possessed with seven evil spirits.

His father, the King, councelled him
against it, yet he could not be per-
suaded, so the favour was granted,
which was, one horse loaded with
money, and another to ride on. Thus
he went forth without any attendance;
and after several days travel he came
to a large market town in Wales, where
he beheld a vast crowd of people gathered together. The King's son de-

manded the reason of it, and was told that they had arrested a corps for many large sums of money, which the deceased owed before he died. The King's son replied, it was a pity that people should be so cruel; but go and bury the dead, and let the creditors come to my lodgings and their debts shall be discharged; accordingly they came, and in such great numbers, that before night he had almost left himself pennyless. Now Jack the Giant Killer being there, and seeing the uncommon generosity of the King's son, desired to be his servant; it being agreed on, the next morning they set forward, when riding out at the town's end, an old woman cried out,—he has owed me two pence seven years, pray sir, pay me as well as the rest; he put his hand in his pocket and gave it her, it being the last he had left; then turning to Jack, he said, take no thought, nor care, let me alone, and I warrant you we shall never want.—

Now Jack had a small spell in his
pocket, the which served them for refreshment; after which they had but
one penny left between them. They
spent the forenoon in travel and familiar discourse, until the sun grew
low when the King's son said, Jack,
since we have got no money left,
where can we lodge to night? Jack
replied, master, we will do well enough,
for I have an uncle who lives within
two miles of this place, he is a huge
and monstrous Giant, having three
heads, and he will beat five hundred
men in armour, and make them fly before him. Alas! said the King's son,
what shall we do there? he will eat us
up at one mouthful; nay, we are
scarce sufficient to fill up an hollow
tooth. It is no matter for that, says
Jack, I myself will go before and pr e
pare the way for you, tarry here, and
wait my return.

He waited, and Jack rode full speed
and coming to the castle gate, he im-

mediately began to knock with such force, that all the neighbouring hills resounded. The Giant roared with a voice like thunder,---Who is there? None but your poor cousin Jack. And what news, said he, with my cousin Jack? He replied, dear uncle, I have brought heavy news, Cod, what. I pray thee what heavy news can come to me? I am a Giant with three heads, and besides, thou well knowest that I can fight five hundred men in armour, and make them all fly like chaff before the wind. Oh! said Jack, but there is the King's son coming with a thousand men in armour, to kill you, and destroy all you have. O! my cousin Jack, this is heavy news indeed, but I hav a large vault which is under ground, where I will run and hide myself, and you shall lock, bolt, and bar me in, and keep the key till the King's son is gone.

Jack having now secured the Giant, returned and fetched his master, and both made merry with the best dainties the house afforded. In the morning, Jack furnished his master with fresh supplies of gold and silver, and having set him three miles on the road out of the Giant's smell, he returned and let his uncle out of the hole, who asked Jack what he should give him for his care, seeing his castle was not demolished? Why, said Jack, I desire nothing but your old rusty sword, the coat in the closet, and the cap and the shoes which you keep at your bed's-head. Aye, said the Giant, you shall have them with all my heart, as a just reward for your kindness in protecting me from the power of the King's son; and be sure that thou carefully keepest them for my sake. for they are things of excellent use. The coat will keep you invisible, the cap will furnish you with knowledge, the sword cuts asunder whatever you strike, and, the shoes are of extraordinary swiftness. They may be serviceable to you, so take them

and welcome ; Jack took them and
immediately followed his master.

CHAP. VII.

Jack saves his Master's Life, and forces
the evil Spirit out of the Lady.

JACK having overtook his master,
they soon arrived at the lady's
dwelling, who finding the King's son
to be a suitor, prepared a banquet for
him. which being ended, she wiped
her mouth with an handkerchief, saying, you must shew me this to-morrow morning, or lose your head ; and
then she put it into her bosom. The
King's son went to bed right sorrowful, but Jack's cap of knowledge in-
structed him how to obtain it. In the
middle of the night she called upon
her familiar to carry her to Lucifer.
Jack wipped on his coat of darkness
with his shoes of swiftness, and was
there before her; but could not be
seen by reason of his coat of darkness.

which rendered him perfectly invisible
to Lucifer himself. When she came
she gave him the handkerchief, from
whom Jack took it, and brought it
to his master, who shewing it the
next morning to the lady, saved his
life. This much surprized the lady,
but he had a harder trial to undergo.

The next night she salutes the
King's son, telling him, that he must
shew her the next day the lips that
she had kissed last, or lose his head.
So I will, replied he, if you kiss
none but mine. It is neither here nor
there for that, says she, if you do not,
death is your portion. At midnight
she went again, and chid Lucifer for
letting the handkerchief go, but, said
she, I shall be too hard for the King's
son; for I will kiss thee, and he is to
shew me the lips I kissed last, and he
cannot shew me thine. Jack standing up with his sword of sharpness cut
off the Devil's head, and brought it
under his invisible coat to his master,

who laid it at the end of his bolster, and in the morning when she came up he pulled it out by the horns, shewing her the Devil's lips, which she had kissed last. Thus answering her twice, the enchantment broke, and the evil spirits left her, when she appeared her former self, both beauteous and virtuous. They were married the next morning, and soon after returned with joy to the court of King Arthur, where Jack for his good services, was made one of the Knights of the round table.

Thus ends the first Part, which leads to the second, where you may have a further account of the valiant exploits and bold adventures of this noble hero Jack the Giant Killer.

End of the First Part.

THE
HISTORY
OF
Jack & the Giants.

Part the Second.

COVENTRY:
Printed and Sold by J. Turner.

THE SECOND PART

OF THE

HISTORY

OF

JACK and the GIANTS.

CHAP. I.

Of the success of Jack's Petition to pur-
sue divers Giants.

JACK having been successful in all
his undertakings, and resolving
not to be idle for the future, but to
perform what service he could for his

King and nation; humbly besought his majesty to fit him out with a horse and money to travel in search of new and strange adventures. For, said he, there are many. Giants yet living in the remote parts of Wales, to the unspeakable damage of your majesty's subjects, therefore, may it please you to encourage me, I do not doubt but shortly to cut them off root and branch, and so rid the realm of all those Giants and monsters in human shape.

Now when the King heard his noble proposition, and considering the mischievous practice of those blood thirsty Giants, he furnished him with necessaries for his progress; after which Jack took leave of the King, and all the Knights of the round table, and departed, taking with him his Cap of Knowledge, his Sword of Sharpness, his Shoes of Swiftness, and his invisible Coat, the better to perform the enterprises that lay before him.

CHAP. II.

CHAP. II.

Of Jack slaying a monstrous Giant, and
thereby delivered a Kuight and his
Lady from Destruction.

JACK travelled over high hills and
great mountains, and on the third
day came to a large spacious wood,
through which he must pass; where
on a sudden he heard very dreadful
shrieks and cries; whereupon casting
his eyes around, he beheld a very monstrous Giant dragging along a worthy
Knight and his beautiful Lady, by the
hair of their heads, with as much ease
as if they had been a pair of gloves.

Their sighs melted Jack into tears
of pity and compassion, upon which
he alighted from his horse, and tying
him to an oak tree, and putting on his
invisible coat, under which he carried
his infallible sword, he came to the
Giant, and though he made several
strokes at him, yet by reason of his

largeness he could not reach the trunk
of his body, but only wounded his
thighs in different places; at length
giving him a swinging stroke with both
his hands, cut off both his legs just
below the garter, so that the trunk of
his body not only made the trees to
shake, but the earth to tremble with
the force of the fall, by which the worthy Knight and his Lady escaped his
rage.

Then had Jack time to talk with
him; so setting his foot upon his
neck, he said, "Thou barbarous and
savage wretch, I am come to execute
upon you the just reward of thy vil-
lany," and with that he run him quite
through the body, when the huge
monster sent forth a hideous groan,
and so yielded up his life and breath to
the hands of the victorious Jack the
Giant Killer, whilst the noble Knight
and his virtuous Lady were both joyful
spectators of his sudden death and
their deliverance.

The courteous Knight and his fair
Lady not only returned him hearty
thanks for their deliverance, but also
invited him to their house, there to re-
fresh himself after this dreadful encounter; as likewise to receive an
ample reward by way of gratitude for
past services. No, says Jack, I cannot
be at ease till I find out the den that
was this monster's habitation.

The Knight hearing this, grew sorrowful, and replied, noble stranger, it
is too much to run a second hazard:
this monster lived in a den under yonder mountain, with a brother of his,
more fierce and cruel than himself;
therefore, if you should go thither and
perish in the attempt, it would be a
heart-breaking both to me and my
Lady, so let me persuade you to go
with us, and desist from any further
pursuit.

Nay, says Jack, if there be any
other, I say, if there be twenty, I
would shed the last drop of blood in

my body, before one of them should escape my fury: and when I have finished this task, I will come and pay my respects to you.

He then took particular directions to find their habitation, so mounted his horse, and left them to return home, while he went in pursuit of the deceased Giant's brother.

CHAP. III.

Of Jack slaying the other Giant, and cutting off both their Heads.

JACK had not rode above a mile and a half before he came in sight of the cave's mouth. Near unto the entrance of which he beheld the other Giant, sitting on a huge block of fine timber, with a knotted iron club laying by his side, waiting for his brother's returning, laden with his barbarous prey. His goggle eyes appeared as it

were like terrible flames of fire; his
countenance was grim and ugly, and
his cheeks appeared like two flitches
of bacon, the bristles of his beard seemed to be like very thick rods of iron
wire; and his long locks hung down
upon his broad shoulders like curling
snakes or hissing adders.

So Jack alighted from his horse, and
put him in a thicket; then with his
coat of darkness, he approached somewhat nearer to behold the figure, and
said softly, O! are you there? it will
not be long before I shall have you
fast by the beard.

The Giant all this while could not
see him, by reason of his invisible coat,
so that coming close up to him, Jack
struck a blow at his head with his
sword of sharpness, but missing something of his aim, he only cut off the
nose of the Giant, who missing it,
roared out like loud claps of thunder.
And though he turned up his glaring
eyes, he could not see whence the blow

came that had done him this unkindness; yet nevertheless taking up his
iron club, he began to lay about him
like one that was stark staring mad.

Nay, said Jack, if you are for that
game I will dispatch you presently, for
fear of some accidental blow; then as
he arose from the block, Jack made no
more ado, but run his sword up to the
hilt in the Giant's fundament, where
he left it sticking a while, and stood
with both his hands a kimbo, laughing to see the Giant caper and dance
the canaries with the sword in his
a—e, crying out, he should die, he
should die, with a griping in his guts.

After this, Jack cut off his head,
and sent it, together with that of his
brother, to King Arthur, by a waggon he hired for that purpose; together with an account of his prosper-
ous succeeding in all his undertakings.

CHAP. IV.

Of Jack's searching the Giant's House
and delivering many.

JACK having thus dispatched these
two monsters, was resolved to
enter into the cave in search of the
Giant's treasure; he passed along
through a great many turnings and
windings, which led him at length to
a great room paved with free stone, at
the upper end of which was a boiling
cauldron, and on the right hand stood
a large table, whereon he supposed the
Giants used to dine.

When he came to an iron gate,
where a window was secured with bars
of iron, through which he peeped, and
there beheld a vast many miserable captives, who seeing Jack at a distance,
cried out,—Alas! alas! young man,
art thou come to be one amongst us in
this most miserable den? Aye, said

Jack, I hope you will not tarry here
long; but I pray what is the meaning
of this captivity? Why, said one poor
old man, I will tell you, Sir,—We are
persons that have been taken by the
Giants that hold this cave; and we are
kept till such time as they have a fancy
for a feast more than ordinary, and
then the fattest of us all is slaughtered
and prepared for their devouring jaws.
It is not long since they took three for
the same purpose. Full many is the
time they have dined upon murdered
men.

Say you so, says Jack, well, I have
given them such a dinner that it will
be long enough 'ere they have occasion
for any more. The miserable captives
were amazed at his words. You may
believe me, says Jack, for I have slain
them with the edge of the sword, and
have sent their monstrous heads in a
waggon to the court of King Arthur,
as trophies of my glorious victory:
and in testimony of the truth of what

he said, he unlocked the iron gate, setting the miserable captives at liberty, who all rejoiced like condemned malefactors at the sight of a reprieve.

Then leading them to the aforesaid room he placed them round the table, and set before them two quarters of beef, with bread and wine, upon which they feasted plentifully.

Supper being over, they searched the Giants coffers, the spoil of which Jack equally divided amongst the captives, who gratefully thanked him for their happy deliverance.

The next morning they departed to their respective habitations, and Jack to the Knight's house, whom he had before delivered from the hands of these monstrous Giants.

CHAP. V.

Of Jack's Entertainment at the Knight's House.

IT was about sun-rising when Jack mounted his horse to proceed on

his journey, and by the help of directions he came to the Knight's house
about noon, where he was received
with all the demonstrations of joy
imaginable, by him and his Lady;
who in honourable respect to Jack,
prepared a feast, which lasted many
days, inviting the nobility in those
parts, to whom the Knight relating the
courage of Jack, and by way of gratitude presented him with a ring,
whereon was engraved the picture of
a Giant dragging a Knight and his
Lady, with this motto round it.

We were in sad distress you see,
　Under a Giant's fierce command;
But gain'd our lives and liberty,
　By valiant Jack's victorious hand.

Now among the assembly then present, were five aged gentlemen, who
were fathers to some of those miserable
captives whom Jack set at liberty;
who understanding that he was the

person who performed such wonders, they immediately paid him their venerable respects.

After this the mirth increased, and the smiling bowls went round to the victorious conqueror.

But, lo! in the midst of all this mirth, a dark cloud appeared, that daunted the hearts of the assembly; for a messenger came, who brought the dismal news of, that Thundel, a Giant with two heads, who having heard of the death of his two kinsmen, was come from the north to be revenged on Jack, for their death, and was within a mile of the house, the country people all flying before him like chaff before the wind.

When they related this, Jack was not a whit daunted, but said, Let him come, I have a rod to pick his teeth. Pray, Ladies and Gentlemen walk into the garden, and you shall be joyful spectators of the Giant's death and destruction.

CHAP. VI.

Of his overthrowing the Giant, and cutting off both his Heads.

THE good KNIGHT's house was situated in an island, encompassed with a moat thirty feet deep, and twenty wide, over which lay a drawbridge; Jack employed two men to cut it on each side, almost to the middle, and then dressing himself in his coat of darkness, he went against the Giant with his sword of sharpness, yet as he came close to him, the Giant could not see him, by reason of his invisible coat; yet, nevertheless, he was sensible of some impending danger, the which made him cry out :——

Fe. fa, fum,
I smell the blood of an Englishman,
Be he alive, or be he dead,
I'll grind his bones to make me bread.

Say you so, says Jack, you are a
monstrous miller indeed.—To whom
the Giant replied, art thou the villain
that killed my kinsmen? Then I will
tear thee with my teeth, and grind thy
bones to powder.

You will catch me first, says Jack,
and so put on his shoes of swiftness,
and run from him : the Giant followed
after like a walking castle, making the
earth to tremble at every step.

So Jack led him a dance, that the
quality might see this monster in nature ; so to finish the work, Jack ran
over the draw-bridge the Giant pur-
suing him with his club ; but coming
to the middle, with the very great
weight of his body, and the vast steps
he took, it broke, and he tumbled into
the water, and rolled about like a
large whale.

Jack standing by the moat, laughed
at him, saying, you told me that you
would grind my bones to powder.

The Giant fretted to hear him scoff

at him; and though he plunged from place to place, he could not get out to be revenged upon his adversary.

Jack at last got a cart rope and cast it over the Giant's two heads, and by the help of a team of horses, he dragged him out of the moat and cut off both his heads in the sight of all present, and before he eat or drank, he sent these after the others to King Arthur's court, and then joined with them in pastime.

CHAP. VII.

Of Jack's coming to a Hermit's House, and what happened there

AFTER some time spent in mirth, Jack grew weary of it, and taking his leave, he went in search of a new adventure. Through many groves he passed, till coming to a mountain, he rapped at the door of a lonesome house, when an ancient man with a head as white as snow, arose and let him in.

Father, said Jack, have you any con-
veniency for a benighted traveller,
who has lost his way? Yes, said the
old man, if you will accept of such
accommodations as my poor house
affords.

Jack returned him thanks for his
civility, wherefore, down they sat, and
the old man began as follows:—

My son, I am sensible thou art a
conqueror of Giants, and on the top
of this mount is an enchanted castle,
maintained by a Giant named Galligantus, who by the help of a conjuror,
gets many a Knight into his castle,
where they are transformed into sun-
dry shapes and forms; but above all,
I lament a Duke's daughter, whom
they took from her father's garden,
and brought her through the air in a
chariot, drawn by two fiery dragons,
and securing her within the garden
wall, transformed her into the shape of
a hart; and though many Knights
have strove to dissolve the enchant-

ment, and work her deliverance, yet none could accomplish it, by reason of two fiery griffins which had destroyed them at their approach, so soon as they had fixed their eyes upon them; but you, my son, being furnished with an invisible coat, may pass by them unnoticed, and on the gates of the castle you will find engraved in large characters by what means the enchantment may be broken.

The old man having ended his discourse, Jack gave him his hand, promising in the morning to venture his life to break the enchantment, and free the lady, and likewise those that were partakers with her in the same calamity.

CHAP. VIII.

Of Jack's Conquest over Galligantus and the Conjuror: with the freedom of many Knights and Ladies.

HAVING refreshed himself with a morsel of meat, he lay down, and in the morning put on his invisible coat, and prepared for his enterprise. When he had reached the top of the mountain, he discovered the two fiery griffins, between whom he passed without the least fear or danger, for they could not see him, by reason of his invisible coat.

As soon as he got past them, he cast his eyes around him, and saw a golden trumpet on the gate, under which these lines were written :—

Whoever doth this trumpet blow,
Shall soon the Giant overthrow;
And break the black enchantment strait,
And all shall be in happy state.

Jack had no sooner read this motto but he blew the trumpet, at which time all the foundations of the castle trembled, and the Giant, as well as the Conjuror, was in a terrible confusion. biting their thumbs, and tearing their hair, knowing that their wicked designs were at an end; when Jack standing

at the Giant's elbow, with his sword
of sharpness cut off his head. The
Conjuror seeing this, he mounted immediately in the air, and was carried
away in a whirlwind.

Thus was the whole enchantment
broke, and every Knight and Lady,
who had been for a long time transformed into beasts and birds, returned into their former shapes again —
And as for the castle, though it seemed to be of vast strength, yet it van-

ished away as smoke in the air; whereon a general joy appeared among the Knights and Ladies.

This done, Galligantus's head was likewise conveyed (as quick as possible) to the court of King Arthur.

The next day, having refreshed all the Knights and Ladies at the old

man's habitation, they set forward for the court of King Arthur; when coming to the King, and having related the passages of his fierce encounters, his fame run through the whole court; and as a reward for his services, the King prevailed on the aforesaid Duke, to give his daughter

in marriage to Jack, protesting there
was no one so deserving of her as he.
The Duke consented, and they was
married, to the joy of all the court.
The King gave him a large estate, as
a reward for past services done to the
nation, where he and his Lady lived
the residue of their days in joy and
content.

End of the Second Part.

Turner. Printer, Coventry

Traditional Faery Tales

Sir Henry Cole

Preface

Sir Henry Cole (1808-1882), under the pseudonym "Felix Summerly," initiated the Home Treasury Series in 1843 "to cultivate the Affections, Fancy, Imagination and Taste of Children." As the father of a family of eight, he deplored the unavailability in suitable form of the traditional fairy lore and legend. Instead, young minds were assaulted by a barrage of factual, informative but stultifying books, typified by the works, genuine and spurious, of "Peter Parley"—the pseudonym of the prolific American writer Samuel Griswold Goodrich (1793-1860). In the original announcement of the Home Treasury, Cole characterized his intent as "anti-Peter Parleyism." His rival protagonist ironically derided the "captivating luxuries" of the Series.

In addition to content, Cole was concerned with aesthetic presentation, defying the assumption "that the lowest kind of art is good enough to give the first impressions to a child." In this pursuit, he employed the distinguished typographer of the Chiswick Press, Charles Whittingham, and utilized the talents of the "old masters" and "the best modern artists . . . in creating a taste for beauty." Three members of the Royal Academy are represented in *Traditional Faery Tales*: "Little Red Riding Hood" was illustrated by Thomas Webster, "Beauty and the Beast" by J. C. Horsley, and "Jack the Giant Killer" by C. W. Cope. Among Sir Henry's most ardent admirers were the two daughters of his close friend William Makepeace Thackeray, who warranted "the mere sight of the little books . . . as good as a nosegay."

The Home Treasury was published by Joseph Cundall, a man of taste and enterprise, until 1846 when it was taken over by Chapman and Hall; the single exception was *The Mother's Primer*, contributed by Sir Henry's wife, Lady Marian Fairman Cole ("Mrs. Felix Summerly"), and published by Longman, Brown, Green, and Longmans.

In a contemporary review, the *Athenaeum* praised the Series as "rich in profit as well as pleasure," judging its appearance "splendid enough to have been stolen from an Alhambra alcove," and terming the editor's preface "cheerful and wise."

Cole's two-volume autobiography, *Fifty Years of Public Work* (1884), reveals an amiable, energetic, and dynamic Victorian. He enjoyed the friendship of such prominent men as Thomas Love Peacock, John Stuart Mill, and Charles Buller, as well as the firm confidence of the Prince Consort, in whose memory Cole proposed the Royal Albert Hall, opened in 1871. The success of the Great Exhibition of 1851 owed much to his organizational skill. After serving in the Record Office, Cole moved to the Treasury, where he introduced penny postage. Several of the best guide books of the day (Hampton Court, Westminster Abbey, the National Gallery) were written by him. He established the nucleus of the Royal College of Music, the Victoria and Albert Museum, and the School of Design. Cundall's Home Treasury Office was responsible for issuing the first English Christmas card, designed for Cole in 1843 by J. C. Horsley. In 1875 Cole was knighted for his unstinting public service.

"Felix Summerly's Home Treasury" precipitated the ascendancy of fancy over fact that was to reach its height by the end of the nineteenth century. The format of the Series varied widely. Single or collected editions were available—in paper or board covers, or cloth bound, with or without gilt, plain or colored. The price ranged from a modest one shilling to a lavish guinea edition. Numbering was capricious. Cole's autobiography lists the following twenty items (the last four of which are novelties rather than books).

1. *Holbein's Bible Events.*
2. *Raffaelle's Bible Events.*
3. *Dürer's Bible Events.*
4. *Traditional Nursery Songs.*

PREFACE

5. *Ballad of Sir Hornbook.*
6. *Chevy Chase.*
7. *Puck's Reports to Oberon.*
8. *Little Red Riding Hood.*
9. *Beauty and the Beast.*
10. *Jack and the Bean Stalk.*
11. *Cinderella.*
12. *Jack the Giant Killer.*
13. *Home Treasury* (i.e., *The Mother's*) *Primer.*
14. *Alphabets of Quadrupeds.*
15. *The Pleasant History of Reynard the Fox.*
16. *A Century of Fables.*
17. The Little Painter's Portfolio.
18. Colour Box for Little Painters.
19. Tesselated Pastime.
20. Box of Terra Cotta Bricks.

Michelangelo's Bible Events and *Whittington and His Cat* both appear on variant listings.

Margaret Crawford Maloney

MARGARET CRAWFORD MALONEY has written intro-ductions for several facsimile editions from the Osborne Collection of Early Children's Books and contributed the preface and biographical notes for The Fantastic Kingdom: A Collection of Illustrations from the Golden Days of Story-telling *(Ballantine, 1974). She first joined the professional staff of the Boys and Girls Services of the Toronto Public Library in 1964 and for the past seven years has been a librarian with the Osborne Collection.*

SIR HENRY COLE and JOSEPH CUNDALL

Selected References:

Cole, Henry. *Fifty Years of Public Work of Sir Henry Cole . . . accounted for in his deeds, speeches and writings.* [Edited and completed by A. S. and H. L. Cole.] Two volumes. London: G. Bell, 1884.

Darton, F. J. Harvey. *Children's Books in England.* Second edition. Cambridge: University Press, 1958. See pp. 241-243.

McLean, Ruari. "Joseph Cundall: a Victorian editor, designer publisher," *Penrose Annual* 56, edited by Allan Delafons, pp. 82-89. New York: Hastings House, 1962.

McLean, Ruari. *Victorian Book Design and Colour Printing.* Second edition, revised and enlarged. London: Faber & Faber, 1972. See Chapter 12: "Joseph Cundall, publisher and book designer" (pp. 140-153).

McLean, Ruari. *Joseph Cundall: A Victorian Publisher. Notes on his life and a check-list of his books.* Pinner: Private Libraries Association, 1976.

Whalley, Joyce Irene. *Cobwebs to Catch Flies.* London: Elek, 1974. See pp. 20-21.

SHE LISTENED BUT HEARD NO ANSWER HER
HAND WENT "TAP: TAP: TAP: AGAINST
THE DOOR A SECOND TIME.

The Home Treasury.

The Traditional Faëry Tales of

Little Red Riding Hood

Beauty and the Beast &

Jack and the Bean Stalk.

Illustrated by

Eminent Modern Artists, & Edited

By Felix Summerly.

LONDON:

Joseph Cundall, Old Bond Street. 1845.

Little Red Riding Hood.

PREFACE.

WITH which of the northern nations of Europe, Saxons, Franks, Northmen or Normen, the Traditionary Tale of Little Red Riding Hood originated, I have not been able to ascertain. As far as I can learn, the earliest publication of the tale was made by Charles Perrault, a member of the French Academy, and a celebrated literateur of his day. He published this, with some other like fictions in the year 1697, under his son's name of Perrault d'Armancour. The title was " Le Petit Chaperon Rouge." From this period there have been countless successive republications. A French edition of Perrault's Tales of the date of 1698 is in the British Museum, which has the double title of " Contes de ma Mère L'Oye," and " Histoires ou Contes du Temps passé." When the earliest version appeared in English I know not ; and I should be happy to receive any communications on the subject. I have before me not less than five *penny* editions of a very primitive sort, printed almost on brown paper ; with wood cuts that might be taken as blocks belonging to Pfister of the fifteenth century, or any other early wood engravings. The books are without date : but do not look more than fifty years old.

LITTLE RED RIDING HOOD.

IN a little thatched cottage near the forest in Hampshire, which is called the " New Forest," there lived a hard working, industrious couple. The husband was a faggot maker, and the wife used to spend all her spare time from her household duties in spinning thread, for these good people lived a great many years ago when there were no large towns in which thread was made by steam engines.

The cottager and his wife had only one child, a little daughter, who at the time of this story, was about eight years old.

She was a handy little maid, and it was her wish to do every thing she could to assist her mother. She was an early riser, getting up as soon as the sun began to shine, in order to make use of the whole daylight for her work, as the family were obliged to put out their lights when they heard the curfew bell toll. She helped her mother in getting ready her father's breakfast before he went to his work. After breakfast she was busy in putting every thing tidy and orderly in the house. She would then go on short errands for her mother; sometimes to take her father his meals to him in the forest, when he was too busy to come home; sometimes to inquire after the health of a sick neighbour: sometimes to see her good old grandmother, who lived three miles off near another part of the forest.

When she had done all her errands and

whatever else her mother wished, she would
then try and learn to spin, and to mend and
darn her father's clothes. When she had time
to spare she attended to her garden, out of which
she often gathered a few herbs to present to
her father for his supper, when he came home
from his work hungry and tired. At other
times, she was at work making little presents
for her playfellows, for she was a kind and
thoughtful child. She was always light-
hearted and happy, and thoroughly enjoyed a
good hearty game of play. All her young
friends were very fond of her, and were eager
to do any thing to please her.

It was the child's great delight to be useful
and helpful to her parents, who were very
fond of her; not because she was so useful
to them, but because she was generally so
very good and obedient. Her parents dearly
loved her, and so did all her friends and

B

acquaintances, and no one better than her dear old grandmother.

Her grandmother, who was old, had herself made for her a little red hood, such as was then worn in riding, which she gave to her as a present on her birth-day, when she was eight years old. It was a nice comfortable little hood, and so warm and pleasant to wear, that the little girl never went out without her red hood, when the weather was wet or cold.

The little red hood always looked so bright and smart among the green trees, that it could always be seen a long way off. When the neighbours used to spy out the red hood far off among the trees, they would say to one another, " Here comes Little Red Riding Hood," and this was said so often, that at last, the little girl got the name of " Little Red Riding Hood," and she was seldom called by any other name. Indeed, I have never

SHE TAUGHT HER HOW TO PRAY.

been able to learn what her other name was. But every body knew of her by this name; and so by the name of " Little Red Riding Hood" we too will call her.

Her grandmother did many other and better things for her grandchild than making her a " hood." She taught her how to knit, to spin, to bake bread, and to make butter— how to sing, so that she might join in the music in the Church—how to be good natured, and kind, and charitable—how to be courageous and honest, and to speak the truth at all times—how to be grateful—how to love and worship God—and to pray for God's blessing and providence.

This good woman fell sick, and as she had no one to sit with her and attend to her, Little Red Riding Hood, was sent to her every day for this purpose by her mother.

At last the grandmother seemed to be getting well, owing, I have no doubt, to the patient nursing of her good grandchild.   Still she was very weak.   It was in the Autumn of the year, when honey is taken from the hives of the bees.

This year, Little Red Riding Hood's bees had made some delicious honey, and as soon as it was put into pots, her first thought was to take some to her grandmother.   Having got up very early one morning she said to her mother,

" Pray, dear mother, let me take a pot of honey to grandmother this morning."

" So you shall," answered the mother, " and also a nice pat of fresh butter.   Put on your little red hood, and get a clean cloth for the butter, and your little basket ready."

Little Red Riding Hood was full of glee at the thoughts of going, and was ready dressed in a few minutes, with the pot of honey and pat of butter nicely packed in the basket. She did not stay for her breakfast, but started at once, intending to breakfast with her grandmother.

The morning was beautifully bright. The sun had just risen, making the dew drops on the trees glitter and sparkle like gold; and the gossamer swung from the boughs like webs of silver. The skylarks were cherrupping over her head. The air was filled with the fragrance of the wild thyme as it crunched beneath her tread. She tripped along with a heart full of joy, not thinking of the weight of her basket, which was rather heavy for such a little girl.

When she came to a part of the forest which was rather dark and overshadowed with the trees, a very large wolf suddenly stepped out.

Little Red Riding Hood was startled, but continued to walk on quickly. The wolf followed her and overtook her.

Upon coming up to her he grinned maliciously, his evil eye stared. He showed his sharp white teeth and looked most cruel and frightful. He looked as if he would eat her up. The little girl began, as you may suppose, to be frightened.

Hark! what are those sounds? It is the whistle and singing of some of the faggot makers going to their work.

How different the wolf looks now! how demure! he hides his teeth! walks gently along and seems quite another animal. The wolf, who was as cunning as he was cruel, hearing that people were near, at once changed his savage look into one of as much kindness as it was possible for him to do. Presently up came the faggot makers; and the wolf

slunk by the side of the little girl as though
he were afraid of them.

" Good morning, Little Red Riding Hood,"
said one of the faggot makers.

" You are up betimes.   Where are you
going thus early ?"

" To see grandmother," replied Little Red
Riding Hood.

The wolf actually came close to the child's
side, and rubbed his head against her hand
as though he was very fond of her and knew
her.

" Why here's a wolf!" exclaimed one of
the men.

" As I am alive," cried another, " I think
it must be the very wolf that stole my sheep
the other night."

" No, upon the honour of a wolf," said the
treacherous knave very quickly ; which was
a falsehood, for he *had* stolen the man's sheep.

" Come, let us kill him," they all exclaimed.

" No, no, don't kill him," said Little Red
Riding Hood. " Perhaps he is innocent—
and I don't think he can be so very savage,
for he did not touch me before you came
up."

" Well, well, child, we'll let him go this
once for your sake," said they, " but we advise him to be on his good behaviour."

So they wished the child " good morning,"
and went away.

As soon as they were gone the wolf put his
paw to his heart, and said, " Many thanks,
dear little friend. I am very grateful to you
for your protection of me, and I will not fail
to remember it. I wish you a very good
morning."

So he pretended to walk off, when suddenly,
however, he returned, and he said in a soft

bland tone. " I think you said you were
going to see your grandmother—Where does
the dear creature live?"

" In a little cottage which is covered with
woodbine and jessamine, not far from Copt-
hurst Gate," answered Little Red Riding
Hood.

" How do you get in?" said the wolf.

" By tapping at the door, and Granny, if
she is at home, will tell you to pull the latch,
and the door will open."

" Good bye, good bye," said the wolf eagerly, and ran off into the forest.

As soon as he was gone, Little Red Riding
Hood began to pick some sweet purple and
white violets for a nosegay for her grandmother, when she thought to herself, " I wonder why the wolf asked me any questions
about Granny? Being a stranger, I think I
ought not to have told him."   And she began

c

to be afraid of the wolf's mischief. Indeed,
it was a fault of Little Red Riding Hood that
she was sometimes too fond of talking: and
when she thought upon this matter, more and
more she felt that she had done wrong in
telling the wolf anything. The best thing she
could do, she said, will be to hasten onwards
as quickly as possible.

The wolf, when he left her, darted through
the forest, bounding over the furze and bram-
bles, and ran as hard as he could until he
reached the house of the grandmother. He
tapped at the door, and the grandmother,
who was in bed, called to him to come in,
not knowing it was a wolf. The sly wolf said,

" Are you alone, madam ?"

" Yes, quite alone," was the answer.

So he rushed in and flew upon the bed,
tore the grandmother out of it, and ate her
up in a few minutes.

When he had finished his meal, he thought to himself, " Little Red Riding Hood will soon be here, and she will make a most delicious feast. But I must hide myself from her until she is fairly inside of the cottage." He then went to the press in the room, and took out one of the grandmother's night gowns and night caps, and put them on as quickly as he possibly could, and jumped into the bed.

Presently the garden gate was opened, and there came a little quick footstep across the pebbled walk leading to the cottage door, and then a gentle tap, tap, tap, at the door.

It was Little Red Riding Hood. She listened, but heard no answer. Her hand went tap, tap, tap, against the door a second time.

" Who's there?" said the wolf, trying to speak like the grandmother.

" Only Little Red Riding Hood."

" Pull down the latch, and come in, my child."

So Little Red Riding Hood entered, but it struck her ear, that her Grandmother's voice was very hoarse this morning. As she entered, she said,

" I am afraid, dearest granny, that your cold is worse this morning."

" Much worse, dear," said the wolf very gruffly under the bed clothes.

" I have brought you a pot of my virgin honey, which will do your cold good; and mother has sent you a little pat of fresh butter, some of the first we have had made from our new cow's milk."

" Put the things down, child, and come into bed to me, for I have been wretchedly cold all night."

Little Red Riding Hood thought it rather strange that her grandmother should tell her to come *into* bed, instead of sitting by the side of the bed as she had been used to do. So she went to the bed side, and gently pulling aside the curtain saw a head, which though in her grandmother's night cap, did not altogether seem like that of her grandmother's. She thought it was something like the wolf's head—Could it be the wolf? she asked herself. Poor thing! she could hardly help screaming out for fright, but she stopped herself, and said, "Granny, what large ears you have!"

A gruff voice said, "The better to hear with, my dear."

It did not sound like the grandmother's voice, so she said faintly, "Granny, what large eyes you have!"

"The better to see you with, my dear."

Her voice faltered still more, and she said, "Granny, what a large nose you have!"

" The better to smell with, my dear."

Little Red Riding Hood felt almost sure it was the wolf. Her tongue could hardly speak. She trembled from head to foot—at last she muttered in a whisper, " Granny, what large teeth you have !"

" The better to eat you up."

And saying this, the wolf sprang out of the bed, and in an instant devoured **Little Red Riding Hood.**

This is the traditional ending of the Tale—but it is a grievous one, which most children dislike.—And as I have heard a version related, in which poetical justice is done to the wolf, I insert it for those who prefer it :

He seized Little Red Riding Hood, and she screamed. Suddenly a loud rap was heard at the door. Again she screamed—and in rushed her father and some other faggot makers, who, seeing the wolf, killed him at once, and released Little Red Riding Hood.

These were the faggot makers she had met in the wood. They, thinking she was not quite safe with a wolf, went and told her father, and they all followed her to her grandmother's house and thus saved her life.

THE END.

"The Beast had disappeared and she saw at her feet "one of the loveliest princes that eye had ever beheld".

Beauty **and the** Beaſt.

PREFACE.

ERSIONS of this tale under very different shapes are met with throughout all Europe. Sweden, Italy, France, Germany, have all their 'Beauties and Beasts.' In the German popular stories translated from Grimm, "Beauty and the Beast" is the "Lady and the Lion," obtained partly from Hesse, and partly from the Schwalmgegend (see German popular Stories, translated from the Kinder and Haus-Märchen collected by M. M. Grimm. London. Vol. I. p. 153, and note p. 232).

Every age modifies the traditions it receives from its predecessor, and hands them down to succeeding ages in an altered form, rarely with advantage to the traditions themselves. The modern English versions of Beauty and the Beast, adapted " to the manners of the present period," are filled with moralizings on education, marriage, &c.; futile attempts to grind every thing as much as possible into dull logical probability ; and the main incidents of the tale are buried among tedious details of Beauty's sisters and their husbands. I have thought it no sin to get rid of all this, without regard to Mrs. Affable, and to attempt to re-write the legend more as a fairy tale than a lecture.

BEAUTY AND THE BEAST.

 " EAUTY" was the youngest of the three daughters of a Merchant. She had been called "Beauty" from her birth, on account of her surpassing loveliness. Her features were not only handsome in themselves, but they were rendered still more so by the charming modesty, kindness, and frankness which were always beaming in her face. She was beloved by all who were able to value her merits, and was most dear to her father, who had lost his wife, for she was his chief and best companion. Her two sisters were also beautiful in their forms, but their minds were wicked and corrupt. As long as their speech was not heard and their manners

not known, they appeared to be handsome, but
their beauty seemed to vanish after a little acquaintance with them. They were vain, haughty,
and untruthful. The Merchant was once very rich.
He was the owner of a large fleet of ships which
used to sail all over the world, carrying from one
port to another the goods which each nation wanted.
His vessels went to India for silk, to South America
for gold, to England for iron and tin, to Russia for
tallow, and so on. Sometimes all his ships would
meet together in one port in order to exchange
their various cargoes. It so happened, that when
they were all assembled for this purpose in the
Persian Gulf, a most frightful storm arose, and
the whole of the merchant's fleet was lost. Some
of the ships sunk at once to the bottom of the sea;
others were blown by the wind upon rocks, and
dashed to pieces by the mad waves. In a single
night, the Merchant was reduced from riches to
poverty. In the midst of one of the most splendid
feasts with which the Merchant had ever delighted
his friends, a breathless courier rushed among the
glittering throng and announced the sad disaster of

the loss of his ships. The poor Merchant was ruined!

Not in a noble palace, but in a small mean cottage now lives the Merchant. He is not attended by troops of servants as formerly, yet he is not wholly neglected, for Beauty watches and supplies all the wants of her still dearest father. This sweet creature soon forgot her grief at the change of fortune. The loss of jewels and fine clothes caused her no pain. She found it quite as easy to be happy without luxuries as with them. Her goodness and lively kindness seemed even greater than before. Beauty's happy contentment did not overtake her sisters; they pined sullenly at their altered state, despised their mean clothing, refused to help in the necessary work of the house, leaving all the drudgery to their over kind sister, and even reproached their own father for their misfortune. They were truly miserable. Their unhappy minds affected their looks; and whilst their handsomely formed foreheads gradually became wrinkled with frowns, their well turned mouths contracted with peevishness. In short, their beauty passed away,

and positive ugliness took its place. Beauty's
looks were not only preserved by her cheerfulness,
but they became even more lovely.

Beauty had always doted on flowers; when she
came to the cottage she became her own gardener,
and the bouquets with which she enlivened her
little sitting room, were not less fragrant in perfume,
or less brilliant in colour, than the rare flowers
which had been supplied to her when she was rich.
Her garden was a pattern of neatness and tasteful
arrangement; and as there was no gardener to trim
the box trees into the shapes of peacocks and griffins,
as heretofore, her good taste suffered them to grow
in their natural forms.

All sorts of flowers bloomed in her garden except
roses; and strange to say, though she often attempted to cultivate them, and planted them without number, they always vanished the night after
they had been brought into the garden. At first
it was thought that the garden had been robbed,
and a watch was set to detect the supposed robbers.
The roses vanished, but no robber was found, and
and not even the print of a footstep could ever be

seen on the flower-bed. Beauty wondered at the mysterious disappearance of the roses, whilst her sisters laughed her to scorn, and even accused her of carrying them away in trickery. Beauty at last got tired of losing her roses, and gave up planting them.

After the Merchant and his daughters had lived in the cottage for about twelve months, good news was brought to him of the safe arrival in a distant port of one of his most precious cargoes, which had been thought to have been lost when the great shipwreck of his vessels happened. It was necessary that the Merchant should go to the port in order to claim his ship, and he resolved to start out the next day for that purpose. He called his three daughters together to tell them of the news; the two eldest were quite overcome with joy, at the prospects of better fortune, but Beauty, though she was glad for her father's sake that he was richer, remained silent. She had become so contented with her present state that she did not welcome another change.

" Tell me, daughters," said the Merchant, " what

presents shall your father bring for you on his return from his journey."

" Bring me," said the eldest, "jewels rich and rare; a watch encircled with diamonds, which plays the most seraphic music; a girdle of the purest crystals, bracelets studded with the most precious cameos, and a chaplet of rubies; you may also bring any pearls of the size of walnuts, if you meet with them, and—

" Hold, sister," said the second, " you will ruin our father before it comes to my turn. My wishes are not so extravagant;—I will only ask for a few of the most splendid Persian turbans, two or three dresses of the richest point lace, a variety of Cachmere shawls, and a tortoiseshell cabinet inlaid with gold, to hold them all. She paused, as though she were thinking to add something else, when the Merchant turned to Beauty and said, " Well, Beauty, and what shall your present be ?"

" I wish for nothing, Father, but your safe return."

" Nay, child, you must make a request."

" Well then, dearest Father, as roses wont grow

in my garden, bring me a rose, if it comes in your way."

The sisters laughed outright with disdain at her modest request.

On the morrow, the Merchant started on his journey. Beauty was in tears at his departure. Not so her sisters, who could not suppress their joy at the prospects of their new finery, and seemed to care but little for their father's absence.

The Merchant arrived in safety at the port, and found his vessel more richly freighted than he had looked for. He arranged all his business to his mind, and made the purchases, extravagant as they were, which his eldest daughters had requested. He mounted his Arab steed, and commenced his journey homeward. Towards evening, he reached a forest of pines and cedars through which lay his way. The horse took the beaten path. The evening was most sultry and oppressive. The sun descended below the horizon, leaving his mantle of the intensest crimson, fringed with golden brilliancy, behind. The stillness was quite painful. The Merchant was so wrapt up with his thoughts of home, that he forgot to guide his horse, and left him to take his own way. The animal's noiseless tread as his hoofs sunk into the fibrous ground, did not awaken the merchant from his trance. The scene grew gloomy. Presently thunder sounded as if booming in the distance. Leaden looking clouds, folded one on another, covered the amber tinted sky, and large drops of rain fell upon the Merchant before he was roused from his own thoughts. He looked about him, and instantly saw that he had lost his road. Should he go on, or turn back? should he turn to the right or to the left? he asked himself. On all sides the forest seemed equally dark and impenetrable. Up came the distant thunder, roaring—crash! crash! as if the heavens were split. Long streams of lightning flooded the forest with lurid light, revealing the huge copper-coloured arms of the cedar trees, on which their dark foliage swayed to and fro like black plumes. Then came thick darkness again, and cataracts of rain poured down. The horse was stupified with fear, the Merchant hardly less so.

During the lull of the storm a sweet sound was heard, as if it said—

> On ! Merchant, on !
> Thy journey's near done !

And at the instant a small blue light was seen through the trees. The Merchant took courage and clapped his spurs to his steed, urging him in the direction of the light. The horse plunged forward. The light expanded into a large soft flame, and then disappeared. In its place was seen the portal of a magnificent palace. A tablet above the entrance was inscribed in glittering letters,—

> Enter without fear,
> All are welcome here !

The Merchant read the inscription and pressed against the golden gates, which yielded to the softest touch and opened without noise. As he passed beneath the marble archway a long flourish of trumpets saluted his ear, but nobody was to be seen. He found himself in a spacious court yard,

c

on one side of which were the stables. The Merchant dismounted from his horse, which directly trotted off to the stable door, as though he knew the way. He followed the horse into the stable, and when he arrived he was greatly surprised to find him already cleaned and groomed, with a fine crimson horse-cloth thrown over him, and feeding off a trough full of oats and beans. Still no one was seen.

The Merchant quitted the stable, and proceeded across the court yard into a long vaulted passage which was brilliantly lighted. As he passed a door it sprang open into a bath room, in the centre of which a fountain played. The Merchant entered, and before a blazing fire of juniper wood and frankincense, which sweetly scented the room, dry and fine clothes were airing. He threw himself on a couch, wet and weary as he was, but hesitated to touch any thing, until he heard a voice gently saying,

You're a guest for the night,
And all that is right
Will appear to your sight
To be used without fright.

The Merchant stripped himself and entered the
warm-bath, which was of rose-water. Upon quitting
it, his wet clothes had vanished, and other dry garments supplied their place. From the bath-room
he proceeded to the supper-room, and there found a
delicious repast prepared, at which he made a most
hearty meal. When he had satisfied himself with
one dish, it was removed by some unseen hands, and
another of a different kind was placed in its stead.
Thus, venison gave way to roasted peacocks, peacocks
to apricots swimming in iced sherbet, and so on; it
is impossible now to tell you of all the dainties provided for the Merchant's supper. During its progress, his ears were filled with most exquisite music.
When all was finished the Merchant departed for
his sleeping apartment, where he also found every
luxury prepared for his coming. Having offered
up his grateful prayers, and especially for his deliverance during the storm, the Merchant retired to
his bed, and instantly fell into a sweet and refreshing
sleep.

The next morning was as bright and peaceful as
the night before had been dark and turbulent. The

Merchant awoke quite refreshed from his fatigue. Every thing was ready for his toilet and his breakfast. After breakfast the Merchant walked in the gardens of the palace; their size, variety, plantations, flowers, were such as he had never seen equalled. Shrubs and flowers which he had always thought most rare, in this garden appeared to grow almost wild. The flowers made him think of Beauty, and then of her request of a rose as a present. He searched for a rose tree, but could see none. Strange, thought he, that there should be no roses in such a garden! He became quite fatigued with hunting for a rose tree; at last, entering an arbour, he found some roses within it. The Merchant plucked a rose: suddenly a monster seized him. "Ungrateful wretch," said the Beast, "is this the way you repay the kindness you have received? You take refuge in my palace from the violence of the storm, you are treated with the best that I can bestow upon you, and in return you steal my roses! Your life is forfeited for your baseness."

The poor old man trembled beneath the grasp of

the monster. " My Lord !" he said falteringly,
" My Lord—"

" Call me by no such title !" interrupted the
monster, " Call me as I am—call me Beast !"

" Sir !"

" Did you hear me say call me Beast?"

" Pardon me, Beast, I knew not I was offending."

" Were the roses yours?" The Merchant gave
no reply. " Why then did you pluck them?" Still
no answer was returned.

" Answer me instantly !" said the Beast, with
increased anger.

" I cannot !" replied the Merchant, for he did
not wish to involve his daughter in his trouble.

" You cannot? you die this instant, unless you
answer."

" Spare my answer, Beast, spare it, but take my
life."

" It was your youngest daughter who asked for
the rose ! I see your astonishment, but I know all.
Still, as you were too noble to tell, and were ready
to suffer for her sake, I will spare your life for the

present. I will allow you to return home and take leave of your children, but you must return here in a week, or send some one in your stead. Take the rose and begone."

The Merchant stooped to pick up the rose, which had fallen from his hand in his fright, and when he turned to thank the Beast, the monster was nowhere to be seen. The fatal rose seemed at once to wither; the merchant put it into his bosom, and hastened through the gardens into the palace.

The breakfast had been removed, and other kinds of refreshment placed in its stead; but the Merchant had lost all hunger, and he proceeded at once to the stable, where he found his horse already saddled and bridled and restive to be gone. He mounted his steed, which dashed forthwith out of the stable towards the entrance gates. They sprang open at his approach, and when the Merchant had passed through, closed again with a loud clang. The horse flew through the forest, seeming scarcely to touch the ground with his hoofs, and continued going at the fastest rate until he was completely clear of the wood. In the evening the

Merchant, almost broken-hearted, reached his cottage.

Beauty was seated under the cottage porch, spinning; she appeared to be anxiously watching the horseman's approach. The instant she saw that it was her father, she sprung from her seat towards him, and in a few seconds the father and child were locked in each other's arms.

Beauty's face was radiant with joy; the father looked very sad. " Oh father!" exclaimed Beauty with fear and pity, "why that look? tell me, tell me what has happened."

" My poor child, thou art the innocent cause of my grief! Here, my child, take the rose you asked for, it will cost thy father his life!" The Merchant took the withered rose from his bosom, and placed it in Beauty's hand. Beauty took the flower, which began instantly to revive, but she fell fainting to the ground, so much was she terrified at her father's speech. The Merchant carried her into the cottage and related to her all that had occurred since his departure. As soon as the Merchant had finished his account, Beauty's face brightened, and she said smilingly, " O father! you shall not return ; it was for my sake that the misfortune happened. I alone will bear the punishment. Frightful as may be the monster, and terrible the death he may have in store, I will go." No entreaties of the father could alter her mind: her resolution was made. " Your life, dearest father, is more valuable than mine. If you were gone, who would support and protect my sisters ?"

Whilst Beauty was sacrificing herself for the sake of her sisters, they entered, and seeing only Beauty, and her in tears, the eldest exclaimed, " What, crying again, you soft-hearted thing ! You have done nothing but cry since our father left : you are miserable because you did not ask for more than a rose." " A rose, indeed!" said the other sister, " why here's a rose, what a magnificent flower ! It is the largest rose I have seen ! Tell me, minx, where did it come from ?" Saying this, the sister seized the rose, which immediately withered again. The father raised himself from the couch he had thrown himself upon. The two daughters ran to him, and without greeting him, said eagerly,

" Well father, where's my watch ? my shawls ? my
bracelets ? my cabinet ?"

" Pray, sisters, pray sisters," interposed Beauty,
" do not trouble father now : he is full of grief."

" Grief! Has he not brought our jewels or
clothes ?"

" Oh yes, sisters, brought all, but still full of
sorrow."

" How can he be sorrowful if he has brought our
presents ? It is impossible !"

Beauty in the kindest manner, then told them
about the disaster of the rose.

" You wicked child," they answered, " to ask for
a rose ! See what trouble you have brought us to :
you might have caused us to lose our jewels and
shawls ! the Beast would no doubt have taken them,
had he known of them. What a risk for a trumpery
rose ! Let us throw it in the fire for a punishment
to you. They made an effort to seize the rose, but
as they approached it, it glided away from them and
took refuge with Beauty. Then the father interfered,
and commanded his two eldest daughters to be silent,

and not again to mention the subject of the rose to Beauty.

The week had nearly passed, and Beauty was full of preparations for her departure. She went round to take leave of all her friends, leaving with each some little token of her love and kindness. She sought to turn away her sisters' unkindness, and offered them the choice of whatever she possessed. They, finding that she was really going, and believing that she would never return, pretended to be reconciled, and affected great grief; but in their hearts they were glad, for they were full of jealousy at her goodness and superiority over them. The morning for departure came: the Merchant insisted on accompanying his daughter and seeing her safely to the Monster's palace. They both mounted their horses and set off; as soon as they arrived at the cedar forest, the Merchant's horse darted into the midst of it as though he knew the right path, and Beauty's horse followed close to the other. Beauty thought she had never seen a wood so grand and yet so beautiful. The nightingales were singing with the wildest richness. Mournfully streamed

through the air their full long plaints, as if in
unison with the melancholy of Beauty's forebodings ;
and then their sadness broke abruptly into laughing,
chattering jug, jug, turning their grief into joy, as if
presaging happiness to Beauty at last.   All kinds
of perfume scented the air ; first came the soft rich
scent of the cedars, then the pungent freshness of
the citrons, then the verbena sent up its fragrance,
as the hoofs of the horses crunched its leaves in
passing.   The nightingales' music was hushed, and
the light seemed broken into millions of prismatic
colours. A procession of innumerable insects formed
before their horses' heads ; they were all marshalled
in order.   In the van came a troop of Dragon Flies ;
then bands of thousands of little Gnats played the most
martial airs on their tiny trumpets ; Bees followed,
humming the richest harmonies ; afterwards came
ranks of Butterflies, dressed in liveries of all the
colours of the rainbow, sailing majestically along.
And so this procession kept before their horses'
heads until they reached the golden gates of the
palace.   The inscription,

> " Enter without fear,
> All are welcome here !"

glittered more brilliantly than at the Merchant's first
entrance; the gates instantly flew open. Beauty's
horse placed itself at once near some steps of marble with golden rails, in order that Beauty might
alight easily. Having done so, and her father being
dismounted also, both horses ambled off to the
stable. The Merchant and Beauty passed into the
arcade; as before, the Merchant went to his bath,
whilst two humming birds, bearing little torches of
white light, flew before Beauty and lighted her to
her apartment, and then flew away. Over the
door was inscribed "BEAUTY'S APARTMENT." The
door sprung open as she touched the enamelled
handle. The room contained the choicest luxuries
of all kinds; sofas, chairs, stools, and ottomans of
all shapes, high seated, low seated, soft, hard, warm,
cool. Patterns of the most symmetrical forms and
beautiful colours were arranged in harmonious de-
corations on the ceiling and walls. The carpets
were of the richest velvet, the hangings of satin
powdered with golden stars, and the finest lace.
In one recess of the room was a library; in another,
all kinds of musical instruments; in another, cabi-

nets of prints; in another, screens covered with the
finest paintings; in another, materials for needle work.
Adjoining to this apartment were Beauty's dressing
and bed rooms. She entered the former, where she
found every article for her toilet prepared, and a
display of numberless dresses of the utmost splen-
dour and richness. Yet she lacked heart and
courage to touch any thing, and sunk down listlessly
into a chair. She raised her drooping eyes, and
beheld a transparency at the end of the room thus
inscribed:

" Welcome, Beauty, banish fear,
You are Queen and mistress here!
Speak your wishes, speak your will,
Swift obedience meets them still."

Having changed her dress, she went in search of
her father, whom she met in the saloon, into which
her own room opened. Here they found a magnificent feast prepared for them. No attendants
waited, and every thing was brought and removed
by invisible agency. During the repast, most
delightful music was performed.

" Certainly, father," said Beauty, " the Beast

must possess excellent taste, and if I am to be killed, he surely intends first to fatten me!"

A magic flute played a few bars of music, then a voice said,

> " The Beast is near,
> And asks leave to appear."

" How very thoughtful for a master in his own house to make such a request! I tremble at his coming," thought Beauty.

The Merchant then spoke, " Appear, Beast, if it be your pleasure."

A door sprung open at the further end of the saloon, and the Beast entered. He wore a large cloak, which concealed his form; his walk was erect and dignified. The room was so long that Beauty could not discover his features, but as he came nearer, his hideous appearance began to be seen. As the Beast approached, Beauty clung to her father's arm for protection. She could not help hiding her face from seeing the Beast. He saw and pitied her alarm, and at once spoke to the Merchant: " Merchant, you have well redeemed

your word. If this be the daughter who has
come in your stead, I trust, though absent from
those she loves, that we shall find means to sooth
her regrets, if not to make her time pass agreeably.
Of my palace and all its contents she is the
mistress."

The voice which uttered this speech was most
musical, and the kind expression with which it was
said, emboldened Beauty to look up. She gave a
glance, but the exceeding ugliness of the Monster
caused her again to close her eyes.

" I am sorry," said the Beast, " that I am not
able to ask you, Merchant, to stay here as the
guest of your daughter ; on the morrow you must
take leave of each other."

" Your kindness, Beast," answered the Merchant,
"is already much more than we were entitled to
expect, and makes us feel most grateful to you.
We are prepared to submit to your will in all
respects."

Making a low and graceful bow the Beast said,
" Farewell!" and left the saloon. As soon as he
had gone the music recommenced, and a concert

was performed, at the end of which the Merchant
and his daughter retired for the night.

On the morrow the Merchant departed with
great grief, and returned home.

At first Beauty felt inconsolable at being alone.
But she reflected that there was no help for it, and
as she was too wise to give way to her sorrow, she
sought to banish it, and to find means of interesting
herself in various occupations. Whatever she
wished for, seemed to present itself at her command.
There was the garden with all its wonderful beauties of flowers and shrubs. The lake, the fountains,
the gold and silver fish, the aviary with the choicest
of birds for song and plumage. The trees of the
gardens were thronged too with birds. If she desired to sail on the water, she had only to step into
a boat, its sails at once caught the breeze, and it
glided noiselessly over the crystal clear waters. If
she desired to ride, her own horse, richly caparisoned,
left the stable and presented himself at the door.
If she would drive out, a carriage with cream-
coloured long-tailed ponies attended at the terrace
steps. Within doors, too, there was every thing

"Beauty felt his heart still beating".

desirable. A noble gallery was hung with the best
pictures of ancient and modern painters. Another
gallery was filled with sculpture. Her own room
provided the most ample means for the study of
books, the painting of pictures, the playing of
music, the working of tapestry and all kinds of
needle-work; yet the absence of any human being
whatever made the solitude most painful. Long
before the first day had passed, she had felt with all
its force the solitude of the place. She quite welcomed the magic flute, and the sounds—

> " The Beast is near,
> And asks leave to appear !"

and was really glad to answer, " Appear, Beast !"
She shuddered as he approached, but her fear wore
off as the Beast stayed conversing with her. When
the clock sounded ten he bid her a respectful " Good
night." The next day she got more used to the
place, and even looked out for the time when the
magic flute should sound. When the Beast appeared
this evening, she looked calmly at his ugliness.
She was more than ever pleased with his conversa-

E

tion, which was delightfully witty, wise too, and
gentle. Day after day thus passed, the Beast
appearing every evening. His visit became the
object of the day, and had he been uglier than he
really was, I have no doubt Beauty would have
ceased to regard it. Thus the time passed for more
than half a year: when one evening, after Beauty
and the Beast had been conversing most pleasantly,
Beast stopped in his talk and took her hand.
Beauty thrilled, but it was not with delight; he
had never done so before. Beauty quietly withdrew
her hand, at which the Beast sighed deeply, and
suddenly he bid her 'adieu!' Some days after this,
the Beast again took Beauty's hand, and she suffered
it to remain. The Beast then said, " Beauty, will
you marry me?" " Impossible!" replied Beauty.
The Beast groaned deeply, and left as if he felt the
greatest grief. The next night no Beast appeared.
Beauty listened anxiously for the sounds of the flute,
but none were heard. The evening seemed to her
the dullest which she had passed since her arrival
in the palace. The next evening came, and still no
Beast. " What can this mean?" thought she, " is

the Beast never to appear again ? I would sooner
have his presence with all his ugliness a thousand
times more, than this constant absence." She had
scarcely acknowledged the thought to herself, before
the flute sounded and Beast entered. He looked
melancholy and pensive, except when Beauty was
talking to him. At the usual hour he departed. As
he was leaving, Beauty said " I hope Beast, you will
come to-morrow." " It is a great balm to my un-
happiness, Beauty, to hear that my visit is not
absolutely disagreeable to you." The Beast continued his evening visits as before, but he never
again mentioned the subject of marriage, nôr took
Beauty's hand. He was as kind and agreeable as
ever, but oftentimes Beauty thought he seemed very
sad : she feared to ask him the cause. She asked
herself over and over again, " Can I marry him?"
and then the thoughts of his excessive hideousness
rushed into her mind, and she reluctantly answered,
" No."

In the midst of all this new life Beauty did not
forget her own home, and often longed to hear how
her father and her sisters fared. One day as she

was standing before a large mirror, she exclaimed,
"Oh that I could see what my father is about."
At that instant a reflection of her home appeared
in the glass. In one room were her sisters trying
on some new gowns. In another room lay her
father on a bed of sickness, so feeble that he could
scarce hold any thing. Beauty screamed, and
nearly swooned away. At that instant, the magic
flute sounded, though it was but noon, and the
Beast came in. He found Beauty sobbing: he
gently took her hand and said, "Beauty, what ails
you, are you ill?" "No, Beast, no, but I have
just seen the reflection of my old home in the mirror,
and my father, I fear, is at the point of death."

"Then you wish to visit him."

"Oh yes, Beast, it would indeed be a great joy
and comfort to do so; perhaps it may be the last
time I shall ever see him alive."

"Take the rose which your father first gathered,"
said the Beast, "and as long as it is in your possession you have only to wish aloud and your wish
will be gratified instantly."

" Oh Beast! believe me, I am most grateful for
your great kindness."

" There is only one condition I have to make,"
said the Beast, " which is that you are not absent
more than a week. Pray, Beauty, do not make your
absence longer, even that time will appear like
ages to me !"

" You may rely on my return within the proper
time. Farewell ! farewell !" Beauty extended her
hand, and even shed tears at the thoughts of leaving
the good Monster.

" Adieu ! Beauty ! Adieu !" and the Beast took
her hand and pressed it to his lips. He then left
the room slowly and sorrowfully.

When the Beast had gone, Beauty took the rose
and placed it in her bosom. She then said aloud
" I wish I were at home." And saying this she
placed her hand before her eyes to wipe away her
tears ; she had scarcely removed her handkerchief
when instead of being in her own apartment she
found herself at the porch of her father's cottage.
She knocked gently, and the door was opened by

her eldest sister, who started at seeing her, and
said—

"Well, Beauty indeed! who would have thought
of seeing you? we thought you were dead long enough
ago, and perhaps eaten up by your Monster."

Beauty threw herself on her sister's neck, and
not heeding her unkind greeting, kissed her. "How
is my father? is he alive?"

"Alive! yes and much better! but no thanks to
your nursing. We thought you had quite forgotten
us."

"Never! never! sister, I came the instant I
knew of our father's sickness."

"Well, well, go in and see him."

Beauty found her father much better, and both
were rejoiced to see each other again. Beauty's
presence hastened the recovery of the old man, and
she at once took upon herself the office of nurse,
which her sisters willingly gave up to her. The
Merchant became quite well before Beauty had
been at home two days. He delighted in hearing
all her news: she related to him and her sisters
how she passed her time at the palace, and how

kind the Beast was to her. Her account of the
palace and all its wonders made the sisters quite
jealous and anxious to take Beauty's place. The
eldest began to think how she could do so. She
learned from Beauty the means by which she had
come home, and how she still possessed the rose
which ensured the fulfilment of all her desires.
The eldest then basely attempted to rob Beauty of
the rose; as Beauty slept, she took it from her
bosom, and wished herself at the Beast's palace;
but the instant she seized the rose, it withered at
her touch, and instead of being transported to the
Beast's palace, the wicked creature was carried
plump down into the pigsty. She threw away the
rose with horror, and roared out lustily until some
one came to help her. The farming men took her
out of the mire, and wondered very much how she
got there, but not a word would she speak, and
when she was brought into the cottage, she kept a
rigid silence : all the questioning of her father and
sisters could not induce her to tell what was the
cause of her being found in the pigsty.

"This event happened towards the end of the

week when Beauty must depart. The next day
was her last day, and she made preparations for
leaving. She looked with pleasure at the prospect
of seeing her kind friend the Beast again. She
wished to give her sisters some presents before she
left them, and sought for her rose to enable her to
do so, when, lo! it was gone. Beauty searched
after it every where she could think of, but it was
not to be found. She became alarmed, not so
much because she was unable to make her sisters
presents, as that she had lost her power of returning
to the palace according to her promise. Her sister
saw her grief, but had not the generosity to tell her
that she had thrown the rose away. The last day
of the week passed, the day after passed too, and
still no rose was found. Beauty was inconsolable.
More diligent search was made, and without success;
in despair Beauty bethought herself if it were possible that the affair of the pigsty could have any
thing to do with the loss of the rose. As Beauty
wandered disconsolate over the grounds she espied
upon a heap of rubbish, the rose nearly withered.
With feelings of the greatest joy she hastily seized

it, and its faded flowers began to revive; she took farewell of her father and sisters directly, and wished herself back at the Beast's palace.

In an instant she was in her own room. As the evening drew near she anxiously looked for the Beast, but he came not. Weary she sat up all the long night, believing he certainly would come at last, but the sun rose in the morning and no Beast appeared. She was filled with alarm, jaded and worn out with anxiety and want of rest. She passed from one room of the palace to another, from terrace to garden, and from garden to grove, calling for the Beast, but found him not. In her despair she seized her rose and wished herself in the Beast's presence. Oh! horror! there he lay as if dead. Beauty felt his heart still beating. She flew to a pool for some water, the Beast uttered a groan, and looked up. His eye feebly opened, and seeing Beauty he said, " Beauty, why did you return only to see me die? I could not have believed you would have deceived me. It was impossible to survive your absence; but I am happy to see you once again before I die."

F

" Oh! Beast! do not die! what can I do to save you?"

" Will you marry me?" faintly murmured the Beast.

" Willingly, to save your life!" answered Beauty eagerly.

The Beast seemed to revive, and said timidly, " But not otherwise, Beauty?"

" Yes! yes!" replied Beauty, covering her face.

The Beast had disappeared, and she saw at her feet one of the loveliest Princes that eyes had ever beheld.

Loudly roared the cannon amidst the sounds of the trumpets and timbrels, and all the palace seemed suddenly peopled with bustling crowds engaged in festivity.

The Prince took Beauty's arm, and led her into the Palace; where, to Beauty's surprise, she found her father, but not her sisters, who had not been invited to the wedding. They were changed into stone statues, so to remain until they had reformed themselves.

The Prince and Beauty were married that very

day, and lived to a good old age in great happiness.
The Prince explained all his troubles to Beauty;
how he had been changed into a Beast by a spiteful
fairy, who had condemned him to be a Beast until
he found some one who consented to marry him in
his frightful form; and how a good fairy had given
him a magic rose tree, telling him that it would be
the means of releasing him from his enchantment.

THE END.

C. WHITTINGHAM, CHISWICK.

Jack's Triumph.

Jack **and the** Bean Stalk.

JACK AND THE BEANSTALK.

N a small village, at some distance from London, lived a poor widow and her son, whose name was Jack. He was a bold, daring fellow, ready for any adventure which promised fun or amusement. He delighted in scrambling along the steepest and most inaccessible parts of the rocks and cliffs, in search of birds' eggs, or anything else which caught his fancy or his eye ; he cared not a rush for tumbles or disasters of any kind. He would climb to the top of one of the highest trees overhanging some steep precipice, and lying along the swinging branches, wave his hat above his head,

and scream with delight.   All the boys in the
neighbourhood acknowledged him as their
leader in all feats of dexterity and daring.
Many a time he got into sad disgrace for
enticing them from their work to follow him
over hill and dale, through brooks and hedges,
in some wild freak or other.

But it was very idle of Jack to spend all
his time in fun and frolic ; he would not work
or do anything useful, by which he might
assist his mother in earning money to buy
them food and clothing. This was partly
owing to the foolish manner in which his
mother had brought him up, for she had not
courage or good sense to make him do anything which was disagreeable to him : she
was so foolishly fond of him, that she only
thought of the present moment, and as she
liked to see him look smiling and happy, she
did not consider what would be the conse-

quence, when he became a man, of the idleness in which she now indulged him; or how miserable and unhappy an idle, useless person always becomes.

As Jack grew older, and cost more money than he used to do when he was a little child, his mother became poorer every year, so that she was obliged to sell one piece of furniture after another, until she had little else remaining in her house except her bed, a table, and a couple of chairs.

She had a cow, of which she was very fond, and which, up to this time, had been their chief support. It supplied them with milk and butter, which she used to carry to market to sell, after setting aside a small quantity for their own use.

But now the time had arrived when she must part with that too; and as, with tears in her eyes, she brought out the cow to feed it

for the last time, before Jack should drive it
to market, she could not forbear reproaching
him, and saying, " Ah! my child, if you had
not been so idle, and had worked ever so little
to help me, we need not have sold my poor
Brindle. But now it must be sold. It is a
great grief to me to part with her; take her,
Jack, and be sure, that you make the best
bargain you can; she is a famous cow, and
ought to fetch us a good round sum."

Jack, too, felt very sorry to part with poor
Brindle; so he walked along rather sadly for
some time, driving the cow before him : by
degrees he forgot his grief, and then began
to whistle, and loiter to pick blackberries.
On the road he met a butcher, who was carrying in his hat some things which Jack thought
very pretty, and which he thought he should
like to have to play with ; they were speckled,
and Jack could not take his eyes off them.

The butcher, who was a bit of a rogue, saw how eagerly Jack eyed his Beans, and said, " Do you want to sell your cow, my fine fellow !"

" Yes," answered Jack, " I do."

" Well," said the butcher, " I will buy her of you, if you like, which will save you the trouble of driving her any farther ; and as you seem to have taken such a fancy to these Beans, I will give you the whole hat-full, in exchange for your cow."

Jack was delighted, he seized the hat, and ran back to his mother. His mother had so constantly given him whatever he wished for, that he now always expected every whim to be gratified ; and he had become so selfish that he thought of no one but himself. In this instance, he only thought of the pleasure of possessing the Beans, and never once thought of the distress his mother would feel

when he should return without the money
which she so much needed. " What! back so
soon, Jack !" said his mother to herself, when
she saw him running towards her,—" then I
guess you have had good luck ;" and she
called out as he came towards her, " What
luck, Jack ? what luck ?"

Jack was too much out of breath to answer;
but as he ran forward heedlessly, his foot
slipped, and he fell at his mother's feet, while
the Beans rolled out of the hat, and covered
the ground.

"Jack, Jack !" said his mother, " why are
you so careless ? Get up and give me the
money ;" and she held out her hand to assist
him to rise: but Jack, without answering,
turned over on his hands and knees, and
began to pick up the Beans.

" What signify the Beans ?" said his mother
impatiently, " get up and give me the money."

Jack's tumble had sobered him a little, and when he heard his mother ask for the money so impatiently, he felt afraid to speak, and the colour rose to his cheeks as he thought that perhaps his mother would not like his bargain; however, he soon shook off these thoughts, and called out in his usual reckless way, "It's of no use to fret, mother, but I haven't brought you any money."

"Not brought me any money!" said his mother distractedly, "why, Jack, you cannot mean it; then where is my cow?"

"Sold, mother; and see what I have got for it," and he offered the hat of Beans to his mother. His mother sobbed as if her heart would break; and saying, "Of what use are these foolish beans?" she opened the window, and threw them all out into the garden.

Jack burst into tears, and went to bed with a sad heart, feeling at last very sorry for his

B

folly, and wishing that he could do something
to comfort his mother and earn some money
for her.   At last he fell asleep.   When he
awoke in the morning the room had an un-
usual look about it.   He hardly knew if it
was morning yet: some little random gleams
of sunshine played upon the wall, though the
room seemed generally shadowed.   He sprang
out of bed, and walked to the window, and
found, to his great astonishment, that one of
the Beans which his mother had thrown out
into the garden, had taken root, and had
grown up, up, up, until its top was quite
lost in the clouds, and he could not see where
it ended.   The stalks were so closely entwined
that he thought he could easily climb up, and
he felt a very strong desire to do so, and to
see what was at the top.   He scrambled on
his clothes, and was in such a hurry that he
forgot to put his stockings on.   He crept softly

down stairs, in order that he should not disturb his mother so early, and he quietly lifted the latch of the cottage door.

The morning air was cool and fresh, and Jack felt full of spirits and eagerness to mount the Beanstalk. He put his foot on a branch and found that it would bear him—then he tried another—then another—" It will bear me, I find," exclaimed Jack. " So here goes." And he tore off his cloak and flung it down, lest it should be in his way.

Up! up! up! he goes, climbing as nimbly as a squirrel. He put forth all his strength, and got on famously. After some time he rested and looking down could only just see his mother's cottage, but he could see the spires of many churches a long way off. Up! up! again he goes—the Beanstalk seemed to get steeper and steeper, yet he did not reach the top. Jack's heart begins to beat more quickly, and his breath gets shorter. His legs and arms tremble, and his foot often slips. Jack began to despair, and thought he could go no further; but after resting for a short time he resolved not to lose his courage, so he again put forth his strength, and at last he reached the very top. He fell down on the ground quite exhausted. He lay in this state some minutes, when he raised himself to look about him. Every thing looked so dreary and gloomy that he became quite melancholy, and began to wish heartily that he was back again with his mother.

He was exceedingly hungry as well as fatigued. At last he fell asleep, and all at once, he seemed to be carried through the air, until he came to a beautiful garden, where he was placed on a bed of the softest moss; he looked around in surprise, and began to wonder to whom this beautiful place belonged, when hearing a rustling noise, he looked up, and beheld, floating in the air, a slight but beautiful creature, in robes of lily white, spangled with gold, which looked like glistening stars. A long train floated behind her, richly fringed with gold and pearls, and supported by two beautiful little cherubs : her golden pinions struck the air, and her long flowing hair, crowned with roses, danced in the sunshine. As she came near, she seemed to smile sweetly upon Jack, and at last alighting on a rosebud which grew near, she turned to him, and said in a silvery toned voice, " If thou art wise, look and learn."

She waved her wand and Jack saw a magnificent house, in the hall of which he could perceive a crowd of poor people, to whom the master of the house was distributing money, clothes, and food; there was a lady too, with a baby in her arms. The fairy

again waved her wand, and Jack saw an
enormous Giant advance to the door, he was
welcomed like the rest, and feasted with all
manner of dainties. The fairy waved her
wand a third time; all became dark, as if
night had set in, and Jack saw the Giant
stalk stealthily to the room where his host
lay, and with one blow of his club lay him
lifeless before him. The fairy waved her
wand once more, and Jack saw the lady,
whom he now perceived to resemble his own
mother, rush out of the house, with her
baby in her arms, and run as fast as if her
feet were winged, whilst the Giant loaded
himself with bags of money, a golden hen, a
beautiful harp, and every thing that was valuable, and then set fire to the house.

All vanished: Jack started, and opening
his eyes, found that the daylight was nearly
gone; he felt stiff and almost famished with

hunger; looking round the plain he saw a
large house as far off as he could see. He
crawled on until he came to the door, at
which he knocked.

The door was opened by a timid looking
woman, who started when she saw him, and
cried out, " Oh, fly, fly, poor boy, before
my husband comes back, do you not know
that he is a cruel Giant, and that if he find
you here, he will eat you up? Run, child, run
quick!" and the woman pushed him away
gently but earnestly. Jack looked at her
with curiosity; her face was frightfully pale
and thin; her cheekbones projected, while
her eyes were sunken and hollow: she stooped,
and her head drooped like that of a person
who lives in constant fear and dread. Jack
shuddered, but there was a kind, pitying look
about her, which made him determine not to
give up the point.

"I cannot run away," said he, "because I am quite tired out with a long day's journey, and I have had nothing to eat all day; pray, pray, good woman, let me in, you may put me anywhere, if you will but give me some supper and a place to sleep in. There is no other house to be seen, and it is almost dark; pray, good mother, take me in, said Jack taking hold of her gown and looking in her face entreatingly. I cannot go any farther to-night, indeed I cannot."

The woman, who was very kind hearted, saw how tired Jack looked, and how sore and swollen his feet were, she therefore told him, though very reluctantly, that she would do the best she could for him. She brought him into the kitchen, and set before him on a table some bread and meat, and a fine foaming jug of ale. Jack ate and drank, and soon felt quite refreshed: he watched the woman who was basting an enormous ox roasting before the fire, and Jack was just thinking what a large appetite the Giant must have, when the woman suddenly stopped and listened; she started, and saying, " My husband! quick, quick; he comes—he comes:" she opened the door of the oven and bid Jack jump in; but before she could shut it close, the knocker fell with a noise that made Jack's heart leap in his bosom: he could feel the whole house rock as knock succeeded knock—louder and yet louder; for the poor woman could not open the door until she had hastily swept the remains of Jack's dinner into her apron, and thrown them at the bottom of the cupboard. At last she went, trembling in every limb, to open the door.

" How dost thou dare keep me waiting at the door?" bellowed the Giant in a voice of thunder; " I have a great mind to grind thy

c

bones to flour! Woman, tell me what mischief thou wast brewing, whilst I was away."

He raised his club to give her a blow, which she avoided by falling suddenly on her knees before him; she escaped the blow, but the wind which it caused threw her prostrate on the floor.   She raised herself on her knees again, and with many tears entreated his mercy, saying that she was so busy about his dinner, that she did not think it was time for him to come back.

The Giant listened for an instant, and then snuffing up the air and striking his club with force against the ground, cried out, as he gnashed his teeth, and darted fire from his eyes :

> " Snouk but, Snouk ben,
> I smell the smell of earthly men."

Jack trembled in his hiding place ; his heart

beat so violently that he thought he should
be suffocated, as he listened for the poor
woman's answer.

" Oh no," said the wife, trembling more
and more, " the hide of the ox smells very
fresh which I threw out before it was cold."
The Giant was both tired and hungry, so that
when he turned to the fire, towards which his
wife pointed, and saw the fine fat ox, his pas-
sion cooled a little, and he demanded, in an
angry voice, what she had got so wonderful
for his dinner, to keep him waiting at the
door for it. The poor woman, who now
began to breathe more freely, answered that
she would show him soon. Then she made
haste to set before him an immense barrel of
strong ale ; he seized it greedily, and putting
the bunghole to his mouth, drained it to the
bottom, whilst she placed upon the table a
tub of soup. This was followed by eight fine

salmon, which were quickly eaten; then came
an ox, then a sheep, then a sucking pig;
then the wife brought in a fine fat buck.   As
the Giant stuck his great knife into the white
muscle of the haunch, his mouth seemed to
water again.   There was a basket of loaves,
and to crown all a hasty pudding full of plums,
and so large was it, that if all the children you
know had sat down to it, they could not have
finished it at a meal.   She then rolled in two
more barrels of ale and three of mead, the
sight of which so delighted the greedy Giant,
that he quite forgot his anger.   With eager
looks and gaping mouth he swallowed the
contents of one dish after another, laughing
hideously and crying out, " Oh, rare wife,
what next, what next?" until he became so
stupified that he could go on no longer.

When Jack had recovered a little from his

fright, he ventured to open the door of the
oven very gently, in order to get a peep at the
Giant, but he was very near betraying himself, for he was so terrified, he nearly slammed
the door, and could hardly help screaming
out. The Giant seemed to him exactly like
the one he had seen in his dream. The
Giant's enormous head, which was covered
with shaggy hair, just like a black bear's,
seemed nearly to reach the ceiling; his large
eyes were red and swollen with excess, and
seemed to shoot forth sparks of fire; his
huge mouth was tusked like that of a wild
boar, and his teeth grinned fearfully, as he
bolted the enormous lumps of flesh which his
wife placed before him. His legs were extended so far from him that he did not seem
to know where to put them; and when Jack
saw him throw back his head and brandish

his great knife as he began to eat, he shut
the door, and fairly wished himself at home
once more in his mother's cottage.

After the Giant could swallow no more he
called out to his wife. " Wife, bring me my
hen, that I may amuse myself before I go to
sleep."

Jack peeped out again, and saw the wife
place a hen—the same he had seen in his
dream, on the table ; he noticed that when the
Giant said " lay," the hen laid a golden egg.
The Giant repeated the word " lay" several
times, until he had collected as many eggs as
he wanted ; he then called out with such loud
merriment, that it made Jack jump even in
the oven. " Ah, ah, wasn't it the best day's
work I ever did, to knock out the brains of
your master, my pretty hen, and get all the
good things for myself?"

He soon fell asleep, and Jack who watched

him as he lay snoring and grunting in his
chair, pushed open the door of the oven, and
creeping out softly seized the hen off the
table, and putting it under his arm, opened
the door and ran off without disturbing the
Giant.

Away ran Jack scouring along the ground,
till he came to the Beanstalk; he was much
sooner and easier at the bottom of it now than
at its top in the morning; and running to his
mother, he told her all his adventure.

His mother recognised the hen to have belonged to her husband, Jack's father. The
hen laid as many golden eggs as Jack liked,
and his mother before long had another cow
and another house, and every thing which she
desired.

But Jack soon got tired of leading so easy
a life; he told his mother that he must go up
the Beanstalk once more. His mother tried

to persuade him not to go; she said the
Giant would surely eat him this time: " Pray
be content, my dear Jack," said she, " with
what you have already got."

But Jack could not rest, so he got up early
the next morning, and disguising himself that
he might not be known, he climbed the Beanstalk, which it was much easier to do this
time, and went straight to the Giant's house.

He knocked at the door, and when the
Giant's wife opened it, he spoke in a feigned
voice, and asked her for pity's sake to
give him a night's lodging. He found it
very difficult to persuade her; she said a
youth, whom she had taken in once before,
had stolen her husband's hen, and that he
had never forgiven her. However, at last
Jack prevailed, and she hid him in the cupboard; he could not help trembling when
he heard the stalking strides of the Giant as

The Ascent

he approached the door. He seemed more savage to his wife than before, and as he growled out,

> " Snouk but, Snouk ben,
> I smell the smell of earthly men"

he glared so fearfully upon her, that Jack felt as much afraid for her as for himself. She said, however, timidly, " It's a piece of flesh which the crows have brought to the top of the house," and hastened away directly to set his dinner before him.   Jack peeped out of the cupboard, and saw him feed as voraciously as before.

The whole time he was eating his dinner he upbraided his wife because he had lost his hen ; and this time, when he had finished his dinner, he gave her a push which sent her flying before him, and said, " Now bring me my bags of money, that I may count them

D

before I sleep: I suppose I shall lose them next; beware if I do!"

The woman flew up the stairs, but returned very slowly with two immense bags, which were so heavy that she could hardly carry them.

Jack peeped out and saw the Giant open one of the bags and roll out upon the table a quantity of silver coins, which he counted twice over, and then putting them back into the bag, he tied it tightly up; he then emptied the other bag, and Jack saw that these coins were all of gold; the Giant played with them for some time, and then tying up the bag again, he said exultingly. " Wasn't it the best day's work I ever did, to knock your master's brains out, and get all the good things for myself?"

Soon after he fell asleep, and Jack came out softly and seized the bags of money; but

just as he had got hold of them " bow wow,"
barked a little dog belonging to the Giant's
wife, most violently.

Jack felt rooted to the spot : he could move
neither hand nor foot. Still the Giant continued snoring. Jack took courage, and putting the bags of money under his arm, opened
the door, and ran as fast as he could ; he
descended the Beanstalk and was soon at his
mother's door.

His mother was delighted to see him with
the bags of money, which she also knew to be
her husband's : but she said, " Ah, my dear
Jack, in what terror I have been all day, for
fear I should never see you more !"

They were now quite rich, and could buy
whatever they desired, but Jack again became
fidgetty and restless, and again he told his
mother that he must go up the Beanstalk.
His mother's tears and entreaties had no effect,

and Jack, having first stained his face and hands with walnut juice until they were quite brown, and put on another coloured jacket, climbed up the Beanstalk a third time.

He knocked at the Giant's door, but had still more trouble than before to persuade the woman to let him in; she said that the Giant had had his money and a favourite hen stolen by some boys whom she had taken compassion on, and that he was so cross and ill-tempered, that she was sure he would kill her if he found her out again. However Jack begged and prayed so much that she at last let him go in, and hid him this time in the copper; the Giant came stalking in as before, and directly he set his foot in the kitchen he sniffed up the air—and looked cunningly about the room saying very slowly,

" Snouk but—Snouk ben,—Snouk-be-e-n,
I smell—I smell the smell of earthly men."

But his wife said, " It is the young kid which I have been skinning for to-morrow's breakfast." The giant growled fiercely, and taunting her for the loss of his hen and his money, said, " If I lose any thing more, thy life shall pay for it."

When he had finished his dinner he said, " Wife, bring me my harp, that it may play me to sleep." His wife brought a very beautiful harp, which she placed on the table, and to Jack's great astonishment, when the Giant said " play," the harp began to play of itself, the most beautiful music imaginable.

Jack waited until the Giant was fast asleep and snoring loudly, and then crept out of the copper, and taking the harp off the table, he opened the door ; but just as he was going to shut it again, the harp, which was itself a fairy, called out " Master! master!"

The Giant started up, but was so stupified

with the quantity of dinner which he had eaten,
and the ale and mead which he had drunk,
that it was some time before he could under-
stand what was the matter. He tried to run
after Jack, but he could not walk straight, so
that Jack, who ran very nimbly, got to the
top of the Beanstalk first. When he had
descended a little way he looked up, and how
great was his horror to see the huge hand of
the Giant stretched down to seize him by the
hair of his head! He was so terrified, that
his hair seemed to stiffen and stand upright on
his head: he slid and scrambled down the
Beanstalk hardly knowing how, and seeing
the Giant just putting his feet over the top as
if he were coming down too, he called out,
" Quick, mother, dear mother! A hatchet, a
hatchet!"

His mother heard his voice and ran out
directly with a hatchet. Jack seized the

hatchet, and began to chop away at the trunk
of the Beanstalk: when he had chopped it
quite through, down it fell, bringing along
with it the enormous Giant. He fell so heavily
that he was killed in the fall, and lay on the
ground like some huge mountain. Jack cut
off his head.

That night as Jack was asleep in his bed
the fairy appeared again, and said: "Now,
my dear Jack, you may take possession of all
your father's property again, as I see that you
will make a good use of it, and become a
useful and good man. It was I who made
the Beanstalk grow to such an astonishing
height, in order to see whether you would
have the courage to mount it. If you had
remained as idle and lazy as you once were,
I should not have exerted my power to help
you to recover your property, and enable you
to take care of your mother in her old age.

I trust that you will make as good a use of it as your father once did : and now farewell."

What became of the Giant's house, or his wife, or the country at the top of the Beanstalk, I have never been able to learn.

The end of Jack and the Beanstalk.

C. WHITTINGHAM, CHISWICK.